A Witch's Legacy

The Salem Witches - Book Two

Cathy Walker
Author

ISBN 978-1519588197

Book Cover by Cathy's Covers

Lots of love for my husband, Fred. As usual, he motivates and pushes me to continue writing despite my moments of frustration and self-doubt.

Books By Cathy Walker

A Witch's Lament - The Salem Witches Book 1
A Witch's Legacy - The Salem Witches Book 2
A Witch's Light - The Salem Witches Book 3

The Witch of Endor – The Witch Tree Book 1
The Daughters of Endor – The Witch Tree Book 2
Coming in 2024
The Book of Endor – The Witch Tree Book 3
Coming in 2024
Sword Across Time
Solitary Cove
The Crystal of Light

PROLOGUE

Upon the highest of cliffs on a night engorged with conflicting magic, evil intent begat a darkness so imbued with a power that it ravaged civilizations throughout time until coming to rest in Salem, Massachusetts. Twice it appeared, bringing pain and death, but never quite managing to enfold the town entirely or destroy all life. Beaten for now, it roars with rage in the recesses of its own creation. Darkness. Rooted in the mists of time and forged with shadowed morals of greed, lust, and destruction, the darkness shall overcome. For those who mistakenly celebrate its destruction know naught the truth of its beginnings, nor the means of its ultimate extermination. So, in a town an ocean away from the cliffs of its birth, the evil simmers, waiting for the seeds sown long ago to bloom in a final chance to fulfill the challenge thrown to the ancient winds of time.

Excerpt from *Faerie Enchantments and Sorcerer Magick*

Village of Salem 1717

John Hathorne struggled to take a breath. His effort elicited a rasping cough that echoed throughout the dimly lit room and caught the attention of his servant, Caleb, who slept on a feather mattress outside the door. With gray hair sticking out at all angles and nightshirt tangled around him, Caleb stumbled to the bed, struck the flint to light the lamp, and fussed with the sheets.

Frustrated, John feebly attempted to push at Caleb's fumbling hands. "Get away with you, I'm fine."

He wasn't. He was dying. His humble life, dedicated to the service of God and the eradication of evil, would end in this isolated hovel, amidst the dirt of unkept surroundings with a half-wit for company. Why had God deserted him? What horrible act had he committed to earn such a bleak, lonely death? A tendril of anger fired deep in his belly and wound its way up to burn in his throat. He choked, and Caleb immediately offered him a tumbler of water. John smacked the fawning servant's hand and shifted into a position better suited to his purpose, while Caleb scrambled to clean the mess caused by John's thoughtless act.

The end drew closer. It came on the whisper of the wind outside the window and slithered in the shadows, mimicking a serpent waiting to devour him. Mostly, he heard it in the voices haunting him day and night. The wail of souls he'd condemned to death during the witch trials. They refused to die. They did not recognize his judgment of them to be an extension of the Lord's Will, or their sentence of death, a way to release their souls from the grasp of evil upon their physical forms.

A shriek sliced through his head and the pulse of voices raced ever faster, forcing John to cover his ears and block the sounds. Caleb frowned and tried to place a cool cloth on John's forehead, but John shoved his hands away in an unusual show of strength. Damn the fickle will of a harsh God and the pious ignorance of his neighbors who'd condemned him to a solitary existence. They refused to accept why he'd spent the last months experimenting with the very art of witchcraft he'd fought against. It was a means to an end. Nothing more. His simple logic soothed the guilt that dabbling in the dark art might lead to Holy Damnation. It didn't take away the bitter bile of betrayal by those who should have understood his actions.

Anger fueled him, giving him strength to finish his task. "Fetch my box."

Caleb blanched. "Please...no, it is blasphemous. You must not."

"You dare speak to me of blasphemy. I am the great Judge John Hathorne, persecutor of the faithless. I've devoted my entire existence to rousting the Devil's advocates and forcing them to confess and give Glory to God."

A wave of howling rushed into John's brain and he slapped hands over his ears to drown out the noise. Sweat broke out on his forehead and pain built in his chest. He stabbed a finger at Caleb. "Obey me or I shall assume you to be in league with the Devil and condemn you accordingly."

With a whimper, Caleb scampered to a chest stuck in the corner of the small room. Slowly, he lifted the lid and retrieved a wooden box. He stretched out his arms, holding the box away from him, and walked across the room to John.

John reached for the box and nearly fell out of bed. Heart pounding and blood pumping, he lifted the lid and pulled out a handful of parchment papers. Time ran short. He needed to complete his task. A lifetime of rousting evil and battling the Devil's existence on earth had led to this moment, but unless he finished writing out instructions, all would be for naught.

Frantic now, he scribbled the ritual onto thick parchment. He transcribed words and etched diagrams despite the voices raging in his head. He hated them, yet he'd dedicated his remaining life to freeing these lost souls. This spell would allow the chosen one to call forth the essence of John's own soul.

John bowed his head and prayed softly; Help them find peace. He thought he'd fulfilled his life's purpose when he'd condemned the witches during the Salem trials. The convicted souls lingered. He put his hands over his ears in a futile attempt to block them out. The pen fell from his fingers and the voices cried for release.

Give us freedom from this endless damnation!

His tortured mind wavered between past and present. A hazy memory of the old woman on the outskirts of town who'd escaped the persecution of the trials. The constant battering of voices had led him to her house, and she'd opened her door to him with wisdom and resignation gleaming in her eyes.

He'd hesitated at first. The stench of wet wood and stone hit his nostrils, while his throat tightened with the thick dust floating in the air. Sunlight slipped through cracked boards covering the window, illuminating a wooden chair and a table set on a threadbare rug. He nodded, willed himself to enter, and sat.

At that rickety table, the woman had told an incredible tale. A spear of light was created in the heavens and ended in a powerful cliff top battle," she whispered in a voice low and eerie. She leaned forward and whispered in reverent tones about the creation of a book and the forging of a knife meant to lead men on a journey through time. "Of course, these objects might not reappear for centuries," she added, her piercing black eyes shimmered with promise.

He was quiet for a time. Contemplative. Weighing. Judging. Considering her words. Satisfied, she nodded and continued her tale. "There exists a sacrificial ritual that can suspend your soul in a netherworld until the time is right for rebirth in the body of one who is worthy to receive you," she said. "Upon the reappearance of the book and knife, you must steal them and complete your task. Release the souls begging you for release. Only then shall you be free."

The buzzing of voices in his head urged him to comply.

Save us. You condemned us. Now you must save us.

For them, he had followed the woman's advice and immersed himself in this wanton ritual. For them, he would commit a final horrendous act and redeem himself in the eyes of the Lord.

Pain lanced through John and jarred him back to the present. He clasped a hand to his chest and prayed to an absent God that he'd live to complete the ritual. Behind him, Caleb coughed and the dying fire crackled in the fireplace as shadows danced upon the walls. Regret rose, but he suppressed it with the sheer will of a man driven. His purpose was pure and nothing would deter him. Scratching the final words onto parchment, he rolled up one copy and placed it back in the box while keeping the second for his purposes.

"Here. Take this and hide it where we discussed," John said.

Caleb paused. Stark fear etched shadows on his face.

"Do it. Trust that what I do is for the good of others. And hurry, time runs short."

Caleb clutched the box to his chest and sped from the room, faltering in the dim light.

Tension pulsed through John and he considered his next step. The final ritual. An act of betrayal and blood.

Footsteps thumped up the stairs and minutes later, Caleb reappeared in the doorway.

"It is done?"

"Yes."

"Good." Relieved, John lifted a wavering hand and motioned Caleb to his side. "Let us pray.

Caleb knelt by the bedside, bowed his head bowed in an obsequious posture, and prayed for forgiveness of his earthly sins.

John reached for the knife he'd secreted under the blankets, grasped the smooth handle, and drew the blade from the sheath. Caleb's low, rumbling voice covered the rasp of metal against leather. John sent the blade arching downward. He hadn't known what to expect, but the jarring of his arm when the knife plunged into Caleb's flesh shocked him. Caleb's head shot up, eyes brimming with pain, jerked back and forth. His mouth opened and closed in a way that reminded John of a fish. The gurgle of a word half-spoken fell from Caleb's lips and before John changed his mind, he plunged the knife in again. And again. He closed his senses against Caleb's spiral to death.

Warm blood spurted on the bed, and John didn't waste a drop. With the coppery scent assaulting his nostrils, he coated his hands in the red liquid and smeared Caleb's blood on his face and arms. The old woman's instruction specified covering his body with sacrificial blood when he recited the verse would free his soul from the physical. Warm blood spurted on the bed. John gagged. His body shook. Guilt ravaged him. He reached out a quivering hand, picked up the parchment, and recited the incantation. With each word spoken, his blood raced with energy so vigorous John swore he had the power to leap out of the bed. Upon finishing the final verse, Caleb's body slid from the edge of the bed and fell on the floor with a thump.

In that instant, everything changed.

John's chest clutched in a tight band of pain.

A vision of the old woman in the hovel sneered at him and reshaped from hag to creature, its forked tongue flicking at him in mockery. Laments of the innocent morphed into taunts of laughter and ripped a pathway through his head. Lies. All lies. Understanding penetrated the haze of pain. How easily they'd led him on the alleged path to salvation.

Expecting the Light of God to beckon upon his deathbed, he suffered instead with a deep knowing of his failure. He'd devoted himself to a crusade against evil, but had become a person obsessed with a foul purpose. Minion to an ancient evil begat upon the earth long ago.

John had doomed his soul to eternity in the devil's service. He'd also sent a seductive evil to terrorize the world. Weighted with guilt and sucked into a vortex of torment, John's last sight of this world was the bloodied body of Caleb.

John Hathorne's horrified screams carried him across the threshold, before he plunged into unknown darkness.

Chapter One

Unbeknownst to the British tribal chieftain, King Cassivellaunus, he'd married a woman born with inestimable Druid power, but she'd denied her birthright to marry for love. As is the fickle way of fate, their daughter's abilities surpassed her mother's. Upon seeing the babe, Seabhac had recognized the Druid light within the child. An old soul reborn.

Cassivellaunus's daughter, Ainevar, radiated with the Light. Seabach recognized the light of hope and prayed Ainevar's power could ensure a survival of Druid knowledge. From the moment of her birth, Seabhac ceased his wanderings across the great land of Britain and remained close to the child.

Julius Caesar's second invasion negated Seabhac's attempt to woo the tribal leader into handing over his daughter to a lifetime of study. The desecration of land and the murder of innocents allowed no time for lengthy teachings. Amidst the confusion of bloody conquest and disillusionment of Cassivellaunus's surrender, Seabhac acted. Summoning an aura of invisibility mastered only by an Arch-Druid, he hurried to find the child and secreted her beneath his cloak. Soothing her with mind-thoughts to prevent her cries alerting anyone to his actions, he kidnapped Ainevar and bore her to a place to prepare her for her destiny. A place beyond the reckoning of mortal man.

Avalon.

Excerpt from *Faerie Enchantments and Sorcerer Magick*

Standing in shifting shadows of late afternoon sun, Cassandra Raines understood that coming to Salem might have been a mistake. Her usually repressed prophetic powers throbbed with unease and unfurled in a wisp of smoke within her belly. Nothing in her surroundings explained the tug on her psyche or sudden hypersensitivity she'd experienced upon entering the city limits. A strong desire to get into her car and head back to the airport overwhelmed her. She told herself the feelings weren't real. They were simply the product of her stressed mind, prompted by eerie stories of witch trials, evil, and ancient magic. Urban myths, bed-time stories to scare visitors. Nothing more.

The whiff of smoke billowing from the chimneys of the nearby homes and the scent of burning leaves gave her little comfort. A normal Saturday afternoon in Salem, Massachusetts. Although the breeze was cool and comforting, a trickle of fear, strong and vivid, crawled into her belly.

Cassandra sucked in a breath, attempting to regain control of her tumult of emotions, but a rustling noise made her jump. Her eyes searched the garden, trying to find the source. Then dread traced an icy finger up her spine.

Chipmunks scampered off the trees, gathering fallen fruit amidst the garden, their busy chatter mimicking a fervent conversation. Cassandra covered her startled heart with a hand. *Chipmunks, that's all.* Knots in her shoulders slowly released, and she shook off the lingering trace of apprehension.

Hoping to calm her jitters, she inspected the house looming before her and studied the graceful architecture. Upon entering the driveway on Winter Island Road, her first impression had been Georgian Colonial. Closer inspection revealed a fanlight over the front door, Palladian windows to each side of the doorway, as well as an elliptical window in the upper gable and a low-pitched roof, all lending themselves to a Federal style. Painted a pale creamy yellow with chocolate brown crown moldings and window shutters, the house possessed a finely carved balustrade circling the roof, and oozed with dignity, refinement, and money. A lovely house. No hint of danger or menace prowled around its hedges. Only those darned chattering chipmunks.

Her brother, Memnon, had money aplenty and didn't mind spending it. Cassandra smiled with fondness at the thought of how her brother's subtle manipulations had brought her here. She should have suspected his motives when he invited her to Jean Georges, one of New York's finest restaurants. As soon as the quick moving, obsequious server had seated them by a window with a view over the city, Memnon had turned to her, his wavy black hair gleaming in the soft lighting of the crowded restaurant.

"I'm glad you agreed to put work on hold long enough to have dinner with me. I have a business proposition for you."

Cassandra laughed, almost spilling red wine from the delicate crystal glass she held. "You never miss an opportunity to tell me I work too much and now you're presenting me with a business proposition."

Memnon grinned. "Yes, well, this is part pleasure and part business. I think it may do you some good."

Cassandra raised an eyebrow and nibbled on a piece of warm, soft bread the server had brought over and left on their table. "Hmm, sounds interesting."

"It could be. Maybe. Depends."

Before he could explain, the server showed up with their soup. He skillfully placed the bowls on the table and left Cassandra and Memnon with the directive to enjoy and signal if they needed anything.

Cassandra took a spoonful of her butternut squash soup with black trumpet mushrooms and brought it to her lips. The delicious taste filled her mouth, and she rolled her eyes. "Oh, my goodness, this is amazing."

"I want you to decorate a house I had built in Salem," Memnon said casually.

Cassandra almost snorted soup all over the table. "Salem?" She narrowed her eyes. "You employ about a dozen designers, all of them the best. Why not use one of them?"

"Cassie. I want you to do this one. This house is special."

"It's...in Salem," she said slowly. "Not my scene. You know how I feel about witches, magic, and occult stuff. You know I hate to leave New York."

Memnon lifted her hand from the table and cradled it in his. Warmth spread into her fingertips, edged up her arm, and slowed her rapid pulse.

"C'mon. A change of scenery will give you a fresh outlook on life. Chances are you'll be too busy to leave the house. Besides, there's nothing to fear. I'm sure there aren't many witches still living in Salem. Don't be so superstitious."

Cassandra almost laughed, which toughened her resolve.

She pulled her fingers from his, leaned back, and arched her brow. "Even if you offered me a million dollars, the answer would still be no."

Memnon grinned. His white, even teeth contrasted pleasingly with his tanned skin. "Hmm, I doubt it." His hazel eyes twinkled with mischief. "Okay, let's test your theory. I'll pay you a million bucks to decorate the house."

Her jaw dropped. "Come on, Memnon. Not even you can make that kind of offer and mean it." Cassandra's hands trembled. Her spoon clinked against the side of the bowl. Soup sloshed on the linen tablecloth. The server brought their main course while Cassandra considered the ramifications of Memnon's offer.

Memnon leaned forward, his voice low and intense, "It's important to me that you decorate this house, sis. No one else." He straightened and wiped his mouth on the napkin. "I'm not reselling this one. I'm moving into it myself."

A slither of fear squirmed in Cassandra's stomach. She brushed a strand of blond hair from her face and tucked it behind her ear. "So why do you want me to go to Salem?"

"I need your expertise and flair. Plus, you're my sister and you already know my tastes in décor. You're the only one I trust with my new home. So, say you'll do it. For me."

She smiled and shook her head. "Oh, you're good. You know I can't resist when you turn on the charm."

Memnon smiled back. "I've had years of practice. What do you say, sis? Will you do it?"

Cassandra caught the note of sincerity in his voice. She should trust him.

So why did the knots in her stomach tighten?

Tendrils of perception tickled at her spine. Light-headed from the invading sentient of thoughts and sensations, Cassandra struggled to fight them. An internal battle raged within her, mingled with the undesirable power coursing through her veins since childhood.

"Trying to read my mind?" He asked softly, his words filled with empathy.

Cassandra's throat closed. Tears threatened to fall. Damn him.

Crossing her arms, she whispered, "You know I don't do that anymore."

"Then why not visit Salem? Help me out."

Her thin brows furrowed as she licked her lips. Their eyes locked. His eyes big. Round. Pleading. She swallowed and crossed her legs. "It's obvious you're not telling me the entire story. Don't deny it."

His penetrating gaze made Cassandra shift in her chair. He sighed. "How do you know?"

She poked at the cold chicken on her plate, taking the time to bring her roiling emotions under control. Once she had curbed the burgeoning senses whirling in her head, she bit her lip and met Memnon's gaze with a smile.

"Because I know you, dear brother. I've had years of practice as well."

"Touché." A flicker of amusement sparked in his eyes. "Good, then it's settled."

He'd thrown the gauntlet between them.

His obvious deception bothered her. But admitting she knew he'd lied would mean confessing to her mysterious perceptive and prophetic abilities.

Memnon drummed his fingers on the table.

Cassandra knew she'd lived a sheltered life. That's how she liked it. But going to Salem might prove he was wrong about her, and that her psychic powers had died with their parents.

"Fine. I'll go to Salem."

So here she was two weeks later, and she wasn't sure whether she proved something to herself, or her brother.

"He's certainly outdone himself," Cassandra whispered to the wind. Her brother had found the ideal piece of property to build his perfect house. Of course, being in Salem, Massachusetts, detracted from the property's appeal. At least in her eyes. This was the last place on earth she'd have visited if given a choice. In fact, she had trouble remembering the last time she'd left the 212 area code unless motivated by extreme circumstances. New York was home.

A touch of homesickness gripped her heart and squeezed. Salem was so quiet and serene. Clean and charming. Opposite of the town that never sleeps. She already missed the din of the city. Every street bustling with traffic—yellow cabs honking their impatient horns, boisterous restaurants that delivered 24/7, skyscrapers reaching the sky, and crowded subways with an assortment of odors; urine, perfume, sweat, bad breath. Even if it was New York, she felt safe in her small rent-controlled apartment. Thinking of home, of her cozy rooms with beige walls, frilly curtains, and hand carved antique bedroom set, and even of the carefully organized life she'd left there made her stomach churn with anxiety and doubt.

She inhaled the briny scents of the nearby ocean and listened to the waves rolling against the shore. The wind whispered through trees surrounding the property, while bright yellow songbirds darted and swooped across the lawn to land in the highest branches. Cassandra inhaled the earthy scent of recently turned soil and the fragrant aroma of flowering plants. Chipmunks scampered amidst the garden, their busy chatter mimicking a fervent conversation, and she smiled because they seemed intent on showing off for her. Knots she hadn't known existed slowly released across her shoulders and peace brought a languorous weight to her limbs. Being a city person, she wouldn't normally take the time to appreciate such simple pleasures.

Realizing the direction of her thoughts, she gave herself a mental shake. One of the chipmunks stretched a quivering nose toward Cassandra. Shiny, brown eyes glowed with expectation while tiny feet gave a happy dance on the grass.

"He's looking for a treat."

Startled, Cassandra turned to the person who'd jarred her from the solitary moment of peace. With an effort, she forced herself not to gasp in appreciation of the sweaty hunk standing before her. Dark green eyes, with dirty blond hair cropped close to his head, and a powerful body clothed in jogging shorts and a T-shirt. His forehead gleamed with sweat, and he wiped it with the back of his hand. The hunk bent over to catch his breath before straightening up and extending a hand.

"Jerome Phips. I live a couple of houses down."

"Hi. I'm Cassandra."

Jerome gripped her extended hand and gave her a measuring glance. His shirt clung to every muscled contour of his chest. "Pleasure to meet you. Was out jogging with my dog and noticed your car."

He eyed the open, luggage filled trunk. "I thought you weren't moving in for another couple of months."

"I'm not. This is my brother's place. He'll be moving here in the fall. Meanwhile, he talked me into doing the interior design and getting stuff ready for his move."

An excited chatter interrupted the conversation and Cassandra's gaze rested on the chipmunks climbing a blackened tree trunk and dancing around, trying to get Jerome's attention. Laughing at their antics, Jerome reached into the pocket of his shorts and pulled out a fistful of sunflower seeds.

"Don't worry, guys, I've got you covered." He put the seeds in his open palm and held them out for the chipmunks. Much to Cassandra's surprise, one of them jumped into Jerome's hand and feasted on the seeds.

She laughed again. "You're kidding. Do you usually walk around with sunflower seeds in your pocket in case you come across a hungry chipmunk?"

"Always." He offered seeds for the second chipmunk, then shooed them away and wiped his hand on his shorts. "Especially since I used to live here and spoiled these guys."

"Oh. I didn't realize."

Jerome hesitated. His eyes clouded over when he looked at the newly built home. "Yeah, I lived here until someone torched my house." He chuckled. "But my place didn't compare to this one."

Torched his house?

Unbidden, a seed of unease began deep in Cassandra's gut. Orange flames and blackened debris flashed in her mind. Her knees shook and a hot flush moistened her forehead. She focused on suppressing her vision. Forgot for a moment that she was not alone.

"Hey, you look pale. Are you okay?"

Jerome's question helped ground Cassandra in reality. Taking a calming breath, she replied, "Sure. I'm fine." She ran sweaty palms down her pant legs. "Where did you move after your house burned?"

Jerome didn't answer immediately. His eyes glazed over. "Actually, I married the woman two doors down and we live in her house. Her place has a history and certain memories, so we thought living there was better than rebuilding here."

He was so not telling her everything. Her scalp prickled at the explanation given in a monotone voice. She fought to keep control over her burgeoning stream of awareness. Without bidding, her mind sent a mind-feeler straight at Jerome. Her stomach trembled with the effort to recall the shaft of energy without making him aware of anything. If she'd been alone, she'd have sat in her meditative pose, breathed deeply, and cleared her mind until she'd regained control. Difficult to do while being watched.

His eyes blazed into her. A moment passed. He reached out and took her arm.

"You're looking pale again. Maybe you should sit."

Embarrassed, she gave a tremulous smile and lifted her arm out of his grasp. "I'm fine, thank you. It's the long drive catching up to me. I need food and rest."

"You sure?"

"I'm sure. Really. I enjoyed meeting you and I hope I get to meet your wife soon." The words fell out of her mouth in a jumble.

"How about coming over for dinner tomorrow?"

"What?"

"Dinner. Tomorrow. With me and my wife, Skye."

An innocent question asked with clenched hands. Cassandra glanced at the stubborn set of Jerome's jaw and challenging glint in his green eyes.

"Why do I have the feeling that you won't take no for an answer?"

"Because I won't." To emphasize his declaration, he placed his hands on his hips.

"Shouldn't you talk with your wife first? She might have plans or something."

Dinner with strangers meant a stressful evening of chitchat and inquisition. Where did you grow up? What do you do for a living? Do you have any children? An evening of social niceties with a fake smile pasted on her face, all while filtering out stray prophetic readings from anyone close to her.

"No worries. She'll be thrilled to meet you."

"All right. Dinner sounds fine." Not true, she'd prefer being alone to immerse herself in work.

"Great. It's the white house two doors east. Around six will be great."

With a wave, Jerome left through an overgrown path at the edge of the property. His absence prompted the chipmunks to chatter, and Cassandra took a mental note to buy sunflower seeds when she went into town.

The uncomplicated act of feeding the chipmunks might help simplify the rest of her life. Opening the trunk of her Prius, she yanked a suitcase out and let it thump on the ground. She should have asked her neighbor to help unload.

He'd been hunky. Also, disturbingly driven, and intent on dinner arrangements with her as a guest. Not in town for five minutes, and she'd already probed the mind of her neighbor. Hopefully, he'd been unaware of her subconscious attempt to plunder his brain. Cassandra staggered to the house, a suitcase in each hand and a frown creasing her brow. She knew that coming to Salem had not been a good idea.

Chapter Two

The roots of the insidious evil stalking Salem began with Julius Caesar's invasion against the ancient tribes of Britain. His thirst to dominate lent rage to the attacking legions and stained the land with the blood of innocents. Two years in succession, Caesar's ships landed upon the shores of Kent, close to the cliffs of Dover, so famous for their steep, chalk-white cliffs. Twice, he ravaged the land and attacked the people, only to eventually rally his warriors back on the ships to return to Rome, leaving behind a country rift with the scars of battle—both physical and emotional.

Unfortunately, his departure did not mean the end.

The Arch Druid, Seabhac, watched from the highest point of the Dover cliffs as the ships sailed past him to a distant horizon. He understood the survival of all Druids rested upon him. Julius Caesar's invasion counted as a first step. Rome would return to conquer and destroy.

Preparation for the attacker's return would be an enormous task and quite possibly beyond the Druid's ability to accomplish alone. His bones ached and his soul cried for release from a centuries-old life filled with constant trials and heartfelt deaths of countless loved ones.

Seabhac's prophesies never failed, which meant the Roman armies would return. With them, an evil so dark, Seabhac shivered with terror. The Tribal Chieftains of Britain would fall. Fearing the influence and knowledge of the Druids, the Romans would seek out and destroy each member of the ancient order of priests. So Seabhac readied himself for what he must do, not knowing how much time he had.

Excerpt from *Faerie Enchantments and Sorcerer Magick*

Present Day Salem

Pastor Joshua Parris stared across the desk at the man who'd admitted to adultery and kept his expression neutral. He wanted to denounce him as a sinner and banish him from the congregation. With an effort, he smiled, offered advice on how to salvage his marriage, and sent the sinner on his way. Joshua sighed with relief when he locked the front door.

Alone for now, he surveyed his surroundings. Polished to a high sheen and perfectly aligned, rows of wooden benches faced the pulpit where he preached every Sunday. Although a small church with minimal congregation, Joshua took pride in the cleanliness and simplicity he espoused for both his church and his soul.

As Pastor of the small church on the outskirts of Salem, counseling members was one of his responsibilities, but the modern immoralities of people were such a blatant effrontery of God's will that it left him cold. Lately, a slow burning urge raged inside him. Once content with preaching to his modest-sized congregation, he'd developed a need to do more. A desire to become more worthy. He lay awake at night listening to the breeze rustling leaves and the roll of the ocean waves upon the shore, each rhythm of life creating a mirrored rhythm in his mind. Speaking to him. Bidding him to create a place on earth that practiced the word of God without soul-consuming sins eating away at the fiber of society until an empty shell of self-serving deceivers remained.

Joshua pictured the face of each member of his congregation. He shook with lingering disgust while recalling the sins each of them had confessed during their infrequent bouts of conscience.

Evil mongers. All of them.

Thoughts of retribution flooded his brain. Visions of eternal Hell forced him to consider his position as a religious advisor. Pressure built within until he slumped on the floor, his legs too weak to stand. He had a responsibility to maintain subservience. A purpose to ensure that God's will reigned over an ever-decadent society.

"Yes." Joshua jumped to his feet with exultation. He would be the savior for modern times. How? He paced the aisle between pulpits. His feet thudding a staccato beat on the floorboards, his hands clasped behind him.

His ancestor, Samuel Parris, had persecuted sinners accordingly and never let his congregation slide into a cesspool of wickedness. Accusing one's slave of witchcraft and sending the town into a maelstrom of bloodlust wouldn't work in present day. The people of Salem practiced witchcraft too openly. He needed a subtle means of bringing the people into line. Modern society would not tolerate burnings, pressings, and hangings.

Frustrated, he struggled to figure out an answer. He'd finally found a purpose, and it wasn't fair for society to limit his actions. Leeway should be given in the quest to save souls. He needed guidance. He needed an ally.

With that thought, sinister whispers echoed from the shadows.

Chapter Three

Shifting his butt on the hard wooden bar stool, Samson leaned forward on the kitchen countertop and considered Skye and Jerome. A ripple of unease in an otherwise calm day had drawn him to visit his friends today.

"If she's so beautiful, should I be jealous?" Skye stood, hands on hips, raven dark hair framing her face and cascading down her back, the gleam of battle in her blue eyes.

Samson didn't envy Jerome, who stuttered, not sure how to placate his wife. If Jerome was numbskull enough to extol the beauty of another woman with a wife like Skye, then he deserved what he got. With a snort, Samson raised the beer bottle to his lips and gulped the cold brew.

Drawn together by dark destiny and forced to battle evil stalking Salem, Skye and Jerome's love had taken root and grown amidst turbulent times. Trust each other, or die. They'd chosen trust. A year later and Salem's residents still whispered and speculated, but Samson's police report kept the truth buried. Dark. Haunting. Evil. An ancient entity slithering across the mists of time to find a weak-minded person and bind them into enslavement. Samson ensured the truth remained hidden, because even in Salem the most liberal-minded person would disbelieve.

Jerome punched his arm. "Come on, bud, don't look so glum."

Samson detected a quiver in Jerome's voice, a flicker of unease deep in his green eyes. He'd been right to come today. He opened his mouth to speak and snapped it shut at a warning glance from Jerome. Buttering bread and slicing tomatoes, Skye appeared oblivious of any byplay between the two men.

Samson should have known better.

Without losing a beat, Skye sliced into a block of cheddar cheese and said, “Don’t even think you two can exclude me from whatever’s going on.” She pulled china plates from a cupboard, cut the sandwiches, slapped them on the plates, and handed one to Jerome and Samson. She folded her arms across her chest and stared, her eyes sparking with stubborn resolve.

Samson grinned. “Hey, I’m merely picking up on your hubby’s vibes.”

“Thanks pal, put it on my shoulders.” Jerome sighed and reached over to rub Skye’s belly. “Sweetie, nothing’s wrong. Your only consideration is taking care of you and the baby.”

Skye smacked his hand away. “Look, sweetie, being eight weeks pregnant doesn’t make me an idiot, and I would think I’ve earned the right to know if there’s even the slightest chance that thing has returned.” She clasped both hands over her stomach. “Especially now that we have a baby on the way.”

Jerome said, “No, it’s nothing important. In fact, it’s so trivial I’m amazed Samson picked up on my emotions.”

Samson smiled at Jerome’s *you’re an idiot for saying anything* look.

“Well then, there shouldn’t be a problem telling me.” She leaned back in the high-back wooden chair and tapped her fingernails on the tabletop.

Samson smiled. Jerome was a goner.

“It’s just...I don’t know. When Cassandra and I met, she seemed normal, other than being tired and hungry from her trip. I’m sure...almost sure; she used a mind-probe on me. It happened so fast.” He glanced at Skye and back to Samson. “I’m sure it was nothing.”

Samson swallowed a hunk of sandwich. “Assume nothing. Trust your abilities, Jerome. They might be new to you, but they are inherently powerful. That applies to both of you.” He directed an earnest glance at Skye. “I’ve had years to adjust and learn to tap into my abilities, while you two are newborns when it comes to this magic stuff. Now that you've ignited them, use them. If your inner voice is telling you something, go with it."

Skye picked at a stray thread on her shirt. Her words came out faltering. "Should we, uh, you know, be worried?"

"Not necessarily," Samson said. "Look, you two endured an insane, blood curdling test of your abilities, but for hundreds of years, witches in Salem have lived mundane lives with passive powers. Jerome, you most likely recognized certain powers in this Cassandra person. Maybe she performed a mind probe, or threw up a block against the energy emanating from you, which, by the way, overwhelms a person at times."

Jerome ducked his head and mumbled, "Sorry, I'm working on subduing my aura's potency."

"Good. I've told you over and again. Accept and curb your powers, don't let them control you," Samson said.

"You're right. I just..."

Skye placed her hand on Jerome's arm and smiled. "We understand what you're saying, Samson." Her smile turned to a light laugh, and her eyes twinkled in merriment.

"Don't you dare tell him." Jerome threatened.

Skye's light laugh turned into a deep belly chuckle and bloomed into rolling laughter. "O...okay, I won't. But the sight of poor Chance rolling around upside down in the air...I...can't help but laugh." She did. Until tears flowed.

Her infectious laughter caught while Samson imagined Jerome's dog caught in a spell-gone-wrong.

Jerome sniffed. "You can laugh, but poor Chance certainly wasn't."

Skye said, "I think he had the ride of his life, swooping around the living room."

Samson roared. "He swooped? I wish I'd seen that."

Crossing his arms, Jerome stared at Skye and Samson until they stopped laughing. "I hope you two are quite finished."

With an effort, Samson pulled it together. "Yep, I'm done laughing at you."

"Gee, thanks." Jerome bit into his sandwich and chewed with indignant fervor.

Samson said, "Come on, if you can't laugh at friends, who can you laugh at?"

Jerome kept chewing.

"I'm sorry," Samson offered.

"I'm not," Skye said.

Jerome's lip twitched into a smile. "It was kinda hilarious." He reached down and gave Chance a pat on the head. "Sorry for laughing at you, pal." The dog whimpered and rolled over for a belly rub.

"What a spoiled suck." Samson was teasing, although he envied Jerome the friendship and loyalty the dog gave his friend.

He sighed and silently hoped that Jerome's radar had gone into alert over minor magic abilities the woman possessed. His responsibility to Salem's residents meant he needed to be sure it amounted to nothing more.

Casually, not wanting to darken the mood. "I'll check her out."

"You mean run a police check on her?" Skye asked.

"No. That wouldn't tell us whether...well, it wouldn't give us what we need. I'll talk to her; read her energy. Try to clarify what Jerome felt."

"Of course." Skye placed a hand on her stomach.

"Don't worry, Skye, I'm sure it's nothing." Samson hoped not. He didn't want his friends embroiled in another battle with the dark forces, and he dreaded the recurrence of ritualistic murders.

"I'm sure you're right. Hey, since Jerome has invited this woman to dinner tomorrow night, why don't you come? It would give you an excuse to tune in to whatever's going on with her."

Samson pinned Skye with a narrowed gaze. "Hmm. This better not be an elaborate scheme to fix me up. Last time didn't work out, if you remember."

Skye grinned. "That wasn't my fault. I had no idea she was a stripper who—ahem—did a little extra on the side? She appeared quite respectable when I met her at the grocery store."

"Respectable. Right. I nearly arrested her for practically raping me in the car at the end of the date."

Jerome chuckled. "I'd have paid to see that." His face darkened. He crumpled his napkin and threw it to his plate. "I do agree with your plan to check out Cassandra."

A stone of dread dropped into Samson's stomach. Levity aside, this woman coming to town possibly signaled the beginning of another period of darkness for Salem.

Witch Capital of the World. Not an unearned title, by any means.

Jerome's departure left Cassandra disoriented, her stomach roiling and rumbling with unease. Being close to him had triggered deeply suppressed inadequacies she hadn't experienced in a long time.

Damn him!

Based on past situations, disaster followed any reawakening of her suppressed powers.

Restless, she wandered through the house. An earlier search of the upstairs had revealed a bedroom equipped with a bed and dresser—her brother's thoughtfulness. Climbing the stairs, she entered the bedroom, hoisted her suitcases on the bed, and surveyed the room. Same as the rest of the house, the room was unpainted. However, the hint of color reflected on the walls from an outside source drew Cassandra to an enormous bay window. The view was breathtaking. Nearby, softly undulating waves of the Atlantic Ocean rolled onto a sandy shore. The vast display of water shimmered between jewel colors of blue and green. Alive and deceptively peaceful, the ocean gurgled and roared.

Nature's immense might tempered with calming energy accented the water's closeness.

Cassandra cranked a window open and inhaled. An array of scents assailed her. Some identifiable, others not. Salt, of course, along with seaweed and a mild fish odor. Underneath the obvious, Cassandra was aware of the crisp aroma of ocean water. Her senses tingled, each nerve ending more sensitive than normal. Hmm, probably the ionization of the ocean, causing her heightened perceptions.

She unpacked. Her organized way of packing allowed her to hang her clothes and line up her shoes with efficiency. New Yorkers expected certain standards of the person designing their million dollar penthouses, and Cassandra's wardrobe consisted of silk, fine cottons, and high-heels. Since Salem wasn't New York and it wasn't necessary to impress, she'd decided to pack her casual clothes.

Once she'd refolded and arranged her clothes in drawers and set the bathroom up the way she preferred...brush, toothbrush, soap, razor, creams, and shampoo, lined up in order...she took a break.

Ribbons of unease still left her frustrated. Unsettled. To occupy her mind and keep her energy focused on reality, she worked.

Sketchbook in hand, she wandered. Touching her hand to a wall, she soaked up the house's ambience and let the structure speak to her. Relying on feeling, not thought, she took notes, drew sketches, and imagined the house with the right paint, wallpaper, and furniture. Her cell phone rang, and she smiled at the familiar number flashing her.

"Hello, Memnon. Checking up on me so soon?" Cassandra teased.

"Me? No, of course not." Memnon's deep voice radiated warmth and reassurance across the phone. If ever Cassandra felt unsure, shaken, or upset, she merely had to let Memnon's voice wash over her to make everything all right again. She'd never forget how he'd comforted her after their parent's accident. She gave herself a mental shake, not wanting to go there.

"Let me guess. You've unpacked, everything's neatly in place and you've already started working, but you forgot to buy food for the kitchen? Am I close?"

Oops, no getting away with anything, even this far away.

"I had forgotten that minor detail. Don't worry, I'll head out to a grocery store soon...wherever it is."

Memnon laughed. "Make sure you do, sis. I want the house to be perfect, but not at the expense of your health. Leave the work and go get food. You promised not to lose yourself in your work."

A hint of hesitation entered her brother's voice, and the tone tweaked an uncanny surety in Cassandra that he was hiding something.

"Memnon. What aren't you telling me?"

"Uh, nothing. Why?"

If snorting had been in her character, that's exactly what Cassandra would have done. "Memnon, you know you can't hide anything from me."

"So what? If I don't fess up, you'll zap me?" Though Memnon's voice edged on laughter, the words struck knife-sharp in Cassandra's chest. She struggled to catch her breath.

Silence reigned.

"Come on, Cassie. I'm kidding."

"I know...but please stop talking about powers I don't possess."

Memnon lowered his voice to a whisper. "Sis, you underestimate yourself."

Tears threatened, but Cassandra scrubbed her eyes with her free hand and resolved to remain strong. "No, I don't."

"Fine. Then tell me this, while you were going through my house, did you put your hands on the walls and let the house talk to you? Did you allow the energy of your surroundings to direct your design ideas?"

Cassandra paced the wooden floor of the empty living room. The cell phone was hot in her sweating hand. "You know I did, but that's how I stimulate my creative juices. Other designers look at magazines, or imagine color schemes and furniture layouts, but I touch the walls. No big deal."

"Sure. Now tell me the sky's not blue. Look, I'm not trying to ruin your day. Just give yourself a break, forget the past, and accept the present. Even if that means accepting what and who you are."

"What I am?" She stopped pacing, her hand gripping the phone harder. "You make me sound like a monster." Hot tears flowed. Driven by a desperate desire to be normal.

"Cassandra, please don't cry."

"I'm not crying." Her shuddering voice belied her declaration. He was such an insensitive oaf!

Memnon chuckled. "You are so. Cassie, you are not a monster. What you are is special and I wish you'd realize that."

"I don't want to be special. I want to be normal."

"I love you, sis." His words held a depth of meaning. Comfort, acceptance, uncaring regard for the rigid confines of acceptable society."I know you do." Without warning, an overwhelming thought struck Cassandra. She dropped to the floor, her legs collapsing beneath her. "Why, Memnon? Of all the places, why did you build a house in Salem? I need to know."

"I told you. I fell in love with the view. I believe Salem is a wonderful place to build a house and raise a family."

"Why did you hire me? Insist that I come here?"

"Because I wanted the best and you're the best."

She wanted to believe him. She needed to believe him. "You're not trying to do something silly like, oh, I don't know, force me into confronting the past and accepting these mysterious abilities you keep harping on."

"Who me? Never. I merely hired you to decorate a house."

"A house situated in Salem. Witch Capital of the World."

Rustling papers echoed down the phone lines, and Memnon mumbled a hurried apology. "Sorry, gotta get back to work. Talk to you later."

Cassandra sat with the phone to her ear. He'd hung up on her. Bugger.

Damn!

Snapping her cell phone shut, she jammed it into her pant pocket, wishing she hadn't answered his call.

Chapter Four

The whispers woke Joshua. Increased to a chorus of seductive song. Shimmered into his soul and wove through him in a fine silken strand. Smooth. Slippery. Beguiling. Charged energy thumped in his chest, and he fell from his bed. He kneeled, and ignoring the hard wood grinding into his knees, extended his arms.

"Please. I am your servant. Help me save the sinners. Show me the way."

He'd dismissed the voices for weeks. Closed his mind to their promise to fulfill his desires and punish all sinners. Then he wondered why. He could remain a servant of God, or rise to become an extension of God's will. Persecutor of the faithless. With the power promised by the voices, he'd force the world to give glory to God and repent, or die.

A flash of white light blinded Joshua and weightlessness claimed his body. Floating. Yes. Soft light above. The light of God. The Lord had chosen him for a task greater than anyone since Jesus Christ.

A hum replaced the whispers in his head. Growing louder, the humming consumed Joshua and drove him from his apartment to the church. He stepped up on the altar and opened a narrow door leading to a basement in the older section of the building; a small area built on what remained of the original foundation from the 1700s.

He descended the rickety stairs, directed to the far wall by the voices. They bade him raise his hands and run them over the rough-hewn stone walls. Not knowing what he was searching for, he followed directions until his hands came to rest on a loose stone. His search was over. Grasping fingers dug out the dirt around the stone. Breathless. Panting. So ready for what lay in the hiding spot. Finally, he loosened the stone and wriggled it free.

He stopped. His heart thumped and blood pulsed. With a lick of his lips, he reached in and fumbled around in the dark recesses of the exposed niche. Rising dust and a pungent, musty odor did little to deter him. Glory be. His fingers brushed on something. Stretching farther back, he grasped the corner of a box and inched in forward. Careful not to drop the treasure, he drew it from the hole and set it on a nearby wooden table. Honey colored, the rough-hewn wooden chest showed scars of misuse and age. How long was the box sitting hidden, waiting for his unexpected discovery?

Anxious, yet leery, he raised the lid. The box opened with a minimal amount of protest and revealed a pile of neatly arranged parchment papers covered with scribbling and diagrams. Not the world-changing treasure he'd craved.

Until he started to read. The significance of the writing made his hands shake.

Yes. Yes. Yes.

An ally. The renowned Judge John Hathorne himself. Recalling the spirit from past to present would mean a blood sacrifice, but the life of an animal mattered little weighed against the cleansing of the town. Sure of himself as never before, Joshua closed the box and reverently carried it up to his apartment to study and prepare.

Sleep taunted Samson. Tossing and turning until his muscles ached in protest, he gave up and rose with a curse. Tromping into his kitchen, he brewed a cup of hot, black tea, gulped the liquid in one mouthful, and returned to bed. Stretched out and comfortable, he concentrated on breathing techniques while visually isolating each muscle from his toes to his head and making them relax. By the time he finished, the mellowing effect of the tea had worked its magic. He'd have no problem sleeping now.

Later, he wished he'd stayed awake.

Drifting into the Shadowlands of a place beyond anywhere he'd ever been, Samson saw a specter of himself floating in a room that resembled the dark recesses of Salem's past. The musty room flared his nostrils with distaste. The low ceiling made him duck, though he was clearly not corporeal, since no one spared a glance in his direction. Obscurity gave him a chance to observe the group of people and their old-fashioned garments. A sea of black, gray, and white, stiff-necked, body-covering clothing. What one might expect in Puritan times.

Each person sat erect, most of the women with hands folded in their laps and the fire of fear in their eyes. Except the young girls sitting at the front, near a raised dais—their eyes gleamed with wickedness and penetrating satisfaction. Up on the dais, a couple of men glared at a single, frightened woman perched on the edge of a rickety wooden chair. With disheveled hair, grubby face, and torn, dirty clothes, she appeared to have been dragged through mud and thrown into the spotlight of a trial.

Samson's heart froze. Trial?

A voice from the crowd boomed in the small room.

"The Devil hath been raised amongst us and His rage be vehement and terrible. When he shall be silenced the Lord only knows." A pinched-faced man spun around and pointed a finger at the frightened woman. "Witch! I, Samuel Parris, declare to this Court of Oyer and Terminer this woman, Bridget Bishop, be of the Devil."

Spectators erupted into fierce declarations of screams and demands for the execution of the witch. Loathing settled in the courtroom until Samson choked on the pungent energy of abhorrence. While the poor woman hunched her shoulders and cried out her innocence, a man at the head table banged his hand and ordered silence. It took a couple of minutes before people sat down, grumbling all the while.

The man with the gavel frowned and ordered. "Sit, Samuel. I direct examination of this accused witch, Bridget Bishop, to John Hathorne."

John Hathorne puffed his chest and stood, adjusted his jacket, and turned his dark eyes to the accused. Bridget shrank into her seat. Hathorne strolled to her side and stared. Bridget's bony hands clutched at the worn shawl thrown across her shoulders, and she whimpered. Samson pitied the thin woman who trembled in her threadbare clothing.

"Bridget Bishop, what say you? You stand here charged with sundry acts of witchcraft by you done, or committed, upon the bodies of Mercy Lewis and Ann Putnam and others."

Bridget hung her head. "I am innocent. I know nothing of it. I have done no witchcraft."

"Look upon this woman and see if this be the woman you have seen hurting you? Mercy Lewis and Ann Putnam and others do now charge her to her face with hurting of them."

Hathorne pointed at the girls seated at the front of the room and upon his attention, they giggled. One girl hastened to shush the others, and they became serious again.

Hathorne continued his interrogation. "What do you say now you see they charge you to your face?"

"I never did hurt them in my life. I did never see these persons before. I am as innocent as the child unborn."

"Bah! Good Bishop, what contract have you made with the devil?"

Bridget leaned forward and grabbed at Hathorne's sleeve. She implored. "I have made no contract with the devil. I never saw him in my life. But Ann Putnam sayeth that she calls the devil her God."

Hathorne curled his lip and threw her hands off his clothes. "What say you to all this that I charge you with? Can you not find in your heart to tell the truth?"

Bridget trembled and whispered. "I do tell the truth. I never hurt these persons in my life. I never saw them before."

At her denial, the girls who Samson assumed were Ann Putnam, Mercy Lewis and Mary Walcott moaned and writhe. The attention of the entire room focused on their antics. They rolled their eyes and fell to the floor. People murmured and stepped back from the girls as though concerned they would come under a spell. John Hathorne and Samuel Parris exchanged a glance of satisfaction and stood back to allow the girl's theatrics to run its course.

Samson swore and wished he possessed the power to do something. Such an obvious display of poor acting, yet the crowd appeared enthralled. Even Bridget's shoulders slumped in defeat. A tear trickled down her cheek.

The girls finally calmed and sat up, directing accusing glares burned into Bridget.

John Hathorne's bellow reverberated in the room. "What say you now, Bishop?" He pointed a shaking finger at the now silent girls. "There sit the innocents upon whom you have set loose the Devil's evil. Tell us the truth and we shall consider a pardon."

"I am not here to say I am a witch. To take away my life."

"Do you not see how they are tormented? You are acting witchcraft before us. What do you say to this? Why have you not the heart to confess the truth?"

"I know nothing of it. I am innocent of being a witch. I know not what a witch is."

"If you know not what a witch is, how know you that you are not a witch yourself?"

Bridget shook her head, her eyes rounded with confusion.

"Enough. Five people have accused you of dark torture and devil play. Therefore, as judge of this Court, and person responsible for the well-being of Salem, I declare you, Bridget Bishop, to be a witch. I also charge that you be taken to Gallows Hill and hung 'til dead."

People exploded when Bridget collapsed to the floor in a huddle. Samson swore and moved to help her. His best effort allowed him to drift a few inches forward. Nothing more. History played out before him, while he floated as a disembodied bystander, sickened by the intolerance and narrow-minded judgments he witnessed. The spinning room caught Samson unaware. His disgust turned to icy liquid shooting through his veins when his last view of the past was John Hathorne looking directly at him. Dark eyes swirled with malevolence. A sneer curled Hathorne's lip, and taunting laughter followed Samson on his journey back to reality.

Hathorne's amoral laugh stuck with Samson in his waking state. Until he recognized the sound as the crows performing their usual early morning, caw, caw, caw, outside his window. Although crows possessed a reputation as the messenger of death in various cultures, Samson preferred to think of his living alarm clock much as the Greeks and Celts did; divine messengers and guides. They led souls on their journey to the afterworld and made sure each person didn't stray.

Reassured by the familiarity of his surroundings, Samson jumped from the bed and went to splash cold water on his face. Driven to cleanse himself of the cloying grit of his foray into Salem's loathsome history, he grabbed the soap and scrubbed his arms and chest. Nausea burned his throat.

To read books of the witch trials was one thing, but to experience the persecution of innocent women. To witness cloying hate and jealousy permeate the room and watch a terrified woman subjected to a battery of inane questions with no basis other than some snotty young girls throwing accusations around to gain attention. Granted, the girls themselves were pawns of the ambitious. Weak minded enough to be easily manipulated into doing the foul deeds of certain narrow-minded and greedy townspeople intent on gaining more land, more influence, more power. No matter that their ambitions had destroyed hundreds of lives and ended in the death of 19 innocent people.

Samson's thoughts spiraled into a quagmire of negativity, so he refocused his attention on the mundane decision of what to have for breakfast. The jingling of the phone sent him bounding down the stairs two at a time.

A glance at the kitchen clock showed 6:00 am, and a knot twisted in his gut. Considering he was the Chief of Police in Salem, early morning calls weren't uncommon, but usually meant trouble.

Praying for the best, he answered the phone. "Hello."

"Sorry to wake you, Boss, but I think we have a...problem."

Samson's heart stilled. "Problem? You better be more clear, Jaks."

"We found a body, not human. An animal carcass laid out in a sacrificial manner."

"Where?" Samson spoke sharply. Now was not the time for sensitivity.

"Under one of the old trees in Old Burying Point Cemetery."

Samson swore. "I'll be right there. Make sure the officers on site keep spectators at a suitable distance from the scene. We don't need a public panic."

"Sure, boss."

First, his nighttime visit in the past, and now an animal sacrifice. Samson didn't believe in coincidences.

Chapter Five

Idiots. Cassandra wielded her car expertly around a couple of people yelling at each other. Two cars sat nose first in the one empty spot in the parking lot. From the rising red color on their faces, both people arguing would benefit from walking a block or two to cool down.

Irritated, she suppressed the urge to shout a curse out the window. The uncharacteristic thought mirrored the restlessness twisting inside her stomach, and she drove away from the confusion to find a spot behind the building. Unable to focus on work, she'd hoped that a visit to the Peabody Museum might relax her.

Wheeling around the back of the museum, Cassandra nearly ran into a line of yellow police tape blocking the road. Great. Now what? A uniformed officer motioned her on the sidewalk to detour around the taped off area. Taking care not to scrape the car's underside, she followed the directions. Creeping forward, Cassandra peeked at what lay beyond the tape. A graveyard—an old one by the looks of the chipped, worn gravestones and gnarled trees with their immense trunks rooted staunchly into the earth.

Probably teenagers vandalizing the place. Kids these days didn't understand the idea of respect.

At the corner where she'd swing back to the front of the museum, a flutter of color caught her attention. A nudge in her mind urged her to look. Past the milling crowd and partially obscured by police lay the butchered body of a dog. Yuck.

Unwanted knowledge fluttered an extra heartbeat. Heat built within the core of her belly and images of dark clouds obscured her mental vision. A crack in the clouds opened, leaving a warped tear running lengthwise. Cassandra wanted to block the sight of what lay beyond the widening crack, but the billowing puffs held her attention in a magnetic vice.

NO! She jerked the wheel and slammed her foot on the brakes.

The car bucked to a standstill and Cassandra jammed her eyelids shut, trying to block the incoming visual. Nothing mattered except stopping herself from enduring the sensations whirling in her brain. Her breath hiccupped in her throat. She pinched a piece of skin on her arm to refocus her attention from metaphysical to physical.

"Ummm, is everything all right here?"

A male voice ripped her from her vision. A man stood outside her car window and must have seen her anxiety fit and self-abusive pinch. She lifted one eyelid and peeked at the worried face of an extraordinarily handsome man. Were all the men in this town awesome looking?

She closed her eyes, hoping he'd go away.

"Hey, are you okay? The awesome looking man tapped on the window again.

Putting on the stiff upper lip, don't show any emotion façade she'd developed over the years, Cassandra opened her eyes, rolled down her window and flashed a cheery smile. "I'm fine. Why do you ask?" She spoke the innocent question without flinching or blushing. An accurate test of her powers of deception.

He harrumphed. "Why do I ask? Oh, gee, I don't know. Probably because you slammed on your brakes and almost rammed the building. Or possibly the fact you're sitting in your car alone with your eyes shut and talking to yourself. More likely it's because you're pinching your arm in a self-flagellation manner."

A flush rose up her neck and warmed her face. Her predicament worsened when she glanced at the stranger and melted into the most striking blueberry colored eyes.

Their piercing gaze sent shivers up her spine. In a good way. Not at all similar to her occasional flashes of precognition. The rest of him looked tempting as well. Midnight dark hair, square jaw bristling with a day's growth of stubble. Over six feet of taut muscle and inflamed intent. Tall enough to block the sun. Wide enough to fill her car window.

She managed a weak smile. Followed by a mental, Oh, oh, when she noticed the gold shield strapped underneath his windbreaker. Her heart flipped. A cop. And she'd nearly bashed the wall of the Peabody Museum. He'd probably throw her in jail.

He leaned over and rested his hands on the edge of her window. "Look, lady, are you okay?" His voice soft, yet strong; deep, yet mellow. Steel covered with velvet. A mighty oak capable of standing strong in the fiercest windstorm.

Her dry mouth made it difficult to speak. "Honestly, I'm fine." He raised an eyebrow and Cassandra's heart skipped a beat "It's a female thing. No worries."

"I understand."

Apparently, he didn't, because he leaned closer and scrutinized Cassandra until heat warmed her in a rushing wave of tingles from the pit of her belly to her face. Drawn into the force of his gaze, she stared him down. Confrontation softened to mutual attraction, edged with an indefinable aura of danger. Neither of them wavered. The museum, cemetery, even the chaotic area of the canine's death receded. Samson shifted his feet. The movement brought him closer, and Cassandra's nostrils tingled with a hint of spice.

Her pulse quickened. She licked her lips. Liquid surged in her belly like warm maple syrup. Sweet. Sensuous. So delicious.

Oh, my God. Cassandra, you're making a fool of yourself.

Putting on her best impassive voice, she retorted. "Is there something else, or am I free to go?"

Recoiling as if slapped, the officer stood to his full, intimidating height and motioned her forward with a snap of his hand. "Move along, then."

With a relieved sigh and a pang of regret, Cassandra put her car into gear and moved away from the crime scene. A glance in her rearview mirror showed the officer watching her. He stood statue-still until she turned the corner and disappeared from his sight. Whew. Maybe she'd forget about the museum for today and head for the grocery store.

A tour of a museum viewing the exhibits when her senses roiled in disarray would not work for her. It was more important she return to the house and throw herself into work. Concentrating on what she loved doing might help suppress psychic tendrils winding their way up from where she'd locked them away years before.

Samson watched her drive away. No doubt in his mind, he'd met Jerome and Skye's new neighbor. He'd perceived the trace of magic Jerome had suspected. He guessed her abilities leaned to simpler spells and doubted she performed a mind probe, no matter what Jerome swore he'd felt. Yet, a ripple of energy had disturbed the air around her and hinted at a deeper force.

No. She was probably exactly what she seemed. An exquisite woman exuding an uptight, finishing school demeanor. He'd love to see her hair let down from its tight, twisted bun. He'd noticed the shining sun set off sparks of gold hidden within the strands of white-blond hair. Her sculpted cheeks and full lips faded when compared with her eyes. If she possessed any power, it was contained within those sapphire blue eyes. One glance from her and his heart thrummed a wicked beat.

Dinner suddenly became much more intriguing. If he read Cassandra's schoolmarm manner correctly, she'd be mortified when faced with a reminder of her strange behavior. In consideration of circumstances and surroundings, Samson suppressed the grin threatening his official, stern demeanor.

Okay. Time to get back to business. He hadn't seen the crime scene yet, and now the urge to turn and run burned within him. His feet refused to move. If he turned and walked away, maybe the situation would disappear. By not lending substance to the murder by confirming what he already knew, life might remain normal and there'd be no more death. If...if...if...

Samson clenched his fists and inhaled the crisp morning air before taking those fated steps forward. The officers on scene backed off with obvious relief and left him room to inspect the morbid setting of ritual death. Speculation and suspicion abounded in Salem over anything hinting at the supernatural, but no one wanted the truth. Especially after last year. Samson's report on that unearthly situation had unofficially placed him as the go-to-guy for strange events. Who better than the Chief of Police to discreetly handle witchcraft gone awry or black magic warlocks with ignoble delusions. Keeping Salem safe fell into his job description. He'd admit that. Against purse-snatcher, car thieves, and crazy drivers, maybe, but not an ancient evil that didn't have sense enough to stay dead.

He confirmed his suspicions immediately. It wasn't the ritual, upside down pentagram, or the candles burning to a puddle of wax on the dirt. It wasn't even the butchered body of the poor dog that'd had the misfortune to be chosen as a sacrifice. Nope. Samson knew because the lingering stench of a familiar presence oozed over him the way slime slides in a sewer. His stomach threatened to give up breakfast when the pervasive tendrils of malevolence took hold. Choking back a ragged breath, he stood and backed up. His subconscious registered the worried glance his men exchanged.

It didn't matter. Nothing mattered now except finding out who'd become a receptacle for the evil. It couldn't be Matthew, as he remained a vegetable locked in a high-security mental institute for the criminally insane. His mother, Verity, lived in a downtown apartment. Shriveled, meek, a shadow of her former self, she existed only for her weekly visits to Matthew.

Samson needed to prevent more murders by finding that the evil held enthralled and keep Jerome and Skye away from the action for the sake of their baby. He'd ensure their safety...no matter what.

Chapter Six

Joshua observed the milling crowd at the cemetery. Sickness, disdain, and stimulation churned his gut into a knot. He'd enjoyed killing the mangy mutt. Insistent voices had guided his hands to complete the ritual with precision and surety. All went as expected, and when he'd finished the final step and wiped the blood from his lips, the once distant voices came alive in a roaring crescendo. Joshua pleaded for them to stop and they'd subsided to a more acceptable choir in his mind, leaving a vital piece of Joshua torn to pieces. Inevitable loss crossed his soul and left him changed. More, yet less, than he'd been.

Those same voices now prodded him to move closer. Trying to remain unobtrusive, Joshua wended his way closer to the yellow police tape cordoning off the crime scene. He smiled and let the surge of potent accomplishment pump through him. All this commotion was because of his blood sacrifice. He inhaled the sharp, fear-soaked air and power raged with delight. Heady with the knowledge that his actions incited people to this level of fright, he wondered—if feeding off human terror was this much better than killing a dog, what glory might he experience by killing a human? Recognizing the reality of the situation, the direction of his thoughts horrified Joshua. Killing a dog was one thing. Murdering a human being was a mortal sin. His purpose was to help people find their way to God, not to kill them. Pain streaked through his mind and threatened to drive him to his knees, but an invisible force held him in place. Searing him, the voices cleansed his thoughts of guilt and doubt. A fierce need to extract vengeance on the people of Salem smashed the remaining seeds of Joshua's soul into a memory. He straightened his shoulders, narrowed his eyes, and perused the surrounding people. Filled with renewed purpose, guided by the voices, he gave barely a passing consideration to the ritual's outcome. His attempt to free the spirit of John Hathorne had yielded a cacophony of voices, sure. However, none of them Hathorne.

"Pastor Joshua?"

Though the voice was familiar, Joshua struggled to remember a name. With an effort, he sifted through his brain for the information. Oh, yes. The adulterer. With the sweet taste of revenge raging within him, Joshua wasn't interested in the well-being of a sinner, but he smiled, shook the offered hand, and schooled his features into a facade of interest. "Hello, Eric. How are you?"

Eric twined his hands in the folds of his jacket. "Things are the same at home. Elizabeth gives the kids all her attention and ignores me."

"I'm sure you're exaggerating. You must realize raising children is a time-consuming chore, and Elizabeth deserves your understanding and help."

"She doesn't give me the benefit of understanding, so why should I try to understand her?"

A slow burn began deep in Joshua's gut. This is how society's slide into subversion started. Children raised by morons, who, in turn, grew up to be morons. The decadence of society perpetuated by people like Eric. Joshua turned his lip into a nasty smile.

"I assume you're still indulging in your...ahem...affair."

The blush spreading up Eric's neck was the affirmation Joshua needed for the fires to flame within his mind. Whirling colors of red gave way to darker swirls of black, and the effect sliced through the edges of Joshua's temper. Voices screamed at him.

Sinner.

Adulterer.

KillhimKillhimKillhim

It was difficult to remain calm with the voices screaming from within. To Joshua's warped mind, they made sense. He's killed a dog and look at the result. The cemetery thrummed with terror and confusion from the onlookers. To perform the same ritual on a human might force the people of Salem into awareness of their sins.

He smiled. “Eric, I’ve been meaning to ask for your help with a plumbing problem at the church. Seems the sink in the washroom keeps leaking. I’m sure it’s a simple job.” He shrugged. “But my talents in the plumbing department are shaky and since you’re a plumber by trade...”

Eric’s lip tightened and his eyes narrowed briefly. A heartbeat passed. Joshua’s heart stopped beating and blood turned cold while he waited for the answer.

“Sure, I can probably spare an hour or two tomorrow morning.”

“Yes, that fits into my plans. I hope you don’t mind. I’d understand if you’re too busy.” Joshua slid a hint of sarcasm into his words and was satisfied when the sinner blushed. His guilty conscience, no doubt.

“No, it’s fine. About ten?”

“Perfect. Thanks so much.”

Eric left, and Joshua turned his attention back to the now diminishing crowd. The dog’s body no longer littered the cemetery. Oh, well, the mutt’s death served a crucial purpose. More important matters beckoned Joshua. And he had much to accomplish before tomorrow’s sacrifice.

Samson smiled at Skye while she scooted around the kitchen, preparing lasagna and quite possibly garlic bread. His stomach growled as the spicy scents wafted to where he and Jerome sat drinking beer.

"You guys don't have to stay here keeping me company, you know."

"No, but there's nothing sexier than a pregnant woman in the kitchen." Jerome grinned and slugged back a mouthful of beer, which he promptly snorted back up when the spoon Skye held sailed across the room and struck him in the ear.

"Ow. What'd I do to deserve that?"

"Don't give me your little-boy, who-me? Innocent look. All I can say is it's a good thing I love you so much."

"Gee, you tell a woman she looks sexy and she beans you with a spoon. What's a guy to do to win around here?"

Samson laughed at the light teasing that came so naturally to his two friends. He envied them. He loved his job and found satisfaction in keeping the streets of Salem safe, but his life lacked something. Jerome and Skye's relationship showed him what that elusive something was. Granted, he'd be better off without the sexual energy pumping from them. He'd warned them to dial it down once or twice. Poor Skye had been mortified while Jerome preened like a peacock. Lucky bastard.

Jerome shifted his butt and tapped his fingers on the countertop. Samson knew his friend well enough to expect the coming question. "So, tell us what you found at the cemetery."

The question had hung heavy between the friends since Samson's arrival and he wasn't sure how to answer. A lie wouldn't work, because they'd know he was lying before he finished the sentence. Once he spoke the words, though, the situation became reality. Heck, who was he fooling? The butchered body of the poor dog made it a reality, and keeping silent wouldn't change the facts.

"Samson." Jerome warned quietly. "Don't even think about lying to us."

Samson snorted. "As if." He paused and considered his approach. "Okay. It wasn't a pretty sight. The dog had been butchered ritually, but it might have been the antics of a kid hopped up and drugs and getting a blast by performing an imagined archaic ceremony."

"But it wasn't, was it?" Skye's voice thrummed with resigned dread.

"No. And based on the aura of intent soaking the entire area, I'd say we're dealing with...well, the same entity you encountered last year."

A gasp escaped Skye's lips, and she leaned against the counter, while her face blanched and lips trembled. Jerome was quick to rush to his wife's side and wrap his arm around her shoulder. The face he turned to Samson was one of a man driven by the most basic instinct to protect those he loved. His features hardened with the surety of one used to handling criminals, yet shaken by knowing the power they thought they'd destroyed had returned.

"I hoped...that we'd killed it when Skye used the knife to force the evil from Matthew. We have seen no signs since then."

"An insidious evil that has survived for centuries will not go away so easily."

"Ha! You weren't there, it wasn't easy."

Samson smiled at Skye's comment and the tension eased slightly. "I can imagine it wasn't. I was on cleanup duty, remember." It had taken some fancy paperwork to write that crime scene up with a semblance of reality.

"What do we do now?" Jerome asked.

Straightforward. A trait Samson admired in the men on his force. Technically speaking, Jerome had retired from the police force to stay home with Skye during her pregnancy and attempt a career with his wood carving. So far, he'd sold quite a few carvings and received commissions for more. Jerome's carved wooden statues went for a chunk of money, and Samson didn't doubt Jerome's income so far this year was close to double a regular cop's salary. Oh, well, more power to him.

Samson grimaced. "I have no idea."

Silence reigned while they considered the situation. Samson spoke first. "I think we should avoid this subject during dinner tonight. We don't know anything about this woman and until I investigate her, I think we should keep her outside the loop."

Jerome shifted in his chair and the screeching of wood against floor earned him a raised eyebrow from Skye.

"Sorry." Jerome muttered while throwing a sheepish glance in his wife's direction.

Samson wondered how marriage cowed a man so completely. He snorted and continued. "It seems strange to me that she moves in, next door no less, and this stuff starts happening again."

Skye lathered garlic butter on a loaf of crusty bread and said, "You might be right, but I'll reserve judgment until I meet her."

The singsong tone of the doorbell and the answering bark of Skye and Jerome's dog, Chance, set Skye into motion. "That must be Cassandra, and I don't even have the lasagna in the oven yet." She shooed Jerome and Samson out of the kitchen. "Go let her in. I'll be out in a minute to meet our gorgeous, new neighbor."

Jerome grinned and on his way out remarked, "Hey, no one is as gorgeous as a pregnant woman in the kitchen." He ducked and ran from the wooden bowl on a beeline course for his head.

Chapter Seven

Beyond the mists of Avalon, the world of Britain continued with minor changes in spite of the Roman invasion. Twice attempted with only partial success, Julius Caesar turned his attentions elsewhere and left the Britons alone. Complacency seeped into daily life as the Romans mingled with the Britons. Close to a hundred years passed and the missing girl-child of a conquered chieftain faded into the forgotten realms of the past. As her family withered and died, Ainevar lived an immortal life in Avalon. Over time and through countless age-old ceremonies, the priestesses bound the girl to the land and taught her their ancient ways and rituals. Preparing for the eventual decimation of the Druids by conquering Romans, Seabhac spent his time journaling their history and traditions. His powers and insights being too vast to journal, he knew he'd need another way to preserve them.

Druids lived a long, but not immortal, life, and Seabhac's passing drew nearer with each day's sunrise. Still, the Romans did not return to Britain. On his occasional trip through the mists, his fellow Druids had long since ceased to accept his declaration that the end drew near. Complacently they practiced their craft and lived their lives. Not a one of them saw what Seabhac had envisioned. None made even the slightest attempt to chronicle their traditions, rituals, or beliefs. Druidic philosophy dictated that teaching was an oral practice. Nothing was written down.

Seabhac best efforts did not convince them otherwise. So, he always returned to Avalon, disillusioned, resigned, and alone with his task. Many years he experimented with combining natural elements and focusing his inherent knowledge into a single item in such a manner to enable even an uninitiated novice to retain the Druidic wisdom of the ages. With pointed fervor, he chronicled his findings, weaving magic into each page of his journal. Now was not the time for Druid sensibilities. Time was precious.

Though Ainevar grasped Druid practices and became quite proficient in all aspects of theology, philosophy, healing, ancient law and lunar wisdom, Seabhac knew there'd be no time to teach her the true secret of the Druids; tapping the power of one's own mind to accomplish seemingly impossible feats.

Finally, on a day of sunshine and peace in Avalon, he was successful. With triumph, he admired the knife he'd forged with the help of the Priestesses of Avalon and imbued with Arch-Druid power. The knife that would become the tool of knowledge for Ainevar and ensure the future of all Druids.

But only the mercy of the fates would decide if his plan would bear results.

Excerpt from *Faerie Enchantments and Sorcerer Magick*

Cassandra chewed the last bit of cheesy lasagna on her plate and washed the tasty food down with a mouthful of red wine. With a sigh of satisfaction, she pushed her plate away and smiled at her hostess. "That was the most amazing lasagna I've ever tasted."

Skye laughed, and a light blush crossed her cheeks. Cassandra envied her new neighbor's beauty. Cascades of dark hair, blue eyes, a creamy complexion, a body of toned muscles with a hint of belly to show she was pregnant. Even in her casual attire of jeans and t-shirt, Skye appeared regal. Cassandra sighed and felt gawky in comparison, although she wore a designer pantsuit from one of New York's finest boutiques. Self-consciously, she tugged at her high-collared blouse and shifted in her chair. The movement drew the attention of the police officer she'd hoped never to see again. He fixed his gaze on her as if reading her every thought, which made her even more uncomfortable.

The speculative look in his eyes pierced her finely built defenses and sent a wave of longing rushing through her. His strangely colored eyes stimulated memories she'd buried, ignited feelings that hadn't insinuated themselves in her life for years. She felt helpless against him and compensated by replying to him with a cold, measured tone. Cassandra knew she had sounded bitchy, but better that than to fall into whatever this guy was selling.

She was relieved when Skye stood and cleared the table. It gave her an excuse to escape Samson's pointed scrutiny. Once she was out of range of his overriding magnetism, the heavy sense that had assaulted her upon entering the house, returned. Nausea bubbled in her stomach and rose to her throat. Pervasive and persuasive whispers tempted her, taunted her. Afraid she was losing her mind; Cassandra struggled to remain in the moment and focused her attention on Skye's movements as her hostess scraped food off plates into the garbage. Drawing in the spicy scents of dinner, Cassandra kept herself grounded in the present while the thread of darkness tried to take her elsewhere. Then she heard a single note of music quivering in the darkness. A piano note, deep and mellow, the music grew and blended with the strings of a violin to become a single voice of lyrical, passionate song. With little effort, the music dispelled the darkness and left Cassandra confused. Wrenched apart by two forces battling for supremacy over her emotions.

Based on years of self-denial and hiding her true self from those around her, Cassandra kept a calm facade. So she thought until she realized Skye was darting curious looks in her direction. Ready to give her usual answer of, 'Sorry, just a migraine threatening,' to explain her wavering lapse from reality, it relieved her when Skye continued the polite conversation.

"So, how are you getting along rattling around that vast house by yourself?"

Relieved, Cassandra answered. "My brother does have a flair for the extravagant. It's a good thing he's so rich he can afford to indulge."

Skye smiled. "As a concerned neighbor, I can only hope he has the good taste to match. I can't imagine a house that size being tacky or too flashy?"

"Memnon has impeccable taste—in women, clothes, cars...basically, everything."

"Decorators as well?"

"Some would say so."

Skye cut the chocolate cheesecake and slid a slice onto a waiting plate. "What would others say?

Cassandra paused, unsure how to answer. She'd just met this woman, and it wasn't in Cassandra's character to open up to strangers. But Skye's mellow sense of warmth and understanding drew Cassandra into its comforting embrace. Chipped away at her well-earned ice-queen exterior.

"Others would say my work is too exact and refined, even slightly on the cold side." Cassandra didn't care, because her work was in demand. Cold and refined must be in fashion because she made a lot of money decorating for people who loved the results.

Skye handed Cassandra a couple of plates of cheesecake, grabbed the other two herself, and smiled. "I think you must be good at what you do to exude the refined coldness when you're clearly such a warm, caring person."

Shocked, Cassandra searched Skye's face for signs of sarcasm, because warm and caring were not words normally used to describe her at all. Surprisingly, her hostess looked sincere.

"Don't look so shocked, Cassandra. You might put on a good show with your perfectly fitting designer clothes that do more to hide than reveal, and your tendency to hold people at a distance, but you can't fool everyone." Skye's mouth lifted into a smile, and her eyes twinkled blue. "Now, let's get the men their dessert before they fall into caveman behavior and start beating the table with their fists."

Not sure how Skye had seen through her defenses so easily, Cassandra tried to re-adjust before going back into the dining room. Skye might have breached her carefully constructed walls of self-preservation, but Cassandra wouldn't let Samson see into her thoughts or weaknesses. Her pesky inner voice hinted at the danger in that direction.

Conversation flowed easily and kept to non-threatening subjects. Through it all, Cassandra sensed the underlying thread of darkness interspersed with the occasional hint of the same haunting song that pushed the darkness back. Hard as she tried, she wasn't able to tune out the brief flashes of insight.

"Do you run your own business in New York?" Skye asked.

Her hostess asked the polite question even while Cassandra knew that Skye's mind wandered to her parents and how they'd be pleased with news of the pregnancy.

"You haven't...I mean, have you told your parents about your pregnancy?"

A stab of panic pricked Cassandra, and she searched for the cause. She didn't have to look any further than Jerome's frown and pinched lips.

"No, they're on safari in Africa and out of reach. They'll be home next week."

With Skye so eager to share the pregnancy news with her parents, Jerome's concern scraped across Cassandra's skin. His base, protective instincts came from a gut-deep place. Cassandra shifted, hoping to relieve their intensity. She didn't need to know

Jerome worried for his coming child and ached for his murdered mother.

Samson's thoughts nudged into her overloaded senses, and Cassandra smiled at a remark Skye made about shopping, shipping, or something. Sexual attraction blazed strong and insistent between her and Samson. Damn, why did being in Salem catch her so off guard? And why wouldn't the darned music stop?

"Cassandra?" Samson's voice prodded her back to the conversation.

"Sorry, I was daydreaming." She avoided looking at Samson. Took a chance and glanced his way. Her heart flipped an extra beat. The man was handsome, powerful, and lean. Hard. Body. Wasn't that the proper term for someone like him? If not, it should be. And his face—comparing him to Gerard Butler or Colin Farrell, might begin to do him justice. Oh, she was in trouble. The corner of his mouth lifted in a lazy, knowing smile.

Jeez, everyone around here seemed to know what she was thinking.

"I asked if you planned to do any sightseeing while you're here. Or are you a workaholic?"

Innocent words thrown out in a challenging tone. She enjoyed her work. So what? Cassandra forced herself to breathe, set her features into a mask of indifference, and answered, "Of course I'd love to tour the town while I'm here."

Samson's eyes glimmered with triumph, and Cassandra groaned inwardly. He'd set her up, knowing she'd jump at the chance to prove him wrong.

"Great, I'll be your tour guide. We can start tomorrow."

She had no chance to refuse because Skye spoke. "That's a wonderful idea. No one knows the city better than Samson does. He should though, because he spent years patrolling the streets before becoming Police Chief."

"Personally," Jerome grinned, "I think he slept his way into the job. What else explains him being the youngest Chief ever?"

Skye jumped to Samson's defense. "Jerome, you know he worked hard to earn his position."

The flicker of unease was barely detectable. Would have been, if the inkling of darkness Cassandra had felt all evening hadn't wound itself around her throat and tightened. She covered the choke by faking a cough, but apparently wasn't successful since three pairs of eyes full of questions and suspicion pinned her in place.

"Ummm...piece of cheesecake caught in my throat."

No one spoke, and Cassandra dreaded the silence. They looked at her, waiting, judging, knowing. Receptive rhythms washed over her and the sweet song rang with insistent force. Unlike the darkness that she sensed, this song lured her. Spoke to her. It warded off the suffocating darkness, left her mind clear and balanced. Provided her with sudden prophetic insight.

She flashed on a statement her brother had made when trying to convince her to come to Salem.

"Sis, it's important to me, that's why I'm asking. It's also important for you."

"Important for me? What do you mean?"

Memnon had sipped his McAllen's whisky before answering. "Nothing more than the fact you need a vacation. Going to Salem will give you a chance to work at your own pace and enjoy some off time. No pressure. No hurry."

Cassandra now realized he hadn't glanced at her once while speaking. As usual, she'd ignored her inner voice. He'd been lying to her. Why?

Confused, Cassandra needed to flee this house and people who set her powers of perception into overdrive. She also wanted to call Memnon. Standing, she tripped over the dog lying at her feet and turned to Skye.

"Thanks so much for dinner. It was wonderful. No, no. Don't get up." She waved her hand at Skye, who'd moved to rise. "I can get my sweater on the way out the door." With a nod at Jerome and Samson, she practically ran to the front closet, grabbed her sweater, and tore out the door. She was halfway down the street before she slowed and gave herself a chance to breathe. The haunting song that had taunted her all evening still sounded in her head.

Strangely comforting, the song weaved a blanket of peace and cleared away the perceptive jumble she'd experienced all evening. The crisp night air raised tingling goose bumps on her skin and invigorated her blood to a heart pumping roar. Certainty and a driving desire to confront her brother and discover the truth spurred Cassandra to cover the distance back to her house at a quickened pace. Memnon had no idea what was coming.

Chapter Eight

At first, Samson was too busy watching the retreating butt packed—oh, so snugly—in silky designer pants, to notice the silence in the room. The slamming of the front door jarred him from his contemplation. Self-consciously, he turned to his friends and found them also staring the direction Cassandra had fled.

Attempting to break the awkward moment, he spoke. "I'll be. She up and ran for no reason."

"No. Not for no reason. Didn't you see her face? The anguish in her eyes. She experienced a realization too intense to handle in front of us." Skye narrowed her gaze and stared hard at nothing.

One minute stretched to two, and longer. Samson shot a worried glance at Jerome, who kept a silent vigil over his wife.

"That's it." Skye jumped up, the light of understanding lighting her features. "I'll be right back."

Her hasty flight from the room left a stunned silence, and Samson gulped a mouthful of beer to still his racing heart. He wiped the back of his hand across his mouth. "Am I right in thinking we're not going to be happy with whatever she's doing?"

"Yup." Jerome leaned back in the recliner and sighed. The shadow of worry passed across Jerome's face, and Samson swore silently. Jerome and Skye had been through enough. They deserved happiness and peace.

"Jerome, whatever this is, I'll handle it. You and Skye have more important matters to focus on."

"Thanks pal, but if people's lives depend on what we do, there's no staying out of it for either Skye or myself." He smiled. "We handle whatever the fates throw at us."

Skye's return cut off any reply Samson might have made. He wasn't capable of speech anyway, because when he noticed what Skye held clutched to her chest, his throat closed and his heart stopped beating.

He'd only viewed the book under the glass case where it used to reside in a local store called The Magic Corner. Priceless and purported to be at least 2,000 years old, *Faerie Enchantments and Sorcerer Magick*, supposedly held ancient secrets of powerful magic. The store owner, Nora, had given it to Skye last year with the edict Skye release ownership at the appropriate time.

After using the book in a ceremony to release souls held captive in a ritual knife, Skye had packed it away in her attic. The fact she held it now meant one thing. She meant to hand it to someone just as Nora's instructed. Panic flared and Samson jumped to his feet, waving his hands.

"No, no. You must be mistaken. No way is that thing meant for me."

Skye smiled and sat on the couch beside Jerome. She plopped the leather volume into her lap. "Don't worry, Samson, I'm not giving it to you."

"Oh." Relieved, yet strangely disappointed, he sank into the recliner. "What are you doing with it?" A suspicion rose. He hoped he was wrong.

"It's meant for Cassandra."

"What?" Samson echoed Jerome's exclamation.

"Yes. I wasn't sure at first because I had no idea how I'd know—when, or who—Nora never told me. She just said there'd be no doubt."

"Okay, sweetheart, then how can you be sure now?" Jerome asked the question hovering on Samson's lips.

"The music, and the look on Cassandra's face."

Samson and Jerome shared a quick, doubting glance.

"No, I suppose you two wouldn't have heard it. Actually, I thought you'd turned on the radio when Cassandra and I were in the kitchen, but then I realized the music was coming from inside my head. Cassandra's reaction made it obvious she was hearing the same music. It certainly spooked her. She recovered well, but once I knew that she'd heard the music, it didn't take long to figure out she was the one."

Things were happening too fast. Nothing made sense. Samson hated not being in control. "You can't seriously mean to hand over such a powerful ancient text because you heard music? Skye..." He ran his hands through his hair and stood. "...you know nothing about her. As far as I'm concerned, she's a suspect in the killing of that dog and no way can I let you give her the book."

"Oh, oh." Jerome shifted to the corner of the couch and eyed his wife, who raised an eyebrow and pursed her lips. "You won't let me."

Skye's tone was soft, yet vibrations of raw energy prickled against Samson's skin. Putting up barriers against the minor pain, he admired the ease with which she sent out the darts of magical force. "Hey, dial it down. I'm not the enemy."

Skye's eyebrows lifted with surprise. Blushing, she relaxed, and Samson's pain stopped.

"Sorry. I'm still learning the extent of my abilities."

"I wouldn't want to be on the wrong side of you when you do fulfill your potential. Having said that, I still don't think you should hand something so valuable to a stranger."

"Why not? Nora gave the book to me during our first meeting. It's what works, Samson. The book guides the guardian. It's not my decision."

Frustrated, Samson tried to think of a way to reason with Skye. Jerome offered a solution.

"Hon, why not wait for a day and give Samson a chance to run a check on Cassandra?" He lifted Skye's hand and gave a squeeze. "What harm in waiting one day?"

Skye struggled with Samson's request to wait before handing such an important object to a stranger. Logic won. Or possibly the pleading look in Jerome's eyes to keep the peace between his wife and best friend.

"Fine. You've got until tomorrow night to dig up any dirt you seem to think you'll find. Then I march up the street and hand it to her with my blessing."

"Deal. Besides, what makes you think she'll even accept the book? Especially since she spooked at any mention of witches or magic."

"Then I'll have to convince her, won't I?"

The possibility of a good challenge gleamed in Skye's blue eyes, and Samson felt sorry for Cassandra. The woman had no inkling of what was in store for her.

Chapter Nine

Cassandra worked until the dark of night covered Salem and stilled the ocean waves to a slow, mellow ripple. Upon returning to Memnon's house, she'd called her brother and now waited for his return call. Frantic with unwanted thoughts, she didn't notice the lengthening of shadows creeping across the wooden planked floors of the house. Nocturnal creatures hoo-hoo'd and chirp-chirped outside the open windows. To Cassandra, the night-voices were nothing more than a distant distraction.

Looking down at the sketch she'd made of the living room, she snorted and ripped the page from her book. What drivel. An amateur would have done a better job. Pursing her lips, she concentrated on the blank page in front of her. Nothing. Her jumbled mind refused to create.

Sketchbook in hand, she stood and stretched her stiffening legs. Her brain refused to cooperate. It kept returning to the wave of magic she'd felt rolling off Jerome, Skye and Samson earlier. Which of them had been giving off the pervasive sense of darkness? And where had the lyrical music come from? Haunting. Sensual. Calming.

"No." She threw the sketchbook down and paced the room. "I will not be lured into any of this." Even as she made the declaration, the part of her that had lain stagnant for so many years acknowledged the truth.

She needed Memnon. She picked up her cell phone the same instant it chimed the familiar Fur Elise tune alerting her someone was calling. Since it was the middle of the night, Memnon must be returning her call. Filled with trepidation, not knowing if she wanted the answers to the questions she needed to ask, she answered.

"Hello."

"Hi, Cassandra. What's wrong? I listened to your garbled message about evil, music, lasagna...I'm sorry. None of it made sense."

"Really. Well, welcome to my world. Memnon, I need to know why I'm here." She nibbled her lower lip and scrunched her hand around the phone, not sure she wanted the answer.

Silence. Dead air weighed the distance between them.

"I don't know what you mean. Has something happened?"

His tone lacked conviction and confirmed Cassandra's suspicions. She whispered into the phone, "You know. You can see things...like I used to."

"Like you still can." His voice boomed over the phone. Censuring her. Chastising her.

"NO."

Memnon sighed. "Fine. Deny it. It's not up to me to make you understand."

A pang of guilt stabbed Cassandra. She hated upsetting her brother. A part of her ached to confide in him; share the guilt eating away at her; lean on him and cry for the loss of a child's innocence and the loss of their parents. But she couldn't. The words stuck in her throat and her heart pumped with denial. She struggled to direct the conversation back to him.

"Why, during all these years, haven't you told me that you," she had trouble even saying it, "have powers?"

Memnon laughed. A sound heavy with bitterness and regret. "I hated the thought of you hating me for what I am."

"Oh, Memnon, I'd never hate you. You're my big brother and you've always supported me."

"I couldn't confide in you, Cassie. After the accident, any talk of magic or prophecy sent you into such a state of grief. I worried about your sanity. So, I kept my secret."

Cassandra remembered how fragile she'd been after their parent's deaths and realized the truth of what Memnon was saying. Maybe he'd made the right choice. "What about after? Once time had passed, you should have told me."

"Cassie, I would have if I thought you capable of handling the truth."

Cassandra bristled. "I'm handling it now, aren't I?"

Memnon laughed. This time it was filled with amusement and love. "Oh, my prickly little sister, I suppose you are. But mainly because I sent you to Salem with no warning of what awaited you."

"Why, exactly, am I here?"

"I have no idea. I had a hunch."

"So you bought a house and bribed me into coming all the way to Salem to decorate said house, based on a hunch."

"I'm paying you, and quite a lot more than you're worth, I might add."

"Ha. It's a bribe to get me to stay here."

"Is it working?"

Cassandra considered her recently inflated bank account and the plans she had for the money. She hadn't held Memnon to his one million dollar offer, but she'd doubled her usual fee. She sighed and imagined the Alaskan cruise and the snazzy, midnight blue BMW M6 Coupe she'd been eyeing. Were they worth going through whatever waited for her if she stayed in Salem?

"I guess it's working. Besides, I gave my word."

"Good. I'm glad. So, tell me, what has you up this time of night bothering your big brother?"

"I...it's hard to explain."

"Try. What else do you have to do at this ungodly hour?"

"Work, of course." She imagined Memnon rolling his eyes and stifled a laugh. He nagged her constantly for being a workaholic. Samson had used that word to describe her earlier as well. Without intention, her thoughts turned to Samson's eyes that sparkled with otherworldly colors. Some would consider the feature feminine, if he wasn't so damned masculine.

"Hmm, I'm sensing a strange vibe, sis. I'm getting downright hot here, so whatever, or whoever, it is, stop."

Embarrassed, Cassandra immediately shuffled all thoughts of Samson to the back of her mind. Attempting to distract Memnon from getting too inquisitive, she jumped into work talk. "So, I've got sketches done for all the rooms. I can send them to you, and once you've okay'd them, I can hire painters and order furniture."

"You don't need my go ahead. I trust your judgment."

"If you're going to live here, you really should have a say in the designing."

"Cassandra. I love your work. I trust you. You've got my credit card and no limit, so decorate the way you'd want it if you were living there, and I'll be happy."

"Wow, I wish all my clients were as amicable—and as generous." She started imagining the burgundy and rose color scheme she'd use in the living room.

It wasn't until a couple of minutes later, Cassandra realized Memnon hadn't pushed to learn the cause of her late night, frantic phone call. Probably a good thing, cause she wasn't sure how she'd describe what had driven her from Skye and Jerome's house earlier.

Despite the late hour, Samson placed a call to an F.B.I. acquaintance of his. Agent Jack Johnson had stormed into the Salem police station and demanded cooperation on a kidnapping six months earlier. Keeping curious neighbors away from the van parked on the street and the use of a cell overnight when they caught the kidnapper had been the extent of Samson's involvement, but Jack had said anytime Samson needed a favor, Jack owed him one.

Because Jack's *the F.B.I. is better than local law* attitude pissed Samson off, he'd never collected on the debt. Now he would. After exchanging pleasantries, Samson gave a quick explanation of what he wanted.

"That's a simple request. Simple enough, you should have no problem doing it yourself. What's the catch?"

"Let's just say I want a thorough search and you have access to resources I don't. Databases and records outside the normal avenues."

"Outside...okay, let's make sure our idea of outside normal avenues coincides."

Samson paused in consideration. How to explain anything Jack turned up might be paranormal without sounding like a total psycho. "Ummm, anything unusual or questionable that you may turn up. Any incident shuffled under the rug because no one can explain or understand it. That kind of information."

Samson thought Jack might refuse, but he didn't. "Figures. I mean, considering the town we're talking about, and all. But let me get the spelling right, it's C-a-s-s-a-n-d-r-a R-a-i-n-e-s."

"Yup."

"And you want this right away?"

"The sooner the better."

"You realize I'll have to cancel a date with a sexy broad with big tits to do this. So we won't be even. No, my friend, you'll owe me big-time."

Samson ground his teeth and replied, "My heart aches for you, and I do appreciate the sacrifice."

"You can appreciate it by sending me one of those police baseball caps with the witch crest. Oh, and a bottle of an expensive sherry I hear you're so good at choosing."

"A suck-up gift for your lady friend?"

"You got it. I'll let her think I chose and paid for the best," Jack said.

Big surprise.

"Of course. I'll send them out first thing in the morning."

"Hopefully, I'll have something for you by then. Bye."

Jack hung up and Samson figured he'd better get some sleep since it was 1:00 am.

He tugged off his clothes and crawled into bed, his brain full of thoughts from the busy day. He didn't think he'd be able to sleep and when he finally drifted off, wished he hadn't.

Chapter Ten

Barely aware of the passage of time, Samson drifted on the edges of sleep until he lost all sense of awareness between reality and fantasy. One minute he was sprawled on his bed, the next, standing on a high cliff with the wind whipping from the ocean below. With a moan, he struggled to escape from the dream, but a part of him longed for the salty scent of the sea and the exhilaration of breathing nature's wildness on a craggy cliff top.

In a blast of understanding, he understood his name to be Seabhac, his realm—the earth, skies, and sea. Rain slashed across his face, yet he reveled in the raging storms sweeping power. Waves smashed themselves upon the rocks far below and the spray of their reckless act smacked him with icy cold pellets. Surges of energy roared through him, a last blast of his fading Druid power.

One hundred years since Julius Caesar's second invasion and the knowing of his prediction coming true had called Seabhac through the mists of Avalon. Not surprising, but heart wrenching nonetheless, he'd found the bloody slaughter of many people. Simple peasants cowed into submission and tribal kings either surrendered or killed. Through tales spoken in hushed tones from those left alive, Seabhac had learned of the Roman Claudius's distrust of Druid political and administrative influence. His vow that spurred the Roman into searching the land and killing all Druids in a public and torturous manner.

Seabhac's heart wept with the slaughter. Using his mask of invisibility, he'd waded in the carnage hoping to find one remaining Druid, but the Romans had gutted and hung them in warning to any who might yet follow the old-ways. Everywhere he went, he heard whispered tales of Claudius's Druid-killer. Settled in Camulodunum, Claudius had sent his distinguished and brutal commander, Vespasian, to annihilate the Druids. Purported to be immortal, therefore undefeatable, Vespasian had hacked a swath of death through Britain.

Laden with anguish and mourning the deaths of so many he'd once called friend, Seabhac came to stand upon the steep, chalk cliffs of Dover. Waiting. Knowing the confrontation would be in such a fitting place of towering cliffs. Guardians against approaching enemies. Citadels of time.

Seabhac raised his arms while the storm raged around him. He shouted at the heavens. "I am Seabhac, Arch-Druid and Guardian of the Knowledge. My time of transformation approaches and I beseech the Powers to instill within me the ability to send my soul in another direction. Though my physical body dies, I cannot ascend yet. If I do so, the Druids and all we have studied and learned will no longer exist. Through the decades in Avalon, and against all tradition, I have written the ancient Druid knowledge. Strike me down for this if you so desire, but as Guardian of the Knowledge, it is my duty, nay, my right to protect what has been spoken, but never allowed into written word.

"If I must die, let my soul give life to the journal that holds all. Let me preserve the power until someone deserving of the responsibility appears. Grant me this request or evil will wreak itself upon this land and into the distant future with retribution never before seen. Only Druid knowledge is able to challenge the coming tide of chaos and death."

The earth beneath him undulated. He flew into the air and his body crashed down upon the rocks. Tossed in such a reckless display of petulant power, Seabhac feared his request had been in vain and his death was imminent.

Instead, while dirt and rock rumbled beneath his prone body, Seabhac saw the outline of a person standing on the grassy area edging the cliffs. A flash of lightning streaked across the sky and speared the man in a display of sparks and dancing jags of light. The intruder raised his arms to the storm, and his laughter echoed deep within the deafening roar of slashing rain, rumbling thunder, and jagged lightning.

Seabhac, Arch-Druid, a man seasoned to the magic of other worldly realms and power beyond imagination, shivered with dread.

The man, imbued with the force of lightning shot from above, taunted him. "You think to rule the world when it is not your right. The Romans claim that right. We are superior in might, ability, and thought."

Seabhac's pulse raced in time with the raging wind as he rose, dusted himself off, and turned to face the one who spoke.

The infamous Vespasian. Druid-killer.

Samson woke in a cold sweat with his heart pounding in his chest. "Jesus." He jumped from his bed and stood naked, letting the cool night air refresh him.

What the hell kind of dream was that? Not a dream. Too real.

His pulse still rushed with the fierce taste of fear at the remembrance of the earth trembling beneath him. A sob racked Samson at the memory—Seabhac's memory—of watching family and friends slaughtered and everything destroyed so callously. It was more than Samson could have borne.

He took a shuddering breath. Paced his room. Pondered the dream.

The witch trials dream had been bad, but this one...holy shit.

The heavy cloak of evil still stifled his breathing. Samson stared out his window at the undulating waves of the inky-dark ocean waters.

He loved being near the ocean and never once regretted trading in the apartment over the garage at his parent's house for his condominium. On nostalgic occasions, a visit home for Sunday dinner filled the void. He sighed and wondered what his parents would say about the vivid dreams stalking his sleep.

How was a Druid in early Britain connected to the evil stalking Salem? Other than the book, of course, which had roots in Druidry. But he didn't think it was that old. Was it?

What he wouldn't give for a simple robbery or drunk driver. He wasn't equipped to handle all this ancient evil, end-of-world stuff. Sure, his heightened level of sensory perception picked up a person's thoughts. He read moods, could coax a dying flower into an extended life, and mingle with the occasional pixie. This current situation presented complex magic and ritual way beyond his level of knowledge.

He needed to see the book. According to legend, it held history within its pages and might provide desperately required answers. His problem would be talking Skye into handing the book to him without revealing his dreams.

Exhaustion took over. Conflicting thoughts and ideas drove Samson back to bed, hoping for a few hours of uninterrupted sleep. As he drifted into that hazy state between wakefulness and sleep, a voice whispered in a far off distance.

You are The Chosen.

Chapter Eleven

Joshua woke to dimly lit surroundings, an acrid odor tickling nostrils and something cold and hard digging into his back. What the...

He remembered. He'd come to the basement last night to prepare for Eric's arrival.

Joshua reached out to touch Judge Hathorne's journal. He'd nearly memorized the pages of rambling scribbles on parchment, each word devoted to rituals considered unholy in context, but the motivation behind each word, pure of soul. Hathorne had so desperately wanted to save souls and put his in danger by practicing the witchcraft he decried. He, Joshua Parris, could do no less.

Dusting himself off and shivering in the cold room, he stood and stretched. He'd prepared everything for today's sacrifice. Yet a nagging bit of doubt wiggled in the back of his mind. The dog sacrifice should have returned Hathorne's soul to a state of being—it hadn't. Joshua's actions had let loose a bevy of voices. They prodded him constantly. Even now, they whispered to him the promise of fulfillment. He climbed the stairs and listened to their assurances that Hathorne knew of Joshua's sacrifice and applauded him his bravery and dedication to the word of the Lord.

Joshua opened the basement door and gasped at the assault of heat compared with the cold he left. The change in temperature jolted him and created a brief second of clarity. Conscience flooded with doubt. But it didn't last. The voices screamed at him. Overwhelmed him. Within that moment, Joshua felt small and detached from his body. An observer watching his actions from afar. Fright froze his blood, but the voices soothed him into calmness.

Certainty replaced doubt, and with Eric arriving anytime, things would get even better. Lowly canine blood didn't compare to human blood.

Samson cursed the traffic and laid a hand on his horn again, knowing no good would come of such an action, but it made him feel better. He'd never understand why people insisted on slowing their vehicle to watch someone change a tire.

Come on. Get moving.

He glanced at the bottle of 1988 Bruichladdich Oloroso sherry on the seat beside him. Samson hoped Jack found nothing suspicious in Cassandra's life, because, considering the ties between the past and the book, someone needed to control the ancient text. It would not be Skye, so it might as well be Cassandra. He certainly didn't want the responsibility.

Or did he?

He tried to imagine having all the knowledge of the Druids in his hands. Forgotten rituals, age-old wisdom that had led to a group of people still held in legend even today. Centuries after their destruction. Sure, Druidry had made a comeback, but in Samson's opinion, they barely touched the surface of Druid craft. To compare modern day dabbling in the craft to ancient knowledge was like comparing a puddle to an ocean. Last night's dream gave him insight. Being Seabhac and feeling the power surging through his blood, commanding the elements at will...he'd felt nothing to compare. And he was no amateur when it came to magic. He decided it's better to leave that kind of power to someone less jaded. Personally, he'd be tempted to use the power to wipe out every snot-nosed, lying, cheating, abusive, drunk-driving jerk in Salem.

Or he might be altruistic and do nothing more than use the magic to rid the world of the evil that threatened Salem.

He sighed, knowing he had little choice. Keeping Salem safe fell on the list of his responsibilities. Then again, he didn't relish telling Skye what to do with the book. No way. Just the thought of facing her hormonal indignation set his hand to banging on his horn again. Maybe he'd let Skye give it to Cassandra. It's what she wanted, and who's to say Samson wasn't letting his ego color his desires.

A waft of warm air brushed across his face and a voice whispered, "You are The Chosen."

The Chosen. Damn, that voice again.

Samson didn't want to ponder the meaning of such a mysterious statement and with the traffic clearing, he ignored it to pay attention to the road. Unfortunately, the voice rang through him, not giving up its insistent chant. So, with a deep sense of inevitability, Samson turned towards Winter Island Rd. instead of his condominium. It wouldn't hurt to check if Skye and Jerome were home. If so, he'd think of a way to talk Skye into letting him borrow the book.

He wheeled his hybrid Hummer into their driveway and noticed the car gone.

Hmm, even better. The book should be in the attic, stashed in an old trunk.

He'd read it and if he heard their car; he'd return it to the trunk and make for the kitchen where he'd grab a beer and sit before they got in the door. Neither of them would think anything of finding him there. Samson and Jerome's shared a long history and treated each other's homes as theirs.

Of course, as life dictates, good intentions often go unfulfilled and once Samson lifted the trunk lid and spied the book, caution vanished. He'd have been better off trying to stop the sun from shining than trying to halt the rush of emotion running through him. A hot flush of familiar, unexplainable senses. Similar to one of those dreams you wake from but can't remember, though it tickles the borders of your memory. A flash here, a color there. Vague sensations eluding you the more you struggle to remember.

He touched the leather cover and music filled him. Sweet and calming, it tugged at him. Prodded him gently to a place that existed, yet didn't.

The past maybe. Or another realm in time. He longed to...

"Samson."

Skye's voice broke him from the trance induced state, and he dropped the book. Dust billowed up, tickled his nose, and made him sneeze. Between sneezes and through watery eyes, he noticed Skye standing in the attic's doorway with her arms crossed over her chest. Her foot tapped. Not a good sign. Jerome stood behind her, a huge *you're in trouble now* grin pasted on his face.

Well, there went his intentions of running downstairs and pretending to await their arrival home. Okay, so he'd play cool instead. He finished his last sneezed and stood to face them with a bravado he didn't feel.

"You're home."

"You're home. That's all you can say? I thought we were friends, so why the need to sneak in here?"

Jerome put a hand on Skye's shoulder and squeezed. "Give the poor guy a chance to talk." He narrowed his gaze at Samson. "I'm sure he has a good explanation."

"I don't...I do...I mean, when your car approached I was supposed to race for the kitchen before you found me."

Skye's mouth dropped open, and she gave a strangled gasp. "Oh, well, yes, I can understand how that would have been much better. Sure, as long as we didn't know you'd been sneaking around our attic and..."

She stopped mid-sentence and Samson stood waiting for her castigation to continue. He deserved it. He should have trusted his friends to help him. He should have told them his dreams. They would have understood his need to see the book. Yeah, right.

He realized Skye had become deathly still. Head tilted to the side as if listening to a far off melody heard by her alone. Jerome waved his hand in front of her face and frowned when she didn't respond.

Shit. Samson would never forgive himself if his underhanded act resulted in danger for Skye and her unborn child. He stepped forward, but stopped when Skye broke from her state of oblivion and whispered, "Do you hear the music?"

"Music?" She caught him off guard. Music had prompted Skye's vow to hand the book to Cassandra. He didn't want the responsibility.

You are The Chosen.

Ignoring the persistent voice, he explained. "I wanted to sneak a quick glance. Maybe read a few pages and get an idea if the ritualistic killing of the dog has anything to do with last year's events."

Jerome snorted. "Right. That won't work and you know it, so why try to lie."

Skye laughed. The soft, gentle chortle fluttered around attic like a tiny bird's wings. When she spoke, her velvety voice brimmed with love and understanding. "He's lying because he's afraid." She raised her hand to stop Samson's denial. "You can't fool Jerome and I think you're beginning to realize there's no way can you can dupe me, so you might as well tell us what's going on."

Samson turned to Jerome for support and found none. His friend dipped his chin and pointed at Skye. "What she said."

"Crap." Samson swore, resigned to the inevitable.

"Good, now that's settled, let's go have tea and talk. Oh, and bring the book." Without waiting for a response, Skye turned and trounced down the stairs, leaving Samson and Jerome to follow. With a shrug, Jerome followed his wife. Samson sighed and cursed his decision to come to this dad blasted, dusty attic for a dad blasted, cursed book. He received an answer with the warming sensation in his hands that originated from the book. Tempted to drop the thing on the floor and run for the front door, Samson instead chose to follow Skye and Jerome with book in hand. Skye had spoken, and no way did he want to be the one to piss her off.

Cassandra had spent a restless night. No, a nightmare-filled, emotion-racked night, to be exact.

Draining the last of her coffee from a mug, she poured herself another and set the coffeepot back in place to keep warm. With a sigh, she used her free hand to rub her stiff neck as she stared out the kitchen window. Carpeted with lush green grass, hedged by a plant with reddish-copper, narrow leaves, and alive with birds, the backyard exuded warmth and serenity. So unlike the state of her emotions.

She blamed her restlessness and re-awakening of unwanted senses on her presence in Salem. No, she'd blame Memnon.

He'd coerced her into coming here. He'd lied to her for years about his powers and his reasons for sending her to this place, which he still hadn't made clear.

Witch capital of the world. Humph! Sure, brother dear, and while you're at it, why not kick me when I'm down?

Visions of her dreams prodded her away from the window, set her on an agitated stride across the kitchen floor, and back again. She couldn't shake the sense of something wrong. Based on experience, she guessed her dreams held the answer. She'd been young the last time visions disrupted her life and her interpretation of them had come from a child's view of the world. Not surprisingly, no one had believed her. Damn! After years of shutting herself off, Cassandra's dreams left her no choice but to pay attention.

Visions of blue eyes swirling with elusive depths of purple turned her thoughts to Samson. Breathtaking—in a masculine way—Cassandra would be shocked if he were single. Though, if he wasn't, he wouldn't have been alone at last night's dinner, much less offered to show her around town. Then again, maybe he would have. Some men she'd dated recently, probably weren't capable of spelling the word commitment, let alone know its meaning.

With a sigh for memories best forgotten, Cassandra filled her cup, grabbed a couple of the double-chocolate, macadamia nut cookies she loved so much, and headed for the bedroom. The master suite boasted a small balcony overlooking the backyard and gave a magnificent view of the rocky shore leading to the ocean beyond. No better place to connect with nature and search the inner working of her clouded mind.

Where to begin?

First, she pulled the cushion off one of the lounge chairs and threw it down. She settled cross-legged on the cushion and took a couple of deep breaths to relax the shoulders that had taken residence up around her ears. The caffeine hadn't been a good idea for meditation purposes, but it was too late now, so she'd have to adapt.

She concentrated on letting loose all the knots in her body and didn't stop the mind-focus until everything let go. The sensation was similar to a balloon deflating, but in slow motion. Once relaxed, she cleared her mind of all thoughts and led her focus to last night's dreams.

Too easy. After years of suppression, her senses had been waiting for this moment of freedom. She trembled when the memories of her dream assaulted her. The face of a man, ever changing. Morphing from one set of features to another. Reborn into a new life. No, that wasn't quite right. Cassandra shifted and tried to grasp the vision hovering on the fringes of her mind. A dark cloud. Yes. The beginning. Adrift in the darkness, a cloud shifting within nothingness.

Suddenly, Cassandra realized a vision replaced the memories of last night's dream. Her chest heaved with the force of disconnection. She hovered, suspended in a place with no substance, no confines. She floated in a place so vast her presence was no more than a mere speck. She squinted at the distant horizon, saw vivid specks of bright lights surrounded by black. The panorama continued into infinity.

Realization hit and she panicked. Her breath caught in her lungs, causing her to choke. The Universe. Within her mind, she floated through the universe.

Hold on. Don't lose your place, Cassandra.

She gave up fighting it and let herself enjoy the amazing sensation. Until the cloud appeared again. Its vaporous substance shifted and undulated in a dark dance distorting the stars beyond. The cloud's presence stifled her, gagged her. Unable to handle the pressure any longer, the cloud formed into a spear and shot away. As Cassandra watched its retreat, she realized it headed toward Earth, far in the distance.

With a wrench, she slammed into a jagged cliff. On the sidelines of a battle between two men. No, not men. The rigid, war-ravaged features and dark, dead eyes of the one in Roman clothing attested his lack of morals and humanity. The other man radiated such pure intent and power he had to be more than mortal. Suddenly, the cloud-spear raced from the heavens and pierced the Roman, who glowed with a darkness lit from within. Before Cassandra saw the outcome of the battle, a maelstrom took hold of her mind and whirled her with a ripping fury. Fighting the sense of being shredded into pieces, she watched, as faces, places, and events, all whipped past her at a breathless speed. She experienced emotions of loss and love at a blinding, withering pace and when she wasn't able to handle anymore, time slowed and her vision cleared.

In a dingy room rested a haggard man with a pinched face who held a bloody knife in hand. The body of another man slipped to the floor to lie in an obscene portrayal of death. The eyes of the man holding the knife drew Cassandra's attention. The Roman's eyes. She gasped and found herself racing again through time. She slammed into the present and stared into piercing, empty eyes.

The same ones she'd seen across the span of centuries that her vision had taken her.

This time the man, or creature, wore the clothes of a clergyman. Cassandra's heart pumped fiercely. Blood raced through her. She wasn't religious and didn't understand the differences between priests, ministers, bishops, monks, deacons...whatever. She did know that this man wore a white collar, casual dress shirt, and khaki pants.

He turned. His gaze burned into Cassandra.

Nausea threatened. His face twisted into a sneer and gave way to flashes of blood dripping from a cross. The deep-red substance snaked a path across the floor and collected in a darkening pool at the feet of an unsuspecting person.

The shoes? Knowledge blasted trough Cassandra with the force of a whirlwind. Her favorite pair of Manolo Blahniks.

A scream formed in Cassandra's throat, but didn't break free because everything went blank. She fought for awareness. She struggled to regain her balance. She tumbled and fell until waking with a jolt on the bedroom balcony. She scrambled to her feet, tried to forget the fiasco of shattered, scary visions, and ran to the railing to draw in a lungful of brisk ocean air.

Damn! I don't want to go through this again.

Chapter Twelve

Samson stared at the pages of the book lying open on the kitchen table. He raised an eyebrow at Skye. Her face registered disbelief and confusion. Not a good sign. She must be seeing the same thing as he was. Nothing. Every page of the book, *Faerie Enchantments and Sorcerer Magick*, was blank.

"I don't understand." Skye stammered. "You saw, Jerome, these pages were full of scribbling and sketches. How can they be blank now?"

Jerome shook his head. "You got me."

Frustration flamed in Samson. To be so close to the book and possible answers and then be thwarted. He shifted his butt in his chair. "I don't understand. The book saved your Dad, it helped you rid Matthew of the evil that possessed him, and showed you how to bind the knife to prevent it from trapping any more souls. So why does it choose now to go blank?"

Skye gently closed the book and rested her hands on top of the scarred leather cover. "I'm sorry, Samson. My guess is I was right about passing the book to Cassandra. Plainly, it won't give any information to you, despite what your dreams might have indicated."

With coercion, Samson had shared his dreams with Skye and Jerome.

Who better qualified to give advice and guidance? It didn't mean they had to get involved in anything dangerous. That would be his responsibility.

"Any idea what the voice meant when it said I was the Chosen?"

"It must mean something other than becoming the holder of the book."

Samson sighed. This would not be easy. "Then why did the music play for me?"

"What?" Skye and Jerome spoke in unison.

"You heard music. When?" Skye's glaring expression made Samson shift uncomfortably and he wished he hadn't admitted to hearing music.

"Upstairs, when I touched the book."

"Oh, this so does not make sense." Skye shoved herself back from the table, stood, and paced the kitchen floor, mumbling.

"I know the book is meant for Cassandra, so you shouldn't have heard anything. Of course, since the pages are blank, it's no good to her, so I don't know..."

Jerome moved to his wife and laid his hand on her shoulder. "Sweetheart, there is a simple answer."

"There's nothing simple about this situation, but go ahead and enlighten me."

"A duo guardianship."

"A..." Skye frowned. "I don't know if that's even possible." She threw up her hands. "I know nothing about the book. As for the knife, our ancestors supposedly forged it during the witch trials as a way to transfer power from one witch to another. I have a feeling that's actually when the replica knife was forged. You know, the knife that messed up Verity's ritual so long ago."

Samson spared a quick glance at Jerome, knowing he'd recognize the pain that shadowed his friend's face whenever there was mention of his mother's death.

Skye turned the force of her deep blue eyes on Samson, and he felt the full weight of her power. A power that had matured as recent as last year when Skye moved to Salem and found herself confronted with an age-old evil. If Samson believed his inner radar, an evil older than imagined.

"Now we know this Seabhac wrote the journal, but did you dream anything about the knife?" Skye asked.

"No. All I know is that Seabhac wrote a journal, but there's no way to be certain it was this one." He pointed at the book. "Anyway, who's to say the dream wasn't an over-active imagination instigated by too much beer and wine at dinner and the ritualistic killing of the dog? Seriously, I do have quite an imagination." He said the words, not believing them for a second. Last night's dream had been too real. Too pumped with emotion and vivid senses.

"Nice try, Samson, but it won't work."

Skye turned to Jerome and said, "Has he always been this stubborn and independent?"

"Pretty much. I remember once, shortly after his parents took me in, he so desperately believed he could fly."

Samson groaned. He thought he'd left that embarrassing moment in the past. Leave it to his best friend never to let him forget.

Jerome ignored him and continued. "He took his mom's umbrella, went outside and climbed the woodshed roof. Barely four feet off the ground, it was high enough for what he wanted. Anyway, he opened the umbrella and jumped off the roof. When he hit the ground with a thud, I figured he was done. But no, not our Samson. He spent all afternoon jumping off that roof, each time swearing that this would be the time he'd fly."

Skye laughed. "Didn't you try to stop him?"

"Sure I did. That's where the stubborn comes in. No way was he stopping until he flew and I finally gave up and left him to it."

"So," Skye turned to Samson with an innocent smile, "did you ever manage to fly?"

"I'll never tell."

"Told you. Stubborn as well as cantankerous." Jerome's smile turned to consideration. "What I find most fascinating about the whole dream thing is Seabhac's remarks about his time of transformation, sending his soul another direction, and giving the journal life." All three of them stared down at the journal lying so innocently on the kitchen table. "What did he mean?"

Skye frowned. "We need more information on this situation." She smacked Jerome when he rolled his eyes. "Situation works as a euphemism." She shivered. "I don't want to call it what it is."

Samson agreed. "I understand. If we give it a name, we give it life and substance."

Skye gave him a tremulous smile. "Kind of. Yes."

"Fine. I'll keep you guys updated on whatever happens. Currently, we can't do much of anything. The book is blank. We've got a butchered dog and a halfway believable dream about a Druid who lived centuries ago." He shook his head. "It might all be a coincidence or the book would be letting us know something. Wouldn't it?"

Skye stared at the journal on the table, hoping for answers. Time stretched. A fly buzzed around Samson's face until he swatted it away. The rolling waves of the nearby ocean wafted through the open window. Jerome shifted in his chair. The ensuing squeak made him shoot a sheepish glance at Skye.

When Skye finally spoke, the jolt of her voice sent Samson's taut emotions into a rush of adrenaline. "I don't think we can make any decisions or judgments until we see how the book responds to Cassandra."

On cue, Samson's phone rang. He grabbed it from his pocket, glanced at call display, and pushed the speaker button. "Hello."

Jack's voice sounded tinny on the speaker. "I hope you've got the bottle of sherry on its way."

"I'm leaving for the FedEx office, as we speak. What have you got for me?"

The rustle of paper came across the phone line. A dead minute of heavy silence. "Look, I'm sure you get into some weird stuff, you know, living in Salem and all."

Samson's throat constricted, and he glanced at Jerome and Skye, who both leaned forward to overhear the conversation better.

"Go on." He prompted, knowing he'd seen and heard things stranger than anything Jack's imagination could cook up. He didn't want the strange stuff to apply to Cassandra.

"You don't really believe any of this hocus pocus, witchcraft and devil stuff, do you?"

Samson expelled a breath and counted to five. He didn't have the patience to count to ten. "Spill it, Jack, or this sherry will find a home on my shelf."

"Okay, okay. Your lady friend..."

"She's not mine."

Skye slapped his arm and shushed him.

"Fine. This woman, Cassandra Raines, was normal until age six."

"Normal?" Samson asked, resenting Jack's judgmental tone.

"Ya. Normal. As in playing with dolls, dressing like a princess for Halloween, following her older brother around like a brat...the usual stuff girls do. Anyway, then the stories started."

"What kind of stories?"

"Everything. Teachers complained she disrupted classes with tales of ghosts floating around the room, neighbors stopped letting her play with their kids because she kept scaring them with predictions of sickness and death."

"Fine. Kids tell stories. What's the big deal?"

"Well—and I'm sure this is mere coincidence—it seems quite a few of her predictions came true. By the time she was eight, her parents had moved five times."

"Moved. Why?"

"No one wanted to be around her, and every time something went wrong, Cassandra suffered the blame. The worst case was when a teenage girl ran away from home and they found her in a dumpster not five miles from her home."

"Yes, but you can't blame a child for the actions of some hormonal teenager." Samson was having a hard time understanding how anyone could hold a child accountable for events so much that her parents had to move regularly.

"They blamed her because she told the parents that their daughter was going to run, and then she stated quite clearly, in front of a roomful of people at a Christmas party no less, that the girl would be found dead in a dumpster. She told the tale from beginning to end and then it came true. People thought Cassandra had heard the perpetrator planning the murder and knew more than she let on. No one believed she'd seen it in a dream and was merely telling what she'd seen." Jack snorted. "Can't say as I blame them. The kid had to know the killer. How else was she able to predict the murder?"

Samson imagined one or two ways, but didn't bother to enlighten Jack. Certain people wouldn't see their hand in front of their face if they made their mind up. It didn't exist. "So, is that all?"

"Heck, no. It gets better."

Papers scratched in the background, and Jack mumbled about sloppy police reports.

"Ah ha. Here we go. They didn't believe her. According to the police report, when she was eight, she woke screaming one night and told her parents that she'd seen them burning in the flames of a car crash. However hard she tried to convince them, they left her and her brother with a babysitter and went on a weekend trip to New England. You can guess what happened."

Yes, he could.

And his heart ached for the girl who predicted the death of her parents and could do nothing. The guilt that must have accompanied their death helped him understand how a girl had grown up to be the staid, uptight woman he'd seen last night at dinner. She'd developed supreme control to keep herself from falling apart.

Skye's hand on his arm broke him from his thoughts. Her face mirrored his feelings, and he had the urge to cry for the loss of innocence and burden placed on such a young child.

"Hey, you there, Samson?"

"What...oh, yes, I'm here."

"That's all I found. Weird, but, as I said, your kind of stuff."

Jerome rolled his eyes, and Skye pressed her lips together. Samson imagined she was having a hard time not saying something sarcastic to the condescending jerk on the phone.

"Yeah. Right. My kind of stuff." He replied, but doubted Jack noticed the sarcastic tone. He wished he'd been less generous on the sherry he'd bought, but a deal was a deal so he'd send it and not replace it with a cheaper one.

"Great. We're done. I'll talk to you next time you need the lowdown on a suspicious character."

Not if I can help it. "Yup. Later, Jack." Samson snapped his cell phone shut. "Why do I feel like a slimy snake?"

"Snakes aren't slimy." Skye assured him.

"Fine, so why do I feel as if I've done something wrong?"

"Blame the jerk on the phone." Skye gave him a cajoling grin. "He's worse than slime, he's sludge."

Samson's half-hearted smile encouraged Jerome's remark. "Worse than sludge, he's toe-jam scum."

"Nope." Skye countered. "He's rat crap."

"Worse. He's bat shit."

"He's the pile of manure dragged out of a barn full of cows after they've been crapping inside all winter." Skye sat back and folded her arms across her chest, daring anyone to one-up her.

No one did.

Samson laughed. "Totally disgusting."

"So is your agent friend. After listening to him talk, I empathize with Cassandra. I can imagine the skepticism, rejection, and abuse she must have faced. And her being so young. How her poor heart must have broken when her parents didn't believe in her." Skye placed her hand on the book. "Now you know more, what do we do with the book?"

Samson considered the blank journal and his thoughts raced with the possibilities. He'd desperately wanted to know what was in the book, thinking he might find answers to recent events. Unfortunately, blank pages did him no good.

"It's not for me to decide. It's always been your choice. I guess I tried to force things into my way of thinking and look at the result." He motioned to the blank pages.

Skye nodded. "It's all right. You're torn between wanting to protect the town and having to contend with supernatural forces you can't control. You're making the right decision. Besides, Jerome had a point when he mentioned a duo guardianship." She sighed and pushed the book across the table to Samson. "I think I'll leave it to you to give the book to Cassandra and explain things."

Sparks of dread flared in Samson's stomach, and the taste of bile rose in his throat. A dark sense of the inevitable settled itself into his bones and he wished he hadn't pursued the book so fervently. "Okay. If you think it's for the best."

"I do. And don't look so terrified, I'm sure she won't bite your head off." Skye's attempt at easing tension didn't work. They faced a dark evil that had made its presence known again. What lay ahead was anyone's guess, and the book that had gotten them through last time was blank. Not a good portend for things to come.

Chapter Thirteen

Cassandra grabbed another piece of chocolate and stuffed the confectionery in her mouth. Mmmm, raspberry caramel, one of her favorites. Not satisfied, she snatched a handful of chips and sent them crunching after the chocolate. Next, she needed something to drink, but all the fridge offered was sparkling mineral water. Oh, well. The ensuing swish when she twisted the cap attested to its fizz, and the cool, tickling bubbles soothed her throat.

She put the empty bottle on the counter and surveyed the kitchen disaster resulting from her efforts over the last hour. She'd forgotten the hunger stimulated by a vision and how necessary to refuel with food to maintain strength. She wiped her hands on a dishtowel and realized weight gain hadn't been a consideration when she was younger, but now it topped the list of side effects of her eating binge.

Yikes! Talk about self-centered.

No. Avoidance of the truth, not self-centeredness. Her stomach burned with stress and clenched into a tight knot. Oh, God. She needed guidance. Who? Memnon was the logical choice, but he'd always come to her rescue. She wanted to handle the situation herself. Since she only knew three people in town and Skye and Jerome were expecting a baby—that left Samson.

Argh! Cassandra stuffed another chocolate in her mouth and chomped. Samson was out, because he disturbed her on a level Cassandra wasn't ready to explore. Ignoring him and the shivers he sent down her spine was the best plan.

She sighed and reached for the last chocolate in the box just as the doorbell rang. Cassandra frowned and placed the chocolate back in the box. The paint wasn't due for delivery until tomorrow and she wasn't expecting anyone else. Each step closer to the door notched her tension up. It was possible her meditation session had heightened her perceptions. It might be the raw sexual tension emanating at her through the closed door, but she knew.

Cassandra placed her hand on the doorknob, braced herself, and swung the door open. Even knowing who the open door would reveal, didn't prepare her for the wave of disorienting warmth at the sight of him.

Tall and muscled with a chest that both her hands couldn't span. Lean hips molded by form fitting jeans. Rugged features with a square chin slightly shadowed by the presence of unshaven scruff. Powerful looking enough to be sculpted in stone, he stood on her front step and stared at her. Challenging her in an unspoken battle. Cassandra resisted the desire to touch the whirls of chest hair, staring so blatantly out from beneath the cream-colored shirt.

Oh, oh.

Cassandra had been staring, and if the crooked grin on Samson's face was any indication, he had a good idea about the direction of her thoughts. A warm flush spread up her neck and across her face and with her fair skin.

And there'd be no way Samson wouldn't notice the color change.

"Hi. Am I catching you at a bad time?"

Yes. "No. You're not. Come in." She stepped aside and motioned him in. He was here for a reason, but she didn't remember why. The fact he practically filled the entire hallway wasn't helping her memory.

Stillness pulsated with expectation. Samson frowned. "I'm supposed to give you a tour of the town today, remember?"

Cassandra's brain regained its purpose. "Yes, I remember. How could I forget?" The last sentence was an admonishment to herself, more than a statement to the man disrupting her composure. "Let me grab a jacket and we can go."

"You're wearing that?" Samson's gaze raked her in a disapproving fashion.

Cassandra ran her hands over her Gucci blouse and pants. "What's wrong with what I'm wearing?"

Samson grinned. "Nothing, except that it's kinda dressy for tourist attire." His gaze touched on her Dolce and Gabbana shoes, assessing the heels and stylish looking suede. "And no way will you be able to keep up with me in those things."

Cassandra raised her chin and retorted, "These are my casual clothes, and as for the heels, I wear higher than these every day for work and you have no idea how fast I can move when the need arises." She snatched her butter-soft leather jacket from the closet and snapped it over her arm. Who cared if it was Armani. The casual style of the jacket suited her purposes for the day. Besides, she owned nothing less formal.

"So, if you're ready to show me the town, I'm ready to be shown." With a false bravado, she walked past Samson, her high heels clicking on the marble floor.

Though she'd never admit it to the man who strode beside her with all the grace of a panther, Cassandra wished she owned a pair of shoes without heels. She was certain Jimmy Choo made lower-heeled shoes that would have suited the Olympic trek Samson took her on.

They hit all the touristy places. The Ropes Mansion and Gardens, a couple of wax museums, and Witch Village. Fascinating and fun. Samson made an excellent tour guide, relating witty quips about each place and keeping the conversation light. Cassandra wondered if he'd wanted to lower her defenses before he hit her with the more historic sites.

They started with the Rebecca Nurse homestead. Built in 1678, the restored saltbox design house was in Danvers and belonged to one of the witches accused in the trials of 1692. During the brief tour, Cassandra felt as if she was walking through tendrils of cobwebs. Each one caught on her and left a mental impression of desperation and desolation. By the time they finished, she was eager to get back to the car and sit.

With less than five minutes to recover, Cassandra found herself deposited outside their next destination while Samson parked the car. The Witch House. The only original building still standing that had direct ties to the witch trials of 1692. Feelings of despair washed over her before she'd even entered the building. It battered her senses in rolling waves of emotion.

Wary and hesitant, Cassandra stepped across the threshold. Her breath caught in her throat and left her choking on a pungent taste of decay. Not of the house itself, though. No, the decay was of the spirit. It drifted around the infamous house that had once held trials condemning innocent men, women, and children with false accusations. It hung in the rafters, leering down at tourists with the knowing smugness of conceit. Waiting. Preying on the unprotected souls of innocents who came to gawk at a place someone should have burned to ashes in a cleansing fire.

The touch on her shoulder made Cassandra jump and scream. Her heart pounded, and it took a second to realize it wasn't a ghostly touch, only Samson.

"It's just me. Are you all right?"

Cold heat raced through Cassandra. She whispered, "I'd like to leave...please."

Without question, Samson took her elbow and guided her out the front door. His support was minimal but reassuring. Cassandra knew if she faltered or fainted, Samson would catch her. It was a comforting thought. Other than Memnon, her only reliance had been on herself.

Once settled in the car, Cassandra breathed easier. She hadn't expected the lingering past to overpower her so much.

"So, does that happen to you often?" Samson joked, though his intent gaze belied his words.

Cassandra fumbled to explain. "No. Well, not recently. I mean, not until recently." She rubbed her fingers across her forehead and closed her eyes. "Can we please visit the next place on your list of places to make me suffer?"

"You think I made this happen to you?"

Cassandra sighed and silently cursed her brother, again, for sending her to a place that would set her senses on full alert. "I'm sorry. It's not your fault."

Samson gave her a gentle smile. "I know it's not my fault, but I can help." He countered her disbelieving look with an explanation. "Think about it. We're in Salem, Massachusetts, Witch Capital of the World and I've lived here my entire life. I know every nook and cranny, and every real witch and witch wannabe. I've seen everything you can imagine—good and bad. Who else do you think is better equipped to help you understand what's happening to you?"

Cassandra wanted to confide, but she'd spent most of her life suppressing and lying about her powers. Just because a man with extraordinary eyes and a body that wouldn't quit asked her to confide, didn't mean she would. She'd handle her visions alone. No one had ever believed her, anyway.

Except Memnon.

Granted, he'd sent her to Salem alone to contend with whatever was happening to her. Damn him for his mysterious actions. She should have stayed in New York, where she'd carved a safe life for herself.

"Cassandra, you can trust me?"

Samson's smooth, rich voice jolted Cassandra from her thoughts. She blushed and wondered how long she'd been silent. "It's okay. I'm fine. I'm feeling light-headed, is all. Is there a place we can get lunch? I'm hungry."

Samson didn't move. His eyes narrowed, and Cassandra sensed the battle going on within him. Would he push? Cassandra hoped not. Or she'd be tempted to bare her soul to him. Finally, he shifted and turned on the car.

"Okay. Food it is. Do you prefer Chinese, Italian, or fast food?" He flicked a glance at her. "No, definitely not fast food. You'd never fit in at McDonald's with those clothes."

Cassandra bristled, but kept silent. She'd never admit to Samson, but she'd felt disoriented for most of the day. Her silk and satin clothes and high heels might blend perfectly in New York, but they stood out like a wart on a witch's nose in Salem.

Yikes! Language, Cassandra. Don't get too rural.

She decided to spend tomorrow morning buying new clothes. A few outfits to get her through the short time she'd be in Salem. She spared a glance at the man driving and concluded the shorter her time in Salem, the better. She needed no more disruptions in her carefully structured life.

Chapter Fourteen

Samson worried that Cassandra's cosmic shift had left her too shaken to continue, but clearly not, since she wanted food. He glanced at the woman sitting stiff-shouldered beside him. She'd shut him out as effectively as if she'd slammed the car door in his face.

"Again, I'm sorry. I should have remembered my first visit to The Witch House. Mom set up a shield of protection and allowed me time to adjust to the disconnected energy running rampant."

A quiet quiver shook Cassandra's shoulders. Her blue gaze pinned him from across the front seat. "How do you do it?"

"What?"

"Live in this town with all the...energy...and not let it overwhelm you."

Responding to the plea in her voice, Samson lowered his voice and spoke softly. "I have the advantage of a lifetime of living here. My natural defenses ensure the supernatural threads of energy weaving through parts of the town, no longer earned a blip on my radar—unless I want them to."

Cassandra frowned, crossed her arms over her chest, and leaned back. "I understand."

Not sure what she'd been expecting, he covered the awkward silence with words. "We'll eat at a bistro on Church St. called the Lyceum. It used to be a lecture hall graced by famous people such as Thoreau, Hawthorne, Emerson, and Alexander Graham Bell." Cassandra's jaw loosened and her fists unclenched. Samson stifled a smile. He hoped the high-end bistro might impress and restore the easy camaraderie they'd shared earlier.

Upon arrival, a perky waitress greeted and seated them in a discreet corner. Cassandra's approving at the restaurant décor reassured Samson that he'd made the right choice. They decided upon food, ordered wine, and sat in uncomfortable silence while they waited.

Cassandra fiddled with her napkin and looked anywhere except at him, while Samson admired the woman seated across from him. Stoic, yet churning with emotion. Considering what Jack had told him about Cassandra's past, Samson knew the impassive exterior hid the truth of her nature.

She wouldn't trust quickly or easily.

He'd have to achieve the impossible.

The wine arrived and Samson poured the sparkling, peach-colored liquid into delicate, crystal flutes. He raised his wine glass in a silent salute. Cassandra flushed and sipped her wine. Their eyes met and fire flamed through Samson.

Okay, where had that come from?

Samson's heart pumped with desire and then slowed to normal. Instead of putting Cassandra at ease, he'd made things more uncomfortable.

Thankfully, the food arrived and briefly negated the need for conversation. Samson inhaled the mouth-watering aroma of French onion soup and gruyere cheese. With gusto, he spooned the messy concoction that was one of his favorite, while Cassandra spooned hers with delicacy. Grilled chicken with roasted peppers and mozzarella cheese followed the soup, and it surprised Samson that Cassandra's taste in food shadowed his, just as her enjoyment of said food matched his.

With a satisfied sigh, Samson sat back and threw his napkin down. Food had definitely been the right choice to help loosen Cassandra's inhibitions.

"Tell me about your brother."

"My brother? Why?"

Ignoring the defensive tone in Cassandra's voice, Samson smiled. "Since I'm Police Chief, it's my responsibility to learn everything I can about new residents of Salem."

"I suppose that makes sense."

"Sure does." Cassandra's logical side gave him leverage to grill her for information. Police interrogation had taught him the direct approach was not always the best approach.

Cassandra pursed her lips. "I'm not sure where to start."

"Why not with his name? I assume your parents had a thing for Greek Mythology?"

"You'd think so, wouldn't you?" Her eyes shifted to a subtle blue dullness. "They definitely named me after the prophetess, Cassandra, at the time not knowing the tragic story behind her name." A hint of a bitter smile crossed her lips. "They'd only just started reading stories of Greek Mythology at the time I was born and they fell in love with the name Cassandra. I always wondered if they'd known the entire myth, if they'd still have named me Cassandra."

"You mean, her seeing the future, but being cursed never to be believed."

"Yes. What a horrible way to live your life."

Samson ached at the sorrowful tone lacing Cassandra's simple sentiment. The bewildered girl, grown to a woman so scarred she let no one see her true self. Knowing she'd reject any offer of comfort, Samson sat and waited for her to continue. Being still was one of the hardest things he'd ever done.

As if realizing she'd let her mind wander, Cassandra snapped back to the conversation. "In truth, Memnon's namesake has nothing to do with Greek Mythology, but is a scarcely known historical figure called Saint Memnon the Wonderworker." Cassandra fiddled with the stem of her wineglass. "This is exactly what Memnon is. He's your typical knight of the nobility. A miracle worker."

Samson searched her voice for a hint of jealousy or bitterness. He found nothing but love and respect. "So how does he perform these modern miracles?"

"He buys floundering companies with little hope of recovering, turns them around, and then sells them for a profit. Over the years, he's saved a dozen companies and thousands of jobs."

"That's quite an endeavor."

"Yes. He also donates to charities, volunteers at a homeless shelter, and most recently paid to fence in an outdoor play area at the local Humane Society."

"He sounds like a great guy."

"He's always been there for me."

Noting the confrontational tone of Cassandra's voice, Samson kept his voice even. "I'm sure he has." Doubting his wisdom, he nonetheless asked the question hovering on the edge of his tongue. "Does he have powers as well?"

Samson busied himself with pouring more wine. The action didn't stop him from seeing the shock that etched her face into a stiff mask. She recovered, picked up her now full wineglass, and downed the liquid in one gulp. In contrast to the rapacious draining of her glass, she delicately wiped her mouth with her linen napkin.

"You're confusing me with your local witches."

Samson let out a belt of laughter. "Give me credit. I told you, I've lived in Salem my entire life so, believe me, I can spot a phony a mile away." Elbows on the table, he leaned close enough to see the sparks of ice in the blue of Cassandra's eyes. "You're high on my list of the most powerful, non-practicing witches I've ever had the pleasure to meet."

There. The pink elephant in the room was gone. He'd laid it on the table; bearded the lioness in her den; breached enemy walls; said what needed saying and any other cliché he'd forgotten. Now he'd wait.

Blue eyes flamed and flowed with shadows and slivers of discombobulated energy shot from Cassandra and raked across

Samson's skin. He didn't flinch. She opened her mouth and snapped it shut, her glare freezing in its intensity. Samson couldn't afford to let her deny the truth of his statement. He glared back. The sheer force of their individual auras melded into a swirling vista of rainbow colors easily seen by an adept, but invisible to an untrained eye.

Finally, she dropped her gaze. "One of the most powerful, you say?"

From anyone else, Samson might have thought they were hinting for a compliment, but from Cassandra, he sensed a need for reassurance. Right now, the woman was again a girl who craved acceptance.

Wanting her to laugh, he teased. "Not as powerful as I am."

Cassandra snapped her head up. She searched Samson's face while he worked at exuding calm and humor. The corner of Cassandra's mouth turned up into a hesitant smile.

"Of course not."

Simply spoken, those words held depths of meaning and the beginning of trust. Just having Cassandra admit to having powers—admittedly, in a roundabout way—was enough for Samson. He'd build on that trust for now.

Samson's phone rang. The trilling the theme from the Bugs Bunny/Roadrunner show earned a raised eyebrow from Cassandra and a moment of embarrassment for Samson. He shrugged and answered the call.

Jaks's news gave Samson a pang of regret that fate wouldn't allow him the luxury of earning Cassandra's trust. He should have known. Fate was about to throw them head first into a fateful backlash of ancient curses.

Chapter Fifteen

A person didn't need to be psychic to know the news wasn't good.

Samson's handsome, chiseled features tightened into cold marble. Flickers of sharp light flashed amidst blue eyes, like streaks of lightening in a storm-darkened sky. And he'd turned those eyes to stare directly at her.

Disconcerted, Cassandra turned and made a pretense of studying the restaurant's décor. Samson hadn't said a word after hello, but coldness struck an icy barrier between them. After a screaming silence and an occasional clench of his jaw, Samson snapped his phone shut.

Cassandra braved a peek in his direction. He stared back with a narrowed, accusing glare. To her, it felt as if a vacuum had sucked all oxygen out of the room and left nothing to breathe. Under his scrutiny, Cassandra fought not to sink back into the insecurities she'd lived with most of her life. No one had breached the stone wall she'd built after her parent's accident. Until now. Whatever was wrong, Cassandra was sure Samson blamed her.

In one fluid motion of concise grace, he stood. Threw money on the table. "Come on. Something's come up. I'm taking you home."

"Fine." With trembling hands, Cassandra pushed back from the table and stepped past Samson. Her shoulder brushed against his arm and the motion ignited tiny sparks of electricity between them. Deep in Cassandra's stomach, tremors of desire fanned into a tiny flame. With every grain of willpower she possessed, Cassandra kept her head high and walked out into the sunshine, not caring if Samson followed. She knew he did, because his presence warmed her back as much as the warmth of the sun on her face.

She'd enjoyed Samson's company, and it bothered her the day was ending with tension. His knowledge and humor impressed her. He accepted her without question or disbelief and comforted her after the episode at The Witch House. She'd relaxed in his company, as she'd never done with anyone except Memnon.

Damn the man for finding the crack in her armor, because now the cold looks he shot her direction found a way right through that crack.

Samson held the Hummer door for her while she stepped up, giving an effort not to touch any part of his body. She didn't need the aggravation of conflicting energy.

The low hum of the Hummer's hybrid engine contrasted with the awkward silence. Cassandra snuck a glance at the brooding man beside her. The interior of the Hummer amplified the rage rolling off Samson. Cassandra gritted her teeth and drew energy from her center, sending it to all parts of her body for a shield. A handy thing she'd learned to do as a child and an ability that had proved useful over the years. She hadn't thought she'd need to protect herself against Samson. She closed her eyes and concentrated. Samson's voice broke her from her meditation.

"Are you all right?"

"I'm fine," she snapped at him. He was responsible for her whirls of confusing energy.

"You don't sound fine," he snapped right back at her.

Cassandra crossed her arms over her chest and stared out the window. She wanted to cry. Confrontation of any kind bothered her. She hadn't wanted to come to Salem, hadn't wanted a re-awakening of her latent abilities, and definitely hadn't wanted to meet a man who made her flame with desire one minute and want to rant in anger the next.

Samson mumbled, but she didn't bother asking what he'd said. She listened to the rustle of denim on leather when Samson shifted in his seat.

"Look. I'm sorry, all right."

A tear trembled on Cassandra's eyelid. God, she hated this temperamental side of herself, and wasn't used to the roller coaster of emotions. "It's okay. I'm sure you have a reason to be so..."

"Rude."

"Well..."

"Boorish."

Cassandra's mouth quivered into an almost smile.

"Uncivil. Bad mannered. Neanderthal."

A snort escaped from Cassandra before she covered her mouth. "Keep going, you're getting closer."

Samson concentrated on maneuvering through rush hour traffic and didn't speak again until they stopped at a red light.

"There's a lot going on I can't even begin to explain without sounding crazy or scary. No, strike that—terrifying is a more appropriate word."

Bitterness colored his words. Dark bitterness. Raw anger. The mixed emotions helped Cassandra recognize he'd not been directing his anger at her earlier. She understood little of what had happened since arriving in Salem, and wondered if recent events tied into her dreams. Part of her did not want to ask the question. She really didn't.

But her traitorous other part opened its mouth. "Does it have anything to do with a cross and, maybe, blood?"

Samson's narrowed gaze pinned her to her seat. The light changed and the person in the car behind them honked. Samson flipped the guy the finger and drove on.

Cassandra sat in open-mouthed disbelief. "You gave that guy the finger."

"Yep."

"You're the police chief. What happened to public relations, presenting a positive example for kids, as well as adults?"

"Don't care at the moment."

"Oh."

"So what's this about a cross and blood?"

"I...I had a dream, is all." It had been years since she'd shared her dreams, and she shouldn't have bothered now.

Samson pulled into her driveway and left the engine running while Cassandra climbed out. "I'll be in touch."

With those words, Samson peeled rubber out of the driveway, leaving Cassandra alone and certain that events in her life were reeling out of control while she was merely hitching a ride.

Samson drove like a madman. He shouldn't have taken the time to drop Cassandra at home, but hadn't wanted to subject her to what he was sure to find at the crime scene. A dead dog was one thing, a dead human, another. According to Jaks, the body lay in a ritualistic manner, just as the dog had been. The difference being, whoever the dead person was had earned a prime spot in the middle of Salem Common.

Damn, no way to keep this out of the papers.

He entered the entrance off North Washington Square, across from the Witch Museum, and had no trouble finding the crime scene. With a curse, he drove onto the grass and headed to the gazebo in the middle of the nine-acre park. Carefully, he eased the Hummer through the gathering crowd and gave silent thanks to whoever put up police tape and barriers before the crowd grew too much. With a nod at the patrol officers standing guard, he strode to the gazebo, all the while steeling himself for what he'd find.

Nothing could have prepared him.

Male. Mid-thirties. Protruding tongue. Face blue and engorged. Cuts over most of the body. Male organ missing.

That observation shocked Samson from his aloof observation. Jeez. The murderer had cut off the guy's testicles and penis and laid them beside him. Samson's stomach heaved and he shifted his feet into a defensive stance. One meant to protect his manhood. Purely a reflexive move.

"Someone didn't like this guy."

Samson recognized the voice of the person who stood beside him, so he didn't bother turning.

"Looks that way. So, Doc, any thoughts on which of his wounds actually killed him?"

"Come on, Samson, you know I can't give you a report until I do a full inspection of the body."

"Then give me your unofficial opinion."

Doc pursed his lips and perused the splayed body. Gratefully, Samson watched his officers keeping the newspaper reporters behind the barrier. The starkness of death portrayed by the mangled, naked body would not make an entertaining front-page photograph in tomorrow's paper.

"Your guess would be as good as mine whether he bled to death or the strangulation got him first. He was alive for both."

"How do you know?"

"If he'd been dead from strangulation, he wouldn't have bled so much. If he'd bled to death, he wouldn't have turned blue and had a protruding tongue." Doc gritted his teeth. "Whoever did this might have spent hours cutting. Look here," Doc pointed to a couple of cuts on the victim's torso, "the incisions are small so he wouldn't bleed to death. The killer probably cut off the guy's oxygen, then let him breathe. Cut it off and then let him breathe again."

"Ya. I get the idea, Doc."

"Sorry. I've never seen such a finely executed murder. You know, in the old days, before they perfected the hanging technique, people routinely took anywhere from 10 to 20 minutes to choke to death. Our killer gave the victim a chance to recover and then started all over. Choking and cutting more until...well, you get the idea. Death came slow for this guy."

Samson's gorge heaved with revulsion. Despite his disgust, his gaze fixated on the lewdly sprawled body. That was when he noticed the cross. A small wooden one on a stand you might buy in a tourist shop, but a cross nonetheless. The tiny piece sat in the shadows, partially hidden by the victim's head. Samson squatted for closer inspection, and Cassandra's words smacked back into his mind.

Does it have anything to do with a cross and, maybe, blood?

Pooled on the gazebo floorboards, surrounding the cross stand was a thickening patch of blood. Samson rose and shouted at the nearest officer, "You're in charge. Move nothing until I return."

"But, Chief." The officer's harried glance at the reporters made clear the reason for his protest.

"I'll be right back. Don't move a thing." Samson reinforced his command.

Chapter Sixteen

Cassandra flipped the page and vehemently sketched another interpretation of the guest bedroom. Fingers flew into a furious frenzy of creation, and she envisioned the room fully painted and furnished. While she directed her mind to work, she didn't have to pay attention to the storm gathering. Raging, demanding, crashing through anything in its way, the storm fought for release. Cassandra couldn't give in. She knew the results of giving up control and allowing the sensations to take hold.

Damn, she never should have opened the doorway so firmly shut over the years. The impenetrable walls had kept her sane. Her heart fluttered unevenly, her palms broke into a sweat making it hard to hold her pencil. A slight tremor caused her to erase and redo more than one sketch. Her dream vision taunted her. The icy glare of Samson's face after the phone call haunted her. A cross surrounded by blood.

A cross and blood. A cross and blood.

Her front door slammed shut. Shocked into awareness, Cassandra jumped to her feet.

Cassandra." Samson bellowed from downstairs.

Chalk it up to intuition, foretelling the future, or a good guess. Samson had come for a reason and he'd not even bothered with the basic convention of knocking on the door to announce himself. No, he'd barged right on in and hollered for her as if she'd done something wrong.

She didn't move. Nervous about the coming confrontation. Heavy, determined footsteps thudded up the stairs. Straightening her shoulders, Cassandra stepped out of the bedroom and into the hallway to confront the man Cassandra knew would change her world forever.

"I'm here." She spoke softly, hoping a calm aura would buffer Samson's apparent jagged energy.

No such luck.

His bulk flooded the hallway, and he nearly ran her down in his approach. His already intimidating size appeared more intense, fiercer. Pain and anger mixed together in the depths of his eyes. Frustration melded with condemnation. She shivered. The girl in her cowered in dread of the inevitable.

He reached out and caught her arm in his hand. "You're coming with me. I've got something to show you."

Cassandra resisted, but he pulled and lifted Cassandra to her tiptoes. Unable to resist the bulldozing force of his will, Cassandra gave in and let him lead her downstairs and out to his car. She grabbed her sweater as they passed the front hall, but only because it hung on a hook outside the closet.

Cassandra clung to the edge of the Hummer's seat as Samson wheeled through the streets of Salem. The scowl etched on his face quelled any chance of asking questions. Besides, Cassandra didn't think she wanted the answers. Nearing the downtown section of town, Samson slowed the vehicle and swung into Salem Common. An area of land the travel brochures described as land allotted for public domain centuries ago.

They drove to the gazebo, its arched structure obstructed by a milling, restless crowd. The Hummer jerked to a halt and Samson jumped out. Cassandra's stomach lurched. Stomach muscles clenched with the sense of an age-old malevolence clinging to the air she breathed. Confronted with curiosity-seekers whose gazes burned a hole to the depths of her defenses, Cassandra faltered when Samson dragged her out of the vehicle.

She pulled back, but he was stronger.

The few short steps to the plateau of the gazebo took an eternity. Memories played tricks with Cassandra until the lines blurred, melding past with the present. Day became night, and Samson's face morphed into that of another police officer. One who'd taken a six-year-old, Cassandra, and her nine-year-old brother away from their home to the police station until a relative could claim them. Cassandra hadn't wanted to go with the police officer then, and she didn't want to go with Samson now.

But he persisted.

What Cassandra saw threw her into the past. She froze. Vividly remembered the vision she'd had of her parents laying on the cold, wet pavement amidst the wreckage of their car. Even though she'd seen it in her mind's eye, the accident scene was sharp and cutting as a knife. Blood and rain mingled with dirt and twisted metal, with her parents sprawled in a vista of death. A fateful completion to a ghastly scene.

Samson spoke, but the roaring in his ears drowned him out. Why had he so thoughtlessly dragged her here? Granted, he didn't know about the tragedy in her past. His voice finally punctured her haze.

"Tell me about the blood and cross."

Samson pointed to an area close to the body's head. Cassandra's gaze followed. Reality was nothing like her dream. Stark. Graphic. Grotesque. Blood-soaked wood and grey skin completed the sordid scene. Aware of Samson waiting for an answer, Cassandra shook her head and shivered.

"Damn it..." Samson spoke and fixed a narrow gaze on Cassandra. "Wait a minute. I'm sorry, I never considered how this might affect you. You know, with your parents and all."

Rage shot through Cassandra. She lifted her hand and slapped Samson; the crack echo drew the attention of the nearest police officer whose hand jumped to his gun. A wave from Samson backed him off.

Lethal with suppressed anger, Samson's voice was a mere whisper. "What. Was. That. For?"

Not wanting to make a spectacle for the nearby crowd, Cassandra whispered back at him. "You bastard. You knew about my parents, which means you had me investigated. Then, you brought me here without warning me. What? Did you think I'd break down and confess?"

"Confess? No, I..."

"Unless I'm under arrest, I'm going home." She raised a questioning eyebrow at him.

"You're not under arrest. That's not why I brought you here."

"Fine. I'm leaving. I'll find my own way home." Cassandra wheeled around and left the scene that would haunt her for a long time to come.

"Samson, you can be quite intimidating when you put on your Police Chief demeanor." Skye admonished.

"You weren't afraid of me when we met."

"Yes, but you must admit that our first meeting was under vastly different circumstances. You'd come to help a boyhood friend in a situation you knew to be traumatic."

"I remember. I never expected a late-night phone call with Jaks blubbering about secrets rooms, skeletons, and Jerome being stubborn and pig-headed." He ducked a flying couch pillow. "I certainly didn't expect the skeleton to be your mom." Samson spared a quick glance at Jerome. "I went as a friend, not a cop."

That's when Samson and Jerome had met Skye. Samson looked at them now, so much in love, and thanked the fates everything had turned out so well.

He'd come here looking for advice after Cassandra stomped away from the crime scene. "I totally messed up with Cassandra." What do I do now?"

"Now, you give her time to cool down, then explain things to her and quit playing the Neanderthal." Skye folded a pair of jeans and placed them on a growing pile of clean clothes.

Jerome came into the living room carrying a couple of bottles of beer. Handing one to Samson, he said, "Maybe if we invite her over again and act as intermediaries."

"No, I don't think so." Skye frowned at a wrinkled blouse in her hand and sighed. "I am so not in the mood for ironing." She brushed her hand down the length of blouse that miraculously smoothed to a wear-ready state. Nodding in satisfaction, Skye ignored Samson's snort and Jerome's shaking head.

"My sense is Samson needs to do this himself. He's got to win Cassandra's trust or they'll never be able to work together to stop this evil." Skye placed a hand on Samson's shoulder. "You'll need to do it soon."

Samson sighed. "I suppose you're right. I think I'm better off contending with criminals than women."

Jerome agreed. "Yeah, with a bad guy, all you've got to do is bop him one if he misbehaves. With women...well, there are ways to bring them in line." He wriggled his eyebrows at Skye, who shook her head and kept folding.

"Hey, I don't need details, thanks." Samson protested.

Jerome laughed. The brief, comical respite didn't last as he asked a sobering question. "So what juicy detail did you leave out of your spiel to the newshounds?"

"Detail? What do you mean?" Skye asked as she folded a shirt.

Samson explained. "When we talk to the media, we always leave out one thing only the perpetrator would know. If we get a confession, the missing detail helps to determine if the confession is valid."

"Come on, people don't actually confess to crimes they didn't commit, do you?"

"Ha. You'd be surprised."

"Why?"

"Who knows? A few of them are crazy, some seek the attention, and others are hoping for free room and board." He turned his attention to Jerome. "In this case, we left out the one clue with the potential to incite public panic. Heck, it scares the devil out of me. Scrawled in the victim's blood, underneath the cross were the words,

For his sin
He is slain
Beware your sins
Those who remain.

Skye's face paled. "You'll have every person in Salem looking over their shoulder in terror if that blood-invoked verse gets out."

"For sure." Samson grew pensive. "After the dog I knew there'd be more killings, human, but it still slams right into my gut."

Jerome nodded. "I agree. At least now we have an idea what we're up against."

"Not we. Me." Samson set his empty beer bottle down and stood. "This time, the ride around the carousel is mine." He stood. "And I think I've given our reluctant cohort enough time to cool down. I better get this over with."

Jerome shot Samson a grin. "You know where to come to get your battle wounds healed."

"Ouch. I'm hoping there won't be any, but thanks for the offer."

"Seriously, Samson, if you need anything, you know I'm here for you. I've got your back." With a nudge from Skye, he rectified his remark. "We've got your back."

"I know, Jerome. You always do."

Samson pushed up from the comfort of the couch and rubbed his hands on his jeans. "Okay. I guess I better go mend Cassandra's hurt feelings."

"Not to mention the invasion of privacy issue and the fact you might possibly have made her think you considered her a suspect in the murder."

"I didn't..." Samson realized he had and shut his mouth before giving Skye more ammunition. "Fine. I'll tread carefully."

The knots in his stomach followed him out the door. Better to confront Cassandra sooner rather than later.

Chapter Seventeen

Cassandra fumed. Her focus was non-existent. Which meant she'd littered her sketchbook with half-done scribbling, having no bearing whatsoever on her design work. In fact, now she considered what her flying fingers had created over the last couple of hours, she was horrified.

She threw the sketchpad down and sat trembling. How was it possible to draw such atrocities without awareness of her actions? Macabre scenes of death, each one a different person contorted into a bloody death pose and each of them titled with a single word title. Pride. Avarice. Envy. Wrath. Lust. Gluttony. Sloth.

Even more disturbing, the rendition of Lust showed the murder scenes Samson had dragged her to earlier. Did that mean the other six were murders waiting to happen? If she didn't stay and help, would the responsibility for more deaths be hers?

"NO! I will not go through this again." Sobbing, Cassandra ran upstairs to her bedroom, opened her suitcases, and began to stuff them with clothes. A testament to her state of mind, because usually she perfectly folded and organized her clothes when packing.

She ran through a mental checklist of everything she needed to do. Write a note for the painters coming tomorrow. Leave her design sketches, swatches and contacts behind for the person Memnon would have to hire to finish the job. Oh, yes, she'd call Memnon. But she'd wait until she was home so he couldn't talk her into staying, though she doubted he'd try once he knew her trip involved magic and murder.

Hefting her two suitcases off the bed, she lugged them downstairs, not caring when they thumped against the wall. Primer and paint would cover any marks that she left.

The doorbell rang and startled her into losing her grip on one of the suitcases.

THUD! THUD! THUD!

The noise echoed through the empty house. The front door slammed open and Samson ran in, gun drawn, stance low. Cassandra dropped her other suitcase and jammed both hands straight up. Her breath came in short gasps. The suitcase came to rest at Samson's feet. His gaze flicked between her and the suitcases until realization dawned on him, and he relaxed his stance.

"Jesus, woman." He whistled the exclamation through clenched teeth. "You scared me half out of my wits. What the hell do you think you're doing?"

"Me. Me. What am I doing? You barge into my house like a reckless, gun-toting cowboy and you wonder what I'm doing."

Samson swore again and shoved his gun into his holster. Jerking his jacket in place to hide the weapon. "You're right. I'm sorry."

Thank God he'd put his gun away. Cassandra's quota for excitement had reached the top, and staring down the barrel of a gun did nothing to improve her mood or emotions. A mild tremor quivered deep in her belly and spread to her limbs. She needed to sit. So she did. Right on the stairs.

"Hey, are you okay?" Samson took the steps two at a time and crouched in front of her.

His closeness brought brushes of warmth emanating from his, oh so hot, body. The dark shadow of stubble on his face gave him a sinister appeal softened by his eyes. Cassandra stood on the verge of losing herself in the depths of the colors swirling around like an artist's palette.

He actually looked concerned. Go figure.

"Well, are you?" His deep voice rasped—gravelly yet smooth, strong yet mellow. It hypnotized and comforted.

"Sure, I'm fine." She replied, before appearing like a total idiot.

"Do you need a hand? I'm sure the couch is more comfortable than the stairs."

"No!" She didn't want him to see the sketches lying strewn on the living room floor like cards of death from a tarot deck. "I'm fine. Really." She stood and wished she hadn't because she felt light-headed and had to clutch the railing.

"You are not fine." With one fluid movement, Samson picked her up and carried her downstairs. "Kitchen or living room."

"What?" Light-headed had graduated to melting hot butter. Her buried nose tickled against his neck and she detected rich, earthy hints of cinnamon and another unidentifiable scent. Cassandra snuggled closer and inhaled, attempting to identify the mysterious scent.

Licorice. The man smelled like cinnamon and licorice.

"Fine, the living room, it is."

"What. No." She struggled for release, but he held on tight.

"So," he set her carefully on the couch and indicated the suitcases in the hallway, "you're leaving us already?"

Cassandra sat mute. How to explain her death scene sketches, or convey the absolute terror of two hours lost in morbid creation of such scenes? She pointed a shaking finger at the sketchbook. Tears filled her eyes.

Samson's gaze fixed on the sketches, and he froze. Literally. The temperature in the room dropped, the breeze outside picked up and scattered the leaves across the grass in a mad flurry.

Cassandra had hoped Samson would be different. Clearly, the sketches repulsed him. She probably did as well, considering she'd drawn them. Even in Salem people recognized her as an oddity, an outcast. The best thing for her to do would be to leave.

Samson strode over and snatched the sketches from the floor where Cassandra had thrown them earlier. He studied each sketch. His brow furrowed and eyes blazed while Cassandra watched. His facial expression gave nothing away, and when he slowly lifted the force of his gaze to Cassandra, she was sure he was about to condemn her as a freak.

"These are amazing. I mean other than the content, which is morbidly stomach-turning; you have a great talent for putting life to paper...or, in this case, death."

"You like them?"

"I hate what they portray, but the detail, the beauty of your pencil strokes—you've made these death scenes so real. Not only that, but you have possibly taken us closer to solving the puzzle."

"I'm sorry, I'm confused. What puzzle? Why aren't you clapping me in handcuffs and lugging me off to prison as a murderer?"

Samson placed the sketches on a nearby table and came to stand in front of Cassandra. Gently, he put his hands on her shoulders and stared down at her. "I never thought you were a murderer. I showed you the crime scene to tap into your psychic abilities. I went about it in, what I'm told, a typical Neanderthal manner and I came here to apologize to you." He indicated the suitcases in the hallway. "Were you going somewhere?"

"I...I was leaving." Her lower lip trembled. Whether from stress or relief, she wasn't sure.

Samson reached out and ran a fingertip softly across her lip. "Cassandra. I can't let you go anywhere. You're an intricate part of what's to come—what's already started."

On more sure footing now that she knew he didn't suspect her of murder, Cassandra straightened her shoulders and glared up at Samson. "You can't let me. How do you think you can stop me? Last time I checked it was still a free country."

"Once I tell you a long, strange story, I have no doubt you'll stay. If it makes you feel better, I'll leave the decision up to you. When I've told the tale, if you want to go, I won't stop you. Okay?"

"Sure. I suppose." Her attention strayed to the sketch portraying Lust, and Cassandra knew she had to listen to Samson's story.

Two hours and several pots of coffee later, Cassandra stared at Samson, not sure what to say.

"Are you mocking me?"

Samson's lips curved slowly into a bittersweet smile. "I wish."

"Okay, briefly, an ancient evil came into being somewhere in the past, you're not sure when, it's responsible for the famous witch trials and executions, came back to Salem thirty years ago, killed Jerome's mom, returned again last year, was beaten by Jerome and Skye, and is back for another round of murder. Oh, and let's not forget the knife that supposedly steals souls and can pass on a person's life's knowledge as well as the magic book that writes its own history."

"Yes, that's a succinct rendition of the facts."

Cassandra studied the face of the man who'd finished telling her such a fantastic tale. Solid, rugged, lined with the wisdom and responsibility of life. Eyes that spoke of depths and knowledge beyond the normal. Without realizing at first she was even doing so, Cassandra sent out mind feelers to prod for any sign of subterfuge. Nothing. Everything pointed to the fact that Samson was telling the truth. Besides, the tale fit too perfectly with her vision from that morning.

She gave a ragged, half-laugh. "And I thought I was strange, but you've got me beat to hell."

"I said before. We're in Salem. Witch Capital of the World."

They shared a brief grin until reality hit, and Cassandra asked, "This is scary stuff. How can you be so sure I'll stay? I mean, a person would have to be crazy to get involved."

"You are involved, whether or not you want to admit it. I'm sure you'll stay because as much as you suppress the mystical side of yourself, afraid as you are of letting loose and exploring your psychic gift...yes, gift," Samson responded to Cassandra silent protest, "at heart, you are an honorable person who will always do what's right no matter the cost to yourself."

"I'm not sure I view myself quite so altruistically."

"You don't see yourself the way you are. You shut yourself off so long ago that you've only been living half a life."

His words resonated within Cassandra. He knew her so well, and his matter-of-fact attitude made it seem simple to tear down the walls she'd built and start using her powers again. The idea scared her. Exhaustion and worry did not make now the right time for major decisions or self-analysis. She squinted at the persistent throb pulsing at the nape of her neck.

Samson put his hand over hers. "Look, you're tired and the night is half gone. Why don't you go to bed? I'll see you tomorrow when you're more rested."

"You think I'll sleep with all this information whirling in my head?"

"No." He smiled. "But I was giving you a way out, so you can be alone to consider what I've told you. If your sketches are right, and I believe they are, then more lives are in danger."

"Yes, the sketches, I'd forgotten. What did you mean about them being pieces of a puzzle?"

"The murder scene had one addition you don't know about. Written with the victim's blood were the words,

For his sin
He is slain
Beware your sins
Those who remain.

Its meaning escaped me until I saw your sketches titled with each of the Cardinal Sins. Eric, the dead man, was a known philanderer. You had his death scene titled with Lust."

"I see."

"Your visions are why I took you to the scene. You asked earlier today about a cross and blood. We found those at the scene. That's when I thought of you and wanted your input."

"The cross in my vision was huge, definitely not the one at the scene."

Samson sat up, years of experience making him alert to the intricacies of minor details. "It wasn't? You might have sketched one of the other murder scenes. Tell me more. What else did you see?"

Cassandra rubbed her forehead. Weariness slogged through her. "I don't know. A cross with blood pooled at the base. Fresh blood running a ragged path. That's all I remember." She didn't want to tell him the blood had run towards a pair of shoes she owned. Giving the vision words might lend it substance. This would mean she'd seen herself at the murder scene. Another innocent person dead. She wasn't even sure she was staying in Salem for another day.

"Forgive me. You're tired. I'll leave. I'll talk to you tomorrow." He stood and walked to the door.

Cassandra followed and opened to door for him. "Assuming I'm still here."

"You'll be here."

Cassandra gave a half-laugh. "You have more confidence in me, than I do."

She wanted his approval. Needed him to believe in her, even if she didn't believe in herself. She also hated coming across as weak and indecisive. Her heart thumped with each second of silence.

Afraid to glance up at Samson, Cassandra gasped when he lifted a finger and brushed her hair from her face. In achingly slow motion, he bent over and placed his lips on her forehead. Fire flamed in her limbs. Melted a pathway down her body. Strength deserted her, and she leaned against him for support. Cassandra groaned. His muscular hardness now stretched the length of her body. She brought her hands up to rest on his chest. It was his turn to groan. Then his lips were on hers. Hard, gentle, warm, pressing.

Her lips parted and his tongue flicked into the warm recesses. The kiss ignited desire and left Cassandra teetering on the edge of a precipice. She wanted him more than she'd wanted any man. She pressed closer, craving his touch. Aching for him.

The son of a bitch pushed her away.

"You'll be here tomorrow." He gave her a lazy smile and walked into the encompassing dark of the night. The Hummer door slammed. The engine revved and then purred into the night. He was gone.

Cassandra stood, stunned. Such an amazing kiss, then...he left. Maybe she'd scared him away. Been too forward. Yes, that made sense. Hadn't she learned anything over the years? The only time things went as planned was when she kept control over every aspect of her life. She wouldn't let a man intrude on her carefully constructed routine. Especially not Samson. She slammed the door and wandered back to the living room.

The story, the kiss...too much stimulation wouldn't help her sleep. She cursed Samson as she kicked the couch. Before his visit, she'd planned to leave Salem. Now she wasn't sure. She admired his self-confidence and ability to what he considered right without question. She wanted to pack and run. Samson stayed unwavering in his protection of Salem's people.

She groaned and picked up her phone. Memnon. He was responsible for her being in this situation, she'd damn well wake him in the middle of the night to listen to her bitch.

The phone rang five times before the answering machine kicked in. Not good enough. Cassandra hung up and dialed again. She repeated this four times before a sleepy sounding Memnon finally answered the phone.

"It's about time you got your butt out of bed and answered the phone, brother."

"Cassandra?"

"You know anyone else who calls you brother?"

"No, but...what time is it?"

"Late, or early, depending on whether you're a glass half-full or glass half-empty kind of person."

"Cassandra, don't joke. You didn't call this late to chat. What's wrong?"

Leave it to Memnon to get to the gist of the phone call. He might appear a fluff piece, playboy type to people, but his true self lay under the mask. When things got tough, there's no one she'd prefer having on her side. Well, one other person, maybe.

"Quit pondering and start talking," Memnon demanded.

Cassandra started to cry. Her day had started with her first meditative vision in years and gone on to encompass a horrible murder scene and her thinking that Samson was accusing her of murder. Then the sketches she didn't remember doing and Samson's astonishing story. Fear and weariness wound through her. Dragged her down.

Her brother was the only person she trusted enough to be honest with.

"Memnon, you have no idea the day I've had."

She explained the day's events. Sharing the burden brought relief with each word spoken.

"I see."

Nothing more, just silence at the other end.

"Memnon?"

"Cassie, I am so sorry. It's my fault. I had no idea I was sending you into the middle of such a dangerous situation."

"Why did you send me here, Memnon? If ever there was a time for honesty, now would be that time."

"You're right, but I only know what I've already told you. When I bought the house and sent you there, it was because of a hunch telling me you needed to be there."

Cassandra's heart jumped. The grave tone of his voice made her want to run and hide. How she wished this day had never started.

"Cassie, you have a gift..."

Before Memnon continued, Cassandra cut him off. "It's not a gift. Why do people keep calling it that? It's a curse."

"No. I will not believe that, because if you're cursed, then so am I."

Memnon softened his voice. "Sweetie, I know it's not what you want to hear, but you have to face the truth or you're going to destroy yourself with guilt and grief. Mom and Dad's accident was not your fault. You can't cut a part of yourself off as if it doesn't exist. You're forcing yourself to live a half-life, and not a very fulfilled one either."

Cassandra protested. "I'm happy."

"No, you're not. Cassie. You were such a lively child, full of life and questions, sure of yourself and the world. Your ability to foresee things didn't scare you. It excited you."

"What good did it do me if I couldn't save the lives of people I loved the most? No one would listen to me. They...they laughed at me."

"Not those who knew and loved you. You were young and might not remember, but Mom and Dad nurtured the powers in both of us. They taught us to embrace our heritage and not be uncertain. They loved life and wanted us to live it to the fullest. They also believed destiny had a role for both of us."

He continued in a calmer voice, "That's why they went on the trip, even though you saw a hazy vision of their death. They could no more have challenged the fates, then stop breathing. None of it was your fault."

Cassandra was so confused. She plucked the tassels on the couch pillow and remembered the devastating effect of her parent's accident. She'd blamed herself for not convincing them to stay home, and the guilt grew over time to block any hint of her inherent powers.

"Memnon, I'm tired and confused. None of this makes sense now."

"That's okay. Go to bed and sleep. Tomorrow will be here soon enough and you don't have to decide right away."

"Yes. Yes, I do. People are dying and Samson says I can stop this ancient force of evil. God, when I say it that way, it sounds crazy." She dragged her hand across her eyes.

"Maybe, but I wouldn't dismiss what this Samson character says too easily. I have a feeling..."

"Ha. That's what started this whole thing." Cassandra attempted to lighten the mood.

"Yes, well, go to bed. We'll talk tomorrow."

"Sure. And Memnon, thanks."

"Sorry, sis. I'd have done anything to spare you. Goodnight."

"Night." Cassandra hung up and leaned back on the couch.

So much to consider. Memnon was right, their parents had lived life to the fullest and would hate seeing their daughter wallowing in self-pity. Until Cassandra rid herself of guilt, she'd be of no use to anyone. If Samson believed she could help catch an entity that had adopted Salem as its personal battleground, then Cassandra wanted to help.

And with refreshing clarity, she knew exactly what she wanted to do in the morning.

Chapter Eighteen

Despite the events of the day, Samson went to bed reassured. Cassandra represented a powerful ally, and he didn't doubt she'd make the right decision and stay.

Especially after that kiss.

He hadn't known a simple kiss could backfire against him. He'd wanted to give her a reason to stay. Instead, he'd given himself a reason to make her stay. He wanted her lying beneath him, soft and naked. Moaning for him to make love to her.

He shifted uncomfortably, rolled on his side, and punched his pillow.

Jeez, he'd probably have wet dreams all night now.

He needed to get his mind back to business. Distraction led to deadly consequences. He wondered if he should have told her that the book was blank and maybe shared his dreams. He groaned and rolled to his back. A light breeze drifted from an open window and brushed across his chest.

She'd be ticked to learn he hadn't told her everything, but he hadn't been ready to share that the connection between them was the key to unlocking the book and the answer to destroying the evil. He'd tell her tomorrow, and together they'd find the person possessed and knock the evil from them the way Skye did from Matthew last year. Before another murder. Great. Now he had a plan.

He drifted off to sleep with visions of a blond ice-goddess with eyes the color of the ocean on the warmest summer day.

Within no time, he found himself jerked from his body and deposited on the cliff top he'd left so abruptly in his last dream.

The strange elemental storm raged around him, sending sticks and small stones whipping in disarray.

He shouted above the storm.

"You know not the might of the Druids, or you would not dare stand upon these cliffs and taunt me."

"Bah!" Vespasian spat and lifted his dirty, blood-smeared face. The glare of dark, fanatical eyes burned through Seabhac. "Killing Druids is as simple as stamping on a spider. No challenge. Merely certain death for the spider. The only foreseeable purpose of a Druid is to die so I may take their power for myself."

Shock ripped through Seabhac. Could it be possible this creature had mastered the power of transference? The same ability, he himself spent a century perfecting. If so, it was even more important that he didn't allow Vespasian to kill him. Such a warped person with the power of an Arch-Druid...well, the world should not bear such an abomination.

Seabhac eyed the warrior's bloodied tunic and torn cape flapping ferociously in the wind. Piercing rain spattered upon skin and created red rivulets of blood and dirt down Vespasian's arms and legs. Gray clouds thickened and darkened, their presence casting ghoulish shadows upon the earth.

Seabhac shook with the force of understanding.

This creature was not God's creation.

Nay, spawned in the pits of Hell and suckled at a daemon's breast, Vespasian reeked of evil. Terror knifed its way into Seabhac's soul. His gaze darted over his surroundings, searching for an escape. He wasn't strong enough to fight such power. Ainevar might be. No matter what it took, he had to ensure she received his knowledge. Wisdom should have prevented him from crossing the mists of Avalon to save his brethren. His mistake might prove to be the demise of Druidry, maybe humankind, if he couldn't prevent Vespasian from stripping him of his powers.

Seabhac blocked out the clouds, Vespasian's taunting insults, and mentally gathered every ounce of strength remaining within him. He couldn't fight. Therefore, his option was to flee. In a way only the Arch-Druid himself was capable. It took merely a wave of his hand and Seabhac melded with the surrounding elements. A moment or two and he would no longer be corporeal in the place, negating Vespasian's ability to sap his powers.

Through the haze of summoned magic, Vespasian's features sparked with realization followed by frustrated rage. The Roman chanted, his words cast to the winds of the darkening night. Slithering, soaked with dark magic, the words formed a substance surrounding Seabhac.

Vespasian's spell sucked the air from Seabhac's chest. A connection made. No! Dizzy with weakness, Seabhac's essence dissolved. Far too slowly.

In a motion bent on destruction, Vespasian screamed and raised his sword high. Clenched in hands that had surely seen death many times that day, the sword descended toward Seabhac who gave one last desperate push with everything he had left. His act of preservation might have taken too much out of him. If so, he'd die and leave Ainevar unprotected, her teaching unfinished. Pain ripped through him, shredded him into incorporeal nothingness. He pleaded with the fates for time on earth to complete his task. Whirling through a place between worlds, a place that did not acknowledge time or earthly needs, Seabhac panicked. His silent scream tore the fabric of oblivion. Sure that all was lost, the solid sensation beneath his re-formed body shocked Seabhac.

Recognizing the surroundings as those of his room in Avalon, he wanted to leap with joy, but the intense pain racking every inch of his body quelled that notion. He groaned. Whispers from the shadowed corners caused him to lift his head carefully. A cool cloth brushed his forehead.

"Shh, you must rest."

Ainevar.

Thank the fates for granting his wish.

"Ainevar, listen." He barely recognized his own raspy voice. "My journal. Bring it here."

Ainevar frowned and dipped the cloth in water. "You can write later. Now you must rest." She moved to press the cloth to his forehead, but he stopped her.

"No! I die. We have no time." Struggling to a sitting position, he pointed a shaking finger at his journal. "Bring it. And the knife wrapped in cloth that rests there as well."

Ainevar hesitated, but one glare from Seabhac sent her scrambling for the book and knife. She held them out to Seabhac, but he waved her away. "Hold the book in your hands and give me the knife."

He grew weaker. His time was limited. With hurried intent, Seabhac unwrapped the knife, grasped the hilt with one hand, while his other hand rested on the book Ainevar held.

"You will feel a flash of heat and maybe pain, but do not let go of the book." His gaze pierced Ainevar, who gulped and nodded. "Once the ritual is complete, there will be no time for goodbye, because I will be dead. No, do not fret. It must be done. And you must, beyond all else, believe in yourself." He paused, making sure Ainevar understood.

Though tears fell freely down her cheeks, she gave a nod of acceptance. A stab of pride brought tears to Seabhac's eyes. So many years they'd lived in Avalon. Daily lessons and rituals, nightly talks around the fire pit of fate and wonderings of life, death, and beyond. He'd first loved the girl as if she was his daughter. The decades passed, and she'd grown to womanhood. Seabhac had craved the touch of her as man to woman.

He loved her deeply.

Now, he left her alone to battle an evil so potent, so pervasive, he hadn't managed to defeat it. Yet he expected this innocent woman to do so. Foolish! She is no innocent. Look at her, so brave, so courageous. How many others possessed the strength to survive the tribulations set out by an Arch-Druid? None. Only dear Ainevar.

He continued.

"Upon completion of the chant, my soul will reside within the book and make it a living entity. Look there for the guidance and knowledge you've always received from me." He raised the knife. "I will empower this to protect you because I will no longer be able to do. Keep them with you always. They are the balance of elemental and physical. Intellect and force. Druid wisdom and brute strength. You will need both."

Breathing became difficult and pain lanced his chest. "Ainevar, I love you dearly and one day we will be together again. You are now the Guardian of the Druid knowledge. It is your place to ensure the safety of these objects until you can find a worthy recipient. Only when Druids again walk in light and freedom, will we be free.

Remember, though, these objects have the ability to imbue their holder with powers to heal or destroy. All lies with the intent. Promise me you will endure this task."

In barely a whisper, Ainevar spoke. "Dear Seabhac, you have given me a life of love, wisdom, patience, and knowledge. You trusted and believed in me. You humble me with your love and I promise, with everything that I am because of you, I will keep these safe and use them only for the well-being of all. My life I will give before I let them fall into the hands of evil."

Seabhac remembered how Vespasian's face had twisted into a mask of evil upon Seabhac's escape from his clutches. He recalled the flash of lightning across the sky that lit a path to Vespasian and how the Roman sucked in the jagged bolt as a man thirsty for water drank from a spring. Seabhac feared the strange occurrence and connection he'd felt. He worried Vespasian might trace Seabhac's life force? Concern for Ainevar sent Seabhac's weakened heart into spasms. Death came for him. Time ran short. Calming himself, he chanted the verse of transference. Each word took a piece of him. Each time he spoke, he became less. As he sang the last word of the song, a thought niggled at him. Transference. Lightning rod. Visions of the lightning striking Vespasian. A way to destroy him.

Life seeped from Seabhac's body and panic flared. He needed to let Ainevar know what he'd realized. He struggled to sit, but felt as if he was moving through a lake of ice water. Noooo, his mind screamed. I'm not ready. But death's unforgiving claws clutched and pulled him from his body. He barely managed to whisper, "Evil comes for you, Ainevar. Beware."

Cassandra slept, but not blissfully. Instead, she fell into a dream-induced state. Aware, yet not awake. Able to think and reason, but not as herself. The sensation differed from her earlier meditation. This time, she wasn't watching from a distance as she became the person she dreamed about.

Ainevar shivered as Seabhac chanted his death-verse. His voice exuded rich depths aged with centuries of wisdom and experience, and his words elicited haunting visions of other worlds and unearthly forces.

When Seabhac had appeared, broken, mumbling, and barely alive, Ainevar and the Priestesses of Avalon acted to heal the Arch-Druid, but his spirit wavered between the Netherworld and Avalon. The only thing keeping him alive was his tenacity and will to perform one final task upon this earth. A last task to save Druid knowledge, because, as much as Ainevar had learned over the last century, it wasn't near the wisdom-of-ages held by the Arch-Druid himself.

While Seabhac held the knife and laid his hand upon the book, Ainevar studied Seabhac's precious, if slightly weathered visage. She'd grown to love him over the years. Their souls had bound together with kindred respect, common beliefs, and a need to protect ancient beliefs and ways of the Druids. Now he used his dying breath to ensure the future of the Druids who had condemned him.

She held the book in her hands and Seabhac's voice faded. Ainevar's memories threatened to overtake her, until the book warmed in her grasp. With a jolt of awareness, but not surprise, her gaze lowered to rest on Seabhac's body. His last act was to drop the knife on top of the book and lay his hand upon hers. Her eyes welling with tears, Ainevar leaned over and pressed a kiss to his forehead.

She took a moment to mourn the loss of so great a man, but the low murmur of voices and shuffling of clothes pulled her from her bereavement. Standing, book and knife clutched to her chest, she turned to the Priestesses, who waited respectfully.

"Burn the body immediately."

Her words elicited gasps and protests.

"It must be done." Ainevar threw a longing glance at the man who'd changed her life on so many levels. "Even with Seabhac's soul gone, I sense the slightest flicker within his body. The last ember of a dying fire turning to ash."

Her blazing gaze fixed on the Priestesses, trying to lend strength to her reasoning. "Whoever he battled, whoever is responsible for Seabhac's death trip within the elements to reach us, that person managed a connection. He will follow, using Seabhac's body as his beacon. Without doubt, that person will destroy all within his path, for he can allow none to live who possess power greater than he."

Brighid, the head Priestess, bowed her head in agreement and whispered instructions to a couple of the novices, who scurried off to do her bidding. That done, she moved quietly to stand by Ainevar. Tentatively, Brighid reached out and touched Ainevar's hand. "And you, child, what of you?"

Ainevar smiled at the word child. She was over a hundred years old herself and felt as far from a child as the sun from the earth. Yet, based on the lifetime Brighid had lived, it was an appropriate comparison. Tears threatened, but there was no time to grieve.

"I must flee."

Brighid nodded in acceptance and indicated the book. "If, as you say, this person follows a connection to Seabhac, does that not mean he will be able to follow the book, which now holds Seabhac's essence?"

Ainevar's heart jumped. She'd not considered that. Oh, sweet fates, she was not worthy of the task given to her.

"Ainevar, do not worry, we can mask you upon your leave-taking from Avalon. I promise no one will be able to sense you or the book. The cloak of protection will last until you are far from here and safe." Brighid straightened her shoulders and sniffed. "Come, we have much to do and little time to spare."

The next couple of hours passed in a whirlwind of activity. Priestesses prepared the ritual to bind Ainevar in invisibility, arranged food, clothing, and supplies in two leather bags Ainevar needed to carry until outside Avalon. Across the mists waited a horse of exquisite bloodlines committed to strength, speed, and stamina. Only one task remained.

As the fire flamed hot, so flamed Ainevar's blood. As the last of Seabhac's remains charred and turned to ash, so did Ainevar's heart. As the smoke curled and rose into the skies above, so went Seabhac, Arch-Druid.

No, that wasn't true.

Ainevar patted the pouch strapped to her waist. The supple, worn leather carried the book and knife. Seabhac was with her; committed his soul to guide her. When the last of the Priestesses quieted, their chant and silence fell upon the clearing in Avalon. Ainevar picked up her sacs of supplies and without a backward glance slipped silently into the mists.

Breaking to the other side of the mist—the world she'd left behind so long ago—struck her as strange. Her equilibrium adjusted, yet Ainevar still felt askew with the reality of things around her. Promised by Brighid, Ainevar found a horse tied to a tree. Aglow with a golden aura signifying the horse's magical faerie breeding, the creature turned brown eyes in her direction and within that moment, Ainevar knew they'd be friends. Aware of the need for speed, she approached and rubbed the horse's velvety soft nose. He snuffled in her hand, swung his massive head up and back. With a stamp, the horse shifted to present the stirrup to Ainevar in invitation.

"Thank you, Baron." For at the moment of introduction, she'd ascertained his name. Settling her bags behind her, checking the tightness of the pouch strapped to her side, she took hold of the reins and gave warning to her new friend.

"We must travel far and fast. If you tire, let me know and we will rest."

Baron pranced in agreement, and with barely a nudge of Ainevar's heels to his side, he took off with the speed of a lightning bolt. They galloped hard; the countryside flying past in a whirling blur. Tears from the wind, of course, streamed down Ainevar's cheeks. They stopped now and again for food and rest, but their journey was relentless. Ainevar had no idea if her enemy, Seabhac murderer, had detected her presence once she came crossed the mists, but she didn't sense any darkness following her. Relying on the goodwill of others, she used a mild transformation spell and formed a stone into a coin of silver to leave as a thank you for food or shelter.

Days and nights became weeks and months. Hoping to deter any pursuit, horse and woman left a staggered path behind them, keeping mainly to the back roads and forest paths.

One day, the journey came to an abrupt end. Breaking from dense forest to a sight so stunning, so breathtaking, Ainevar nearly fell from the Baron's saddle. Spread below and stretching beyond the imagination lay a rolling landscape of water. She'd heard tales of water so vast it belied belief, but she'd never thought to see it for herself. Slipping from the saddle, she stepped to the side of the rocky cliff and stared at the crashing chorus below her. Thundering, snapping, roaring, the water smashed into the rocks, split into ragged spears and droplets, then fell back onto itself.

Ainevar's senses roared in unison. She breathed the chill salty ocean air.

She lived.

Seabhac didn't.

The pain cut deep, and Ainevar fumbled to open the pouch and draw the book out. It warmed in her hands. Fright pulsed with the rhythm of her blood. She was alone. Oh, heavens above, she didn't know what to do. Where to go? How to protect what Seabhac had entrusted to her.

Emotions swirled from a place inside her that had remained untouched and protected by Seabhac's care and love. Book gripped in one hand, she struck her arms over her head and screamed her loss to the Heavens. Her wail carried across the water and reverberated on the horizon. She knew not how long she wailed before sinking to the ground and clutching the book to her chest.

Reason returned. Seabhac might not be alive, but he was still with her. Against custom, he'd trained her to fulfill the duties of an Arch-Druid. He'd believed in her and left his essence in her keeping. She couldn't let him down. Without her and the book, there remained nothing of the once proud and powerful Druids. The responsibility rested heavily on her heart.

She sniffed. Wiped her nose. Stood. Stared across the expanse of undulating ocean.

Her whispered words rose to mingle with the maelstrom of whipping winds. "I will make you proud, Seabhac."

Cassandra woke with dried tears on her face and her throat clenched in a knot. Choking out a sob, she rolled from the bed and staggered to the bathroom. Grasping the cool porcelain of the taps, she ran water until it was hot and sluiced the liquid on her face. Fully awake, and not knowing what to expect, she lifted her face and looked into the mirror above the sink. The face greeting her was hers, yet not. After seeing—being—Ainevar and living the roller coaster of emotions, Cassandra felt disconnected from her life and world.

Tentatively, she brushed a finger down her face. Ainevar was her. She'd been Ainevar. Except for minor differences, they might have been twins. Ainevar's hair had been longer, the features of her face more finely cut, lips not quite as full, and her eyes more green than blue. Many of their differences could be attributed to Ainevar's harsher life.

Cassandra shook her head. "What am I doing? It had been a dream. She's not even an actual person."

The face in the mirror raised an eyebrow as if to say, you know better.

Cassandra sighed. "Yes, I do." What she'd experienced had been no dream. Whether a vision or a memory of a past life, she didn't know. But the words, I will make you proud, Seabhac, whispered in her mind until Cassandra knew no choice remained. Seabhac's ancient cliff top battle and Ainevar's flight from Avalon had changed her present day world. Forever.

She smacked her hands on the vanity top. Her dream reinforced last night's decision to embark on an experiment or two of her own today. Salem was a living entity, and she wanted to feel its pulse. She chuckled. A bit of Ainevar must have stayed behind because before last night, Cassandra had never considered the earth a living thing.

Well, it was time to expand her horizons.

Tamping down a pervasive sense of urgency, she dressed in her most casual and comfortable clothes, pulled her hair into a ponytail, applied lip-gloss, blush, and mascara, snatched an apple, her sketchbook, pencils, and sunglasses. By the time she was ready to leave, the mundane tasks had helped her recover a sense of control. With a sigh of inevitability, she set off in her car for a day of discovery.

Chapter Nineteen

Joshua bowed his head in prayer. Except he wasn't praying to the good Lord, as his parishioners might assume. He replayed yesterday's ritual in his mind, his blood tingling with the elation of the kill. By rote, he murmured the closing prayer while his congregation followed along.

Their voices rose in adulation to the Lord. Sinners, one and all.

He knew, because they confessed their sins to him weekly. Risking a peek, he opened one eyelid and tilted his head to view the sea of bowed heads. He suppressed the urge to heave a primal scream of triumph and supremacy. They had no idea. No sense of the recent accomplishments of their quiet, boring pastor. Yes, they talked behind his back. Now he was giving them juicy fodder for gossip.

A sliver of unease whispered through him. It wasn't fair. They'd never know the lengths he was taking to ensure their souls remained safe from evil. Once brought into line by fear of retribution, they'd live their pious lives of prayer, never considering the sacrifice that he made to save them.

Anger at the injustice of bearing such responsibility tore with knife sharp pain. Joshua shivered with the memory of slicing into the belly of the sinner, Eric. He reveled with the eruption of power that had accompanied the bloody death and ritual bathing in blood. The thick walls of the church's basement had effectively stifled the screams of torture. The absence of anyone near the church on a Saturday morning gave no audience to the sobs and final moans of a dying man.

The cloaking spell in Hathorne's journal allowed Joshua freedom to walk past people in the Common with the body slung over his shoulder. A couple of people frowned with his passing, maybe detecting a glimmer of his presence. He'd laid the body, set the scene, and waited for discovery of the body. Joshua stifled a smile when he recalled the woman's terrified scream and panic that followed as morbid curiosity drew people to the death scene.

He snorted. Realizing the sound carried across the room built for optimal acoustics, he covered with a cough and finished his final word of prayer. Immediately, shuffling began as people readied to leave. Ungrateful imbeciles. They didn't have the decency to let him finish before wanting to rush away.

"Excuse me." His bellow jolted his parishioners into sitting back in their seats.

Good. It was time they showed respect. "I'm sure most of you are aware of the unfortunate death of one of our own."

Murmurs crossed the room in a wave. Joshua drew the emotion in with a breath and let it sink into his belly. Time to choose my next victim. "At times such as these we need to draw together as a congregation and lend strength to one another."

He viewed the faces below him. Many shone with empathy, others with uncertainty, but there was one...

"I'm sure you all feel Eric's loss, and under such tragic circumstances." He shook his head, feigning disbelief, all the while watching his quarry to make sure he hadn't mistaken the look. No, there it was. A glimmer of impatience. A hasty glance at his watch.

"Eric was not perfect, none of us are."

A roll of the eyes.

"If we can bow our heads for one minute of silence in remembrance."

A silently mouthed curse word.

Joshua took the minute to consider his prospective victim. The expensive suit, gold watch, perfectly gelled hair, tanning salon tan, and diamond pinky ring. Oh, yes. Pride goeth before a fall.

Or, better yet, pride and arrogance goeth before death. He raised his head and released his congregation. With voices raging in his head, Joshua offered goodbyes at the door. He even managed to be civil and shake hands with his next victim.

"Thanks for coming today, Randy. I understand how precious your time is."

"Sure. I know how important my being here is to the collective. Since I'm such an important member of the congregation, I attempt to be here."

Important member. Effort to be here.

Joshua wanted to scream at the man's egotistical assumptions. He ground his teeth to help control the rise of anger and self-righteous piety threatening to overwhelm him.

Arrogant bastard.

Joshua breathed deeply and smiled. Timing was everything. Planning garners the most desirable circumstance. Proper props and ritual ensure access to power. Act not in haste.

All these quips from Hathorne's journal reverberated in Joshua's mind as he bid Randy farewell. With the last person gone and the church to himself, Joshua elated in the silence and the knowledge that the next time they gathered, they'd be offering a prayer up for another of their own. Meanwhile, he needed animal blood to prepare for the next human sacrifice.

Chapter Twenty

Cassandra plopped her butt on a bench, slipped off her shoes, and rubbed her aching feet. The morning had passed quickly, but not easily. During her visit to the older sections of town, she'd sensed energies beneath Salem's surface of touristy glamour. Disjointed whirls of dark sorcery mingled with lighter, more non-threatening threads of magic. She soaked in the ambience of historic homes seeped with tragedy, aching with the imprint of life and death.

At first, she picked up a mild crackle of disjointed energy. Certain areas of town, she'd found slightly out-of-step with surrounding buildings or landscape. Opening her senses and focusing on these anomalies, she'd cracked the surface and caught glimpses of a world existing beyond the vision of most people. She toured through houses such as The Derby House and The House of Seven Gables, and acclimated herself to the constant barrage and thickening visibility of entities that swirled and whirled on a plane only slightly removed from human beings.

The knot in her throat slowly dissolved when she realized none of them meant her harm. They merely existed because they didn't know what else to do. They had nowhere to go, or possibly didn't know how to release themselves from the world and go beyond.

Even so, by noon she was shaking with the intense onslaught of otherworldly energies and needed to take a break. She stopped at a small café on Essex St. for a coffee and bagel. Parking her car, she walked past the Peabody Essex Museum and to the Old Burying Point Cemetery, where they'd found the dog a couple of days ago. The place she'd met Samson.

Without the confusion of a curious crowd, presence of police cars, flashing lights, and yellow tape slashing across gravestones, the cemetery became a different environment. The eerie quiet and aged sense of history wound around the landscape like early morning mist in the deepest forest glade.

Cassandra stood by the stone fence that showed the entrance to the cemetery. She inhaled sharply to adjust her awareness of the surroundings. She stepped forward and noticed a mild wind the ruffled the limbs of the cemetery's ancient, gnarled trees. Goosebumps rose on her arms and crept down her torso. Her legs shook, and she fought the urge to cry. Why, she didn't know. It was as if all the people buried in the Old Burying Point Cemetery whispered their tales of suffering and death to her.

Row upon row of grayish, cracked, and tilting headstones gave silent testament to a lengthy history. Regret. Anger. Pity. Defeat. Desperation. Resignation. All these emotions and more washed over Cassandra in an undulating wave that left her weak. Yet, each footstep became stronger, more sure. Each story of a past life and death reinforced within her a deeper understanding of herself. On a level unseen, Cassandra knew that by relating their stories, the spirits also gave their trust.

Cassandra wandered for 10 minutes or more. She belonged here more than anywhere else in Salem. She grinned and didn't even want to know what that statement said about her.

It was a shame so many of the headstones hadn't weathered the centuries well. Crumbling, leaning, and worn, many of them were barely distinguishable as anything other than a decaying mass. Cassandra ran her fingers gently over a few of them as she passed, noting each detail, experiencing each sensation sharp and sweet.

Vandalism was an obvious problem, and Cassandra gave a silent apology for the disregard people showed for such a hallowed place that should have garnered respect. Echoes of ancient voices moaned, threading within the creaking of the old tree limbs and rustle of leaves upon the patchy dirt.

Cassandra noticed a walled courtyard surrounded by empty stone benches. Closer inspection revealed each bench bore a name and date. With rising nausea, Cassandra recognized the names as those of the accused witches executed during the witch trials. A stone memorial for the falsely executed. A cenotaph of remembrance for Salem's history of intolerance and violence.

She bowed her head and offered a brief word of love to the restless spirits. A soft touch upon her shoulder and waft of warm breeze across her face acknowledged her words as accepted and appreciated.

Suddenly needing movement and the reassurance of life, Cassandra sat up and glanced down at the slender gold watch on her wrist. She couldn't believe how much time had passed. Two hours, not the ten minutes she'd thought.

How had she lost so much time?

Her heart thumped, and she risked a harried glance around the cemetery to see if anyone was around. Thank goodness she was alone.

With only one place left on her list, Cassandra returned to her car. As with the cemetery, Salem Common presented a far different setting without all the confusion of a murder scene. The peace gave Cassandra a chance to enjoy the atmosphere of the vast park. Lushly green, surrounded by trees and wrought iron fencing, the park lent itself well to an afternoon stroll, picnic, or playtime with your dog. Birds twittered and tweeted, while squirrels scampered amongst the tree branches hiding their hard won nuts and other treasures.

Someone had done a great cleanup job on the gazebo. You'd never know a body had lain there only yesterday. Worn out from the cemetery's echoes of life and death, Cassandra sat on the gazebo steps with a groan. She'd connected to the town's power lines more than she'd ever thought possible. Knew where they lay and how to access them. Memnon would be proud. She gulped a mouthful of invigorating hot coffee and smiled.

Now she'd wait. She would not be alone for long.

Samson approached the gazebo and wasn't surprised at the lone figure perched on the steps. A waif. A pixie. A princess with golden hair. An exquisite faerie bound in an earthly body. No, an Arch-Priestess of the Druids. Yes. That description fit her best. Honorable. Loyal. Bound to the earth.

She looked up and smiled. His heart jumped to his throat. She'd changed. When he'd first seen Cassandra, a murky knot had cut off the flow of life energy to parts of her aura. Now, it was as if the knot had been untied and released vivid colors to even the farthest reaches of her aura. Not only that, but the hard-to-see energy field now extended past the bounds it had before.

Samson stepped within the boundary of her aura and swore he walked into warm wafts of a summer breeze. Neither of them spoke as he sat on the steps and extended one of the two cups of coffee he'd brought with him.

Cassandra accepted with a slight upward curve of her lips. "You knew I'd be here?"

"I figured."

"I see."

With the sun to warm him, the darting birds to entertain, a coffee to drink, and a striking woman beside him, Samson didn't imagine life could get any better. However, the future promised much worse. This moment of bliss was but a sliver in time to enjoy and fortify. He watched in the distance at the constant stream of tourists through the Witch Museum.

"It's a busy place." Cassandra indicated the museum with a nod of her head.

"You have no idea. In peak season the lineups are phenomenal."

"I've been in the store, but haven't seen the show yet. It must be worth seeing if it's so popular."

Samson laughed and took another sip of coffee while considering his answer.

"Depends who you ask and what expectations they hold. Some people love the performance, others walk away disappointed. I've listened to comments it is cheesy, second-rate, and amateurish. I remember hearing one woman complain because she had to sit on a wooden bench to watch the show. She was perturbed there weren't plush, padded seats for paying customers to sit on."

"What do you think?"

Cassandra turned her shimmering blue eyes on him, and Samson wanted to melt. Good thing he was sitting. Bad thing that this woman affected him so much.

"It's a horrible situation being presented in as simplistic a manner as possible so the public gets a glimmer of the past without actually being overwhelmed with the vehemence, terror, anger, and unrepentant murders. I think people who complain about it not being comfortable enough are living in an arrogant world of self-centered denial and people who want a true re-enactment of the past are living in an arrogant world of self-centered denial. One group refuses to acknowledge the horror of the times and the other group couldn't handle the truth if they did live it. I think the people who run the place are walking a razor's edge, trying to show the past without really showing the past. Does that make sense?"

Cassandra nodded, her blond hair slightly shaken loose from its elastic to drift across her cheek. Samson fought the urge to touch the silken looking strand.

"At least the building is magnificent, even if the history it shows is ugly. I'm assuming it used to be a church." Cassandra said.

Samson considered the ecclesiastical stone building with its twin towers framing a large wooden door and arched, rod-iron covered window above. "You'd be right. The style is Gothic Revival, and it's the Second Church Unitarian, built in 1845. Not quite as far back as the witch trial period, but old enough."

"Wow. I'm impressed."

"It is impressive."

"No, I mean you."

Samson shrugged, trying to appear nonchalant while his heart warmed with her praise. "I've lived here my entire life. Besides, I told you before, the town and its people are my responsibility. Knowing everything possible about the town and people grants me an edge." Maybe he sounded self-righteous or moderately arrogant, but he meant every word. People had often teased him for being too serious about his obligations.

Cassandra pursed her lips and considered his words. Samson sensed the struggle to meld her business oriented, logical side with her emerging mystical side, so he remained silent. Until she asked the questions brewing, Samson was content to sit quietly and finish his coffee. The sun crawled across the late afternoon sky, but neither of them moved. The thrum of traffic and beeping of horns increased as the dinner hour approached.

Cassandra's voice smacked into the quiet, and she asked a question Samson hadn't expected. "Tell me about your dreams."

He hesitated. Considered lying, or putting her off with a distraction. She didn't let him.

"Don't even try."

The full force of her determination blasted Samson. He raised his hands as if to ward off the nearly physical assault of her intent.

"Whoa. Dial it down a notch."

Cassandra frowned and gave her head a shake. "Sorry." She took a deep breath, gulped the last of her coffee, and stared him down with a calm demeanor. "You came to me asking for my help. You seem to feel I've a role to play in this ghoulish debacle, so give me all the details. Not a convoluted story you've watered down to pique my interest, but not scare me away."

Samson's lip twitched into a hint of a smile. Women who didn't shy from the truth attracted him. A woman who demanded respect and consideration, who, in the light of even the most daunting circumstances, didn't stand there blubbering like a ninny.

"Okay. First, I have to say that it's my turn to be impressed." He answered her unspoken question. "That you know about my dreams."

Cassandra lifted a shoulder and let it drop. "It's what I do. What I've always been able to do."

Samson thought she was going to share, but her eyes clouded over. She retreated behind her carefully constructed wall and asked. "Your dreams?"

Samson related his courthouse dream, doing his best to leave out the visceral, stark fright penetrating the below ground room. He attempted to describe the archaic witch trial, but his voice faltered at the memory when John Hathorne had pinned him with a penetrating glare oozing with malevolence.

Cassandra wrapped her arms around herself. Relived the dream with him. She laid a hand on his arm and the warmth of her touch comforted Samson and settled his jangling nerves.

"The other dreams I've had, two of them, are different. Rather than watching from the sidelines, I was the person I dreamed about. I lived his desperate drive to ensure the survival of Druid knowledge."

Cassandra stiffened but remained silent.

Samson continued. "In a series of flashes, I watched the invasion of Caesar, the desecration of places held sacred by Druids, and the savage slaughter of all Druids except one."

"Seabhac." Cassandra's whisper blew from her lips in a reverent word.

Samson snapped his head around to stare at Cassandra. "How...oh, I forgot. You're psychic."

"No, that's not it." She didn't explain further. "You forget, Seabhac wasn't the only one left after the slaughter."

"You're right." Samson shot a frustrated frown at Cassandra. "Look, you want the details. I'm giving them to you, but you have to share as well. If it's not your psychic ability, then how do you know this stuff?"

The worn wood of the gazebo's steps creaked when Cassandra shifted. Activity in the Common had slowed to almost non-existent, as afternoon shifted to early evening. Cassandra felt the expectancy palpitate in the air, making her breathless. Samson's psychic radar tuned into Cassandra's struggle. Her distrust of him, his reaction at odds with her need to share. He didn't push, though his belly churned with the urgency to act. He ground his teeth. There'd be another murder, and Cassandra represented part of the solution. Heck, she might even be the salvation of Salem. How could he make her understand?

Her voice barely caused a ripple, so quietly she spoke. "I saw it in a dream."

"What? What did you see in a dream?"

Samson's reaction jolted Cassandra into a standing position. She looked everywhere but at Samson as she wrapped her arms around herself and rubbed vigorously. The words streamed from her lips, each word visibly calming her. "It started with meditation yesterday morning, that's what I'd been doing before you came, then continued last night in my dreams. At first, I floated in the universe, then found myself hovering above a cliff top battle between two men. A storm raged above them, yet left me untouched, and waves crashed against the rocks in the ocean below. I don't know how it ended because my dream yanked from there into a dim, sparsely furnished bedroom where one man killed another with a knife."

Cassandra sat back on the gazebo step. "Then, a furious whirl of energy took me on a tempestuous ride through time until I ended in the present. I believe I was in a church with a man who was a priest or minister."

"How do you know that?"

Cassandra lifted a hand to circle her neck. "He wore a white collar and stood among rows of wooden benches with a huge cross behind him."

"The cross you mentioned with the blood?"

"Yes. But there's more."

Samson didn't doubt the worst was yet to come. "Go on."

"At the beginning, on the cliffs, the storm clouds formed into a jagged spear of lightning and blasted the man dressed in Roman clothing. He had dark eyes, but after the lighting struck him, his eyes whirled with demonic intensity. I can't begin to describe the madness in their depths, but the man in the bed who stabbed the other one, had the same churning glare."

"Let me guess. So did your clergyman."

"Yes. Different men in different centuries, yet they possessed the same chilling expression."

"That happened during your meditation. Tell me about the Seabhac and Ainevar dream?" Samson asked.

"Seabhac appeared in Avalon, barely alive. The priestesses and Ainevar worked to heal him, but failed. His last act was to give a book and knife to Ainevar with the words, 'They are the balance of elemental and physical. Intellect and force. Druid wisdom and brute strength.' When he died, he put his essence into the book."

Samson's mind whirred with the information. Puzzle pieces fit together with a snap and so much became clear. "That explains a lot. We knew the history of the knife as far back as the Salem witch trials, now we know how far back it goes. It also explains the book's strange powers and how it can write and re-form itself."

"You believe *Faerie Enchantments and Sorcerer Magick* is the book from my dream and it's actually magic?"

"Yes. It sounds strange and I haven't told you everything yet." He grimaced at Cassandra's raised eyebrow. "Right now, the book is blank."

"Blank? How? What does it mean?"

"I've seen the book once or twice and writing covered the hundreds of pages. Now, nothing. Skye and her mom used it last year to defeat this ancient force, but not now."

"That makes little sense..." She hesitated, torn by conflicting emotions. "How can that be?"

Samson laughed. "There's not one thing in this entire situation that makes sense. At least not on any normal level. Maybe in an alternate reality. Which is where we need to focus if we're going to beat this thing."

"We." A thrill of fright touched her spine. Her eyes narrowed. She spoke softly. "That's assuming I stay."

"Well. Are you?"

Chapter Twenty-One

Cassandra laughed. "You think I'd have an answer to such a simple question." She crushed her paper coffee cup in a clenched fist.

"It's going to be dangerous, isn't it?"

Samson nodded. "Yes."

"Neither of us has any idea how to defeat this thing, do we?"

"Well, the book..." Samson began and then shrugged. "No, not a clue."

Earlier, Samson had called her an honorable person who'd shut herself away from the world and was only living half a life. Memnon said she possessed a gift and blasted her for her half-life existence as well. Maybe she should listen. Rather than fear her powers, she should use them to help others.

Truthfully, she was tired of running. Worn down from carrying around her guilt. Staying in Salem and defeating the evil might offer the chance to defeat her demons. Besides, the idea of a book imbued with Seabhac's life source and a knife containing souls fascinated her.

"You do know that I have next to no control over my powers, right?"

"I'll help you. I've had experience."

The corner of Samson's lips lifted into a crooked smile, and Cassandra thought she'd agree to anything. But years of denying who she was and what she was capable of was a pattern not easily broken.

She stared into the distance and lifted a shoulder. "I'm not sure. I just can't commit."

She felt rather than saw Samson's frown of frustration. When he spoke, his voice was controlled and quiet. "Fine. I guess I can understand. Meanwhile, at least do me a favor and look at the book?"

Curiosity battled wariness, and Cassandra answered before logic took over. "Sure."

"Great." Samson stood quickly before she changed her mind. "It's in the Hummer."

"You keep an antique book in your vehicle?"

"It's better than leaving it at home." He frowned. "Maybe it's not safe to look at the book in public. I should take you home and let you check it out."

"It's just a book. What do you think will happen?"

His glare seared into her. "Just a book. Come on. You can say that even after your dream and everything I told you?"

Cassandra shuffled her feet and squinted up at Samson, who towered above her, blocking the sun. "For all I know, it was just a dream, and I have no way to verify what you've told me." Cassandra didn't know why, but she felt the need to push Samson's buttons.

Samson snorted. "Thanks. Why not just call me a liar?"

"That's not what I meant."

"That's what it sounded like." He ran a hand through his hair and shifted his feet. "Are you willing to look at the book?"

She stood and brushed the dirt off her butt. "I'll look."

"Fine. Then let's go."

Without waiting for her, Samson set a long-legged stride towards the Hummer, which sat on the edge of the Commons.

Idiot. Why do all men have to be such idiots?

Cassandra stuck her tongue out at Samson's retreating back and leisurely followed. By the time she caught up, he was holding the door open and tapping his foot in an impatient rhythm. She smiled at him and climbed into the masculine, tank-like vehicle.

He climbed into his seat, and she quipped. "Home, James." Samson harrumphed in return, revved the engine and put foot to pedal fast enough to cause Cassandra's head to jerk back against the headrest.

Idiot.

Cassandra crossed her arms over her chest and wished she could start this day over. Heck, starting her life over sounded even better.

By the time they reached the house, the sun had dipped below the horizon and dim shadows of dusk danced across the landscape. An in-between time. A time when nocturnal animals stirred and chased the light loving creatures to lairs and nests.

Cassandra made coffee, set out a dish of crackers and cheese, then sat on the couch and held the silk wrapped book on her lap. Samson's intent consideration annoyed her, so she shot him a frown. With difficulty, she ignored Samson and unwrapped the silk to reveal a leather-bound, timeworn book, complete with frayed edges and faded color. Cassandra's insides frothed with bubbles of familiarity. All sight and sound receded to a distant haze as she focused on the book. Drawn by the weight of the book in her lap, Cassandra reached out with a wavering hand and brushed a finger across the leather.

Fire and ice. Dark and light. The sweet taste of honey and the pungent scent of the earth during fall's cycle of decay. Grotesque bodies, sliced and bloody, assaulted her sight. Cold, stabbing inevitability tore a hole in her mind. Lungs expanded to bursting with the exertion of a harrowing race for life. Then it all snapped shut into oblivious darkness. She floated and then began to shake. A voice called out to her from beyond. Struggling to make out the words, the voice remained distant. The more she strained to hear, the less she heard. The shaking increased until her teeth rattled in her head. Finally, the voice broke through with a bellow.

"Cassandra!"

Her eyelids flew open, and she gasped at the pain of awareness. Clutching the book to her chest, she released her lungs and let the oxygen flow.

"Are you okay?" Samson knelt on the floor. His hands held her arms in a vice grip, and concern etched his face into a frown.

"I'd be fine if you'd let go of my arms."

Samson dropped her arms as if they were rabid. "Sorry. How are you?" He remained kneeling on the floor in front of her.

"Fine. I guess." Cassandra rubbed her arms vigorously where Samson had gripped. There'd be bruises tomorrow. "I went into a vision or trance for a second there."

"A second. Woman, you were a zombie for 10 minutes."

"No. That can't be."

"Trust me. I wouldn't have shaken so hard if you'd only been out for a second. I was ready to call 911, though what good they'd have done, I'm not sure."

He stood. The shadow of his towering height dwarfed Cassandra. She held the book tighter in a gesture of protection, though whether she was protecting the book or thought the book might protect her was the question. Samson took a step back, allowing Cassandra room to breathe.

"I'm fine. Sit." She waved a hand to the chair he'd been before her episode. "Drink your coffee."

Samson sat. Gulped his remaining coffee in one mouthful and set the mug back on the table with a definite thump. "Coffee's gone. Now tell me what happened," he growled.

Cassandra related her experience while Samson stared at her, unblinking. "The book became a doorway and pulled me into the past. If you hadn't shaken me, I'm sure I'd have ceased to exist and become lost in the pages of history. Strange. Not a pleasant experience."

"It's my fault. I should have prepared you for a reaction. The question is, did your journey into the past return the writing to the pages?"

"I hadn't thought of that." She stared at the book. It appeared so innocent, yet offered lifetimes of ancient magic and dangerous pitfalls. "Should I open it?"

Samson reached for the book. "Let me do it. I don't need another near heart attack."

Cassandra handed him the book, slightly reluctant to do so.

Sharing a glance of hope, Cassandra crossed her fingers while Samson creaked open the heavy leather cover. He flipped through page after page, his expression giving nothing away, until Cassandra wanted to burst with anticipation.

"Well?" She prompted.

"Nothing. Nada. Not a thing. Zilch. Zero. Blank. Dammit."

"I'm sorry."

Samson's lips lifted in a parody of a smile. "Don't be. It's not your fault."

"I guess that negates your theory of the duo guardian thing, doesn't it?"

"Not necessarily. Since we don't understand why it's blank, we don't know what will make the writing reappear. And I still believe, based on our similar dreams and our mutual roles in the current murder, we have to work together."

Cassandra didn't want to believe.

Didn't want any role in death or age-old evil.

She didn't say a word, but her changing facial expressions must have clued Samson in to her thoughts.

"Don't tell me you still have doubts."

"No, it's not that I doubt anything you say."

Before she voiced her roiling thoughts, Samson leaned forward and fixed his gaze with hers. "I've been patient, but with people's lives in danger and evil that has survived centuries stalking Salem, you better stop waffling and get with the program."

Cassandra flushed with indignant anger, yet restrained from snapping a retort. A deep part of her agreed with Samson, but years of habit dragged her into a familiar space of non-committed denial. Mental and physical fatigue tugged at her.

Drawing a hand across her eyes, she declared. "I'm tired. I'm going to bed and hopefully have an uninterrupted night's sleep. We'll talk tomorrow when I've had a chance to assimilate everything the last couple of days have thrown my way."

Samson ground his teeth and stood. The blasted man left her standing there and disappeared with a curt goodnight. With a sigh, she cleared the dishes, went upstairs, and fell into bed. Unfortunately, she didn't get the peaceful night's sleep she needed.

Chapter Twenty-Two

With her faithful faerie steed ever at her side, Ainevar roamed the lands of Britain for what seemed an eternity. With the knowing that came from the book, and therefore Seabhac, Ainevar taught Druid ways and did her utmost to ensure even a grain of their past remained alive until such time as the persecution of anyone or any belief not Christian, stopped. She had not known the hard-fisted, fearful reign of the new religion would dominate for so long.

She'd not known her life would be so long. Seabhac's life had spanned uncountable years, but she'd assumed hers would end much sooner. As it was, she outlasted Baron and even the land of Avalon. Her heart ached with the loss of everyone and everything familiar.

Even the land itself morphed into an entity strangely foreign to her. No longer respected and paid homage by the Druids, it was as if Mother Earth rebelled by withdrawing into herself. The land died as people slowly forgot the old ways that had fed the earth. Ainevar experienced more difficulty sensing the power lines or finding a pure place to do ritual.

So, she travelled far and wore herself into a barely living shadow as she struggled to stay ahead of the darkness, pursuing her yet attempted to stay in one place long enough to teach.

She'd never forget the day long ago when her wanderings had returned her to the mists of Avalon. Decades had passed since she'd sensed even the slightest hint of the darkness. Rumor said that Vespasian died many years earlier, and for a short time, the killing stopped. Ainevar took the reprieve as a time to return to the land of mist and mystery.

She wished she hadn't.

Vespasian had obviously connected to Seabhac on the cliff top and followed him to Avalon. The devastation was complete. Untouched by animals having an innate respect for hallowed places, the bones of the priestesses lay scattered around the fire pit, which had been Seabhac's burning place. The bone's stark whiteness contrasted obscenely with the greenness of the grass. Vespasian must have come upon the women before the ritual's end, which meant Ainevar had timed her departure well. Or not, depending on your perspective, she thought bitterly.

"Do not trouble yourself, little one. You did not determine Fate with your actions." A soft touch brushed across her cheek. Whispered words drifted in her mind.

Ainevar startled with surprise. Her gaze searched the desolate field of death, once the most illustrious of all places. Nothing. Not even the stirring of a songbird, or the cackle of a crow. Stillness haunted the echo of Avalon.

"Seabhac." She whispered.

The chill of approaching evening cooled her skin, and she pulled her cloak closer around her shoulders. Baron snickered and stamped a hoof, showing his unease at remaining. So they'd left, and Ainevar felt more alone than ever.

Lifetimes ago for most people, her brief visit had become a distant memory for Ainevar. The voice she'd heard in Avalon never returned, but the book remained strong and true while the knife saved her life many times.

She slumped exhausted at her campfire one night. Alone, aching for the fulfillment of laughter and love, and so tired. Ainevar realized her time of life ran short. Not one person she'd taught over the centuries had shown promise or motivation enough for Ainevar to gift with the full knowledge of the brutally vanquished Druids.

Orange flames crackled and coals glowed with the brightness of a fire long burning. Ainevar poked the fire and it flamed bright, then muted. It threatened to die soon. She'd follow shortly. When she did, no one would remain. All Druid knowledge would pass into memory and weary travelers would tell stories around campfires such as hers. Tales of wonder, but not of truth. A way to waste minutes between dusk and slumber.

She could not die and face the Arch-Druid in the afterlife with the knowledge that all he'd sacrificed, all he'd lived his life and died for, was gone. She could not—would not allow such a thing to happen.

Possibly a transference spell? Seabhac had transferred his knowledge to the book, but not his power, only his power of protection to the knife. She considered the possibilities. Her fatigue grew to excitement. With nerves strung like a bow at full draw, Ainevar paced, and her mind whirled through memories, ancient rituals, and the last minutes of Seabhac's life.

She'd apply Seabhac's spell of transference to an object, perhaps the knife. Except she'd use an enhancement. Seabhac's spell gave Ainevar access to him through the book, but did not give her access to his power. Without the book, Seabhac ceased to exist, as did his knowledge. Ainevar needed to transfer her power to the knife and spell it so that whoever she passed it to would possess the ability to draw power from the knife and integrate it with theirs. Knowledge and power passed from one person to another. That remained the only way to ensure the immortality of the Druid knowledge.

Primal need for Druid survival drove her and Seabhac's ethereal spirit guided her through night into day. Summer sweetness gave way to brisk fall breezes. She foraged for food and dug with frozen fingers for much needed herbs to test in ritual after ritual. With small amounts of food and even less sleep, Ainevar lost weight and tired easily.

Finally, as sharp winter's breath warmed with the stomach tingling scent of spring, Ainevar accomplished her task. She gazed in wonder at the knife. Such a simple item, yet it held the fate of the Druids within the cool steel of its blade. Glorious, with its ebony handle glinting with shards of rainbow colors, yet lethal enough with its blade honed to the sharpest tip.

For her next task, she had to find a worthy recipient to entrust with the knife. Such a person did not exist in Britain. No. Her travels had shown her that much.

Over the centuries, she'd travelled the breadth of the land, reveling in the rocky shores and lush green, inland hills. She'd survived Rome's shaky rule over Britain with its constant flow of disputed and undisputed emperors and false promises. When the Vikings arrived on the southeast shores, she'd fled to the north and held a place until 1070 when the reach of William the Conqueror forced her from her northern home.

Now, with the Norman rule stamped out and the beginning of the reign of a new breed of king, the urge to leave the land of her birth drove Ainevar from deep within. Her long-life had presented no person to take the role as protector of Druid knowledge. Drawn by the barely remembered memory of her first sight of the vast ocean, she set a westerly course.

Travelling by foot, because she'd never found a steed to replace her beloved Baron, it took her weeks to reach the shore. When finally she came, weary, to the water's edge, the salty tang and crisp coolness of the water invigorated her. Ainevar breathed the pungent aroma of the creatures and seaweed living and growing beneath the rolling water. Yes. Her final destiny lay across the water. Past the distant horizon, beyond sight and comprehension, would be born the person who Ainevar could entrust with knife and book. Then she'd take a last breath and join Seabhac in the Netherworld.

With the morning light came a foggy, dream-saturated consciousness. Cassandra rolled from bed and shuffled to the bathroom where she splashed cold water on her face. An act becoming a regular morning routine these days. A glance in the mirror showed a face shadowed with hard choices and too much loss. More Ainevar's face than hers. It worried Cassandra that maybe her dream twin was somehow taking over her waking self.

She closed her eyes, counted to ten, and looked again. Better. The image staring back was hers. Thank God. As she brushed her teeth and hair, Cassandra considered her dream. No. She couldn't fool herself with false belief any longer. Her nighttime adventures went beyond mere dreams and into the realm of the unimaginable. Genetic memory of an ancestor? Possibly even her memories from a past incarnation.

Cassandra mentally chastised herself. She didn't believe in reincarnation. Or did she? Truth be told, she had no idea of her own values, on a moral, religious, or esoteric level.

She plodded from bathroom to bedroom. The realization struck her that she didn't know who she was. How trite? She laughed at people who said they needed to find themselves. A convenient mid-life excuse for having an affair, buying a sports car you don't need, or quitting the job you'd had for years and going back to university. Now, here she was in a crisis of personal faith and understanding.

Cassandra yanked on her pants and buttoned her silk blouse. If she stayed, her motives must be for herself and the people she might help, not because Samson goaded her into it.

Half a life.

Samson and Memnon's words repeated in her mind. She wanted a full life, whatever that entailed. If not now, when? What other situation would give her the opportunity to find herself—she so hated that expression—and grow into her fullest potential. Nothing. Nowhere. It was now. Here. In Salem.

Damn.

What if she messed up and more people died? Cassandra dreaded the responsibility. Couldn't risk anything happening again. Much better for her to leave Salem before things got out of hand. Amidst the irritating voice in her head and battling a mind reeling with conflicting thoughts, Cassandra felt a sudden, powerful urge to talk with Skye. Now she had strange experiences to share. She needed guidance from one who'd been there. Not Samson, who overwhelmed her with his single-mindedness. She'd talk to Skye and then decide whether to stay in Salem. Yes. A solid plan worth following.

Samson stared at the book and cursed for the hundredth time since he'd arrived home last night. Sleep eluded him, driven away by a compulsion to decipher the mystery of the blank book. Nothing worked. The extent of his progress was to stare and curse.

The first ray of the morning sun shone through his partially closed curtains and wavered on the book, flaring the pages into a creamy glow and then subsiding. Samson ran a hand over the pages. His palm prickled with magic, sensed the pulsing energy of ancient knowledge hiding beneath the surface of empty pages.

Damn!

Exhausted and frustrated, he folded the heavy leather cover, effectively closing the blank pages for sight, and set down the book. On cue, the phone rang.

"Hello."

"Hey, boss. Sorry to interrupt, but..."

"I know." Samson ran his free hand through his hair. "You've got a crime scene I absolutely have to see."

"Right. Don't worry, it's not another murder. Not human, anyway. Out at Salem Willows Park. You can't miss it."

"Thanks, Jaks." Samson hung up and gave silent thanks for small miracles. At least missing a pet was not as bad as a family member. Though, remembering the bond between Jerome and Chance, he realized many people considered their animals to be members of the family and the trauma of losing them just as wrenching.

Grabbing his badge, gun, and jacket, he made for the door while slinging his holster over his shoulder and buckling it in place. Knowing he might need to use his gun whether on duty or not, he took the weapon with him everywhere and used a nylon concealment holster as an alternative to the usual duty holster. Besides, he felt bare without it. A wizard without his staff might experience a similar bleak sense.

Driving up Fort Avenue toward Salem Willows Park, he realized only in Salem could a person make a comparison between a gun and a magic staff, and not have it sound strange.

Chapter Twenty-Three

Cassandra knocked tentatively on the door, not sure she even wanted someone to answer. Her thumping heart sent her blood racing and drowned out the sound of the nearby ocean. She hadn't decided to stay, but figured advice from a person who'd been in a similar situation might help.

No one answered the door and Cassandra considered fleeing.

Scaredy-cat.

Memnon's voice taunted her from the past. It had been years since he'd called her that.

"Don't start." Cassandra whispered a warning to a phantom Memnon as she lifted a hand to knock a second time. An excited bark drew her to the back yard instead. She followed a stone path around the side of the house until she came to a wooden gate signaling the end of a huge hedge running off into the distance and curved out of sight down by the water's edge.

Another bark followed by a feminine laugh. Cassandra steeled herself and stepped through the open gate. Chance saw her immediately and ran to her side, stick in mouth and dancing excitedly.

"He wants you to throw it for him." Skye stepped from the deck stairs to the grass.

"Will he let me take it from him?"

"Are you kidding?" Skye laughed. "Yes."

Cassandra hadn't been around dogs much and seeing the stark white glimmer of sharp teeth from behind wet, drooling lips, made her want to retreat a step or two. However, the soft, begging plea in the dog's eyes beckoned her. She reached down. Before she touched the stick, Chance dropped it and danced a couple of anticipatory steps away. Laughing, Cassandra picked up the discarded stick and swung her arm. The stick flipped through the air, and Chance turned into a gleaming, red-gold streak as he raced for the treasure. As fast as he'd left, he returned with the stick and Cassandra threw it again. The game continued five or six times before Skye stepped in.

"Chance, you've had enough attention. My turn. Go lie down."

Cassandra was impressed when the dog dropped the stick, ran up the stairs, and lay in a corner of the deck where he stared over the backyard.

Skye laughed. "He's surveying his domain. I haven't decided if it's a dog thing, or a male thing. Come on up, I've been waiting for you." She gestured to the deck stairs.

Not sure what to make of Skye's remark, Cassandra hesitated for a second before following her up the stairs. The deck ran the length of the house and approximately twelve feet wide. The dark wood gleamed with the obvious care of someone who'd spent time protecting it against the elements. Complete with lounge chairs, table, dog bed, and chew toys, the deck felt homey and comfortable. Especially with the warm breeze drifting from the ocean. It lazily caressed the chimes on the limb of a gigantic oak rising from the middle of the deck.

"You built your deck around a tree."

"Of course." Skye frowned. "Why take it down and displace so many animals. Besides, it's been there for so long, no one even knows how old it is. Who are we to even think about destroying such a guardian of the past?"

Skye placed a hand on the trunk and closed her eyes. Cassandra swore a glow of white surrounded the woman, then disappeared. A chipmunk popped his head from behind an oak leaf and chittered a greeting, his merry brown eyes twinkling.

Cassandra laughed at the insignificant creature. "I understand what you mean about displacing the animals. That little guy is way too cute."

Skye dropped her hand and smiled mysteriously. "He's only one of many who uses this tree. I can offer you cookies and a glass of iced tea. I finished baking the cookies just before you arrived."

Cassandra hadn't noticed the pitcher of iced tea and platter of yummy chocolate chip cookies. "You really were expecting me."

Skye's laugh sounded like the chimes. Musical. "Yes. You're here to talk about your dreams and the book. Oh, and Samson as well."

Cassandra reached out and took the glass of iced tea Skye held out to her, but it was a mechanical movement rather than a conscious one. She gulped a mouthful of the sweet, tart, cool drink and set the glass on the table. "Are all people in Salem so open about magic and psychic abilities?"

Skye settled into a lounge chair and took a considering sip of her drink. Cassandra envied the woman her stunning looks, shining ebony hair, and eyes that shifted from blue to green with each thought.

"I suppose the truth is that there's no time for subterfuge. I am what I am and you are what you are. The sooner you can understand and accept your role in the current situation, the safer Salem and everyone who lives here, will be."

"I suppose you're going to tell me my role." Cassandra sounded bitchy, but didn't care. She was tired of people telling her what to do and how to do it.

"No. That, you need to figure out yourself. I can help." She reached over and laid a hand on Cassandra's arm. "I know what you're feeling because I've been where you are. When I came to Salem last year, I didn't even know I possessed powers." Skye snorted and leaned back. "Within my first few days here, I found a skeleton behind a secret wall in my new house. I met Jerome, who hated me on sight for reasons I'd discover later; my parents were in a car crash, which left Dad in a coma; powers I didn't know I had started causing no end of trouble; Mom told me about an ancient family birth-task that involved curses and a knife. Not only that, but shortly thereafter, this evil that has haunted Salem for centuries almost killed all of us in a ritual meant to transfer enormous power." Skye shivered. "I hate to consider the consequences. So you see, Cassandra, I do understand what you're going through. I also know if you walk away from this town, you're condemning Salem to a time of darkness unseen since the Salem Witch trials of 1692. Possibly even worse."

Cassandra blew out the breath she'd been holding. "I see. And I have no choice in this whole situation."

"Yes, you have a choice. You're free to leave."

"Sure, and be responsible for more people dying."

Skye just smiled and shrugged.

"I'm not even sure how much of this I believe."

Skye chuckled.

"Aren't you going to say anything? Try to convince me to stay?"

"Nope. That's your choice. But while you're here, you can tell me about your dreams, and then I can tell you everything I know about Samson."

Cassandra gulped her iced tea and set her glass on the table. "That's the second time you've mentioned him. I'm not sure what interest you think I have in him, other than his connection to this situation."

"Let's start with the basics first. Your dreams."

Cassandra told her everything.

Samson surveyed the familiarly staged setting of macabre murder. The only difference between the canine death scenes was one took place at the cemetery and this one at the park, near the merry-go-round. Coincidence? Or a twisted scene of portrayal. A warped way of magnifying the monstrous act committed in a place familiar to the laughter of children.

"Where are the damned crime lab guys? And who let those reporters get so close? Get them behind the tape. Now. We're not here for a picnic in the park. It's a crime scene, for God's sake." Samson turned to the young patrolman who'd withstood the worst of the verbal rant. "So where are the crime lab guys? Get them here, now."

The patrolman flushed, punched the radio button, and started talking. Samson didn't bother waiting for the result of the conversation. His verbal lashing held enough heat to light a fire. He didn't need to ensure his command was carried out.

Instead, he crouched by the poor, butchered animal. With an impassive demeanor honed over years of crime scenes, he studied the tableau. Every detail. Every slice of flesh, arrangement of limbs, and blood-drawn symbol, was precise. Laid out exactly as the first scene.

If all else followed accordingly, there'd be a human body laid out similarly tomorrow. His blood turned to ice. What if the next victim was a child? Christ. Futility swept over Samson as he realized the narrow chance of stopping another murder. He rose and turned his back to the frenetic activity. There was no forensic evidence at any of the scenes, so he had no idea where to find the evil, and the book was blank. The only hint of any progress was Cassandra's sketches of the Seven Deadly Sins. Even that didn't give him much to work on. Heck, practically every person in the city of Salem qualified as a sinner if you followed those biblical edicts.

Samson stared out over the Atlantic with an unfocused gaze and breathed the salty tang of the water deep into his lungs. He thought his veins ran with salt water instead of blood and if he were ever cut off from the ocean for any reason, he'd die. For now, he let the weedy, briny scent swirl around inside him, while his aura fed off the undulating waves pulsing with nature's power.

Energized and more able to handle the situation at hand, he considered his next step. An ancient force of evil possessed the murderer; therefore, normal police procedures were useless.

Samson needed to focus his attention on more mystical techniques. *Faerie Enchantments and Sorcerer Magick* held the answer within its archaic pages. The key to Salem's survival lay in unlocking the mystery of the blank book. Time for Samson to take a chance.

Chapter Twenty-Four

Cassandra waited for Skye to speak, but the other woman seemed hypnotized by the rolling ocean waves. She twined her fingers together, shifted in her lounge chair, and watched a silent Skye. A perfectly carved statue of alabaster skin and blue eyes. A stray ocean breeze lifted raven-dark hair from Skye's shoulders and sent it in a playful dance, while Cassandra sipped her now warm iced tea. A gull screeched a single cry and everything fell silent until Skye finally spoke.

"It's all fascinating. Your dreams fill in many blank areas of the knife's history."

"Oh. What blanks?"

"Well, according to Mom, the history was sparse. We believe it was forged in Avalon and given to our ancestors in Salem around the time of the witch trials as a way to transfer power and knowledge from one person to another. A protection during uncertain and barbaric times against losing all the knowledge that took a lifetime to learn." Skye leaned forward, the intentness of her gaze boring into Cassandra. "We didn't know who, or what circumstances dictated the making of such a knife. We also didn't know about the connection to the book. And the poem about the knife gives contradictory information, though it makes sense now."

"What poem?"

"Oh, yes, of course. You wouldn't know." Skye leaned back and closed her eyes. Her voice thrummed with the melody of magic rooted in an uncertain and potent past.

"Shaped from the truest of earth's steel

Forged in fire blessed by the fire Goddess, Brighid
Cooled by the water of the sacred Chalice Well
Breath-blown for purity by Arianrhod, Goddess of air
This knife shall contain the magic of the craft
Perfected by the Goods and passed to each in their line
But beware, Goods from ancient to new
Guard this knife, ritual-bind it and keep it near
For this same magic may be turned for evil purpose
With mere intent and a sacrifice of human blood
This knife of divine creation will instill the wielder
With the powers of the sorrowful witch sacrificed"

Skye's reverent voice tapered off to a whisper by the end of the poem. "See, the confusion was always that if the knife was created in Avalon, how had my ancestors come into possession of it? And if it contained the power of the craft and could transfer the power of a witch, as the poem states, how could it have been created in Avalon before witches existed? Magic, sure, but 'witch' was a term that came into being after Avalon. I think there was also some confusion because an identical knife was forged during the witch trial time period. One meant to be a decoy to help keep the actual knife safe."

Cassandra's interest increased. "Second knife?"

"Yes. Used as a red herring to protect the actual knife."

Skye tugged at her headband and shook her hair free. The dark mass settled around her shoulders, and she rubbed her scalp with her fingertips. "It worked too, until a local woman, Verity Parker, sought to access the power of the fake knife. The result of that fiasco was the death of Jerome's mom during a ceremony gone wrong. The evil festered for thirty years and then came to the surface last year when I moved to town." Chance raised his head and whined. Skye smiled and gave him a reassuring pat.

Now they were getting to the primary reason for Cassandra's visit. "You actually beat the evil?"

"Sure. By using the knife."

"The real one? You know where it is?" Excitement raised the hair on Cassandra's arms and she stifled a chill brought on the incoming ocean breeze.

Skye lifted the corner of her mouth in a slow smile. "Yes to both questions."

"So you think this Ainevar person of my dreams brought the knife across the ocean and ended up in Salem?"

"You're the only person able to answer that question, but it sounds like that's the case."

Cassandra sat back with a thud. The responsibility came back to her again. She watched the sun drop over the ocean, its rays glinting fragments of light on the rolling water. "I'm not sure why I keep having these dreams."

"Dreams have a purpose. You will learn from them."

"Tell me about some of your dreams."

Skye smiled. "I was usually an observer, not the actual person in my dreams. My dream about the knife took place in a jail cell and was a conversation between Sarah Good and her daughter, Dorcas. Sarah spoke of a knife her grandmother had given her. She also made Sarah swear a blood-oath to protect the knife and ensure to only use it for good."

She sipped her iced tea and continued. "Sarah's grandmother was the first of the Good's to possess the knife and swear to the birth-task of protecting it from evil. I got the sense that she'd come into possession of the knife from someone else. Now we know it was likely Ainevar, though a direct connection hasn't been made yet."

"Did your dreams ever stop?"

"I only have them when I need information. I think you'll find the same with yours. Pay attention and open yourself to the flow of energy. I also have a theory." Skye shot a hesitant glance at Cassandra. "Are you up to hearing it?"

"At this point nothing could shock me. Go ahead."

"It's more a feeling than anything based on fact, but I think your dreams are past life memories. Either you were Ainevar, and that's why you're living the dream, or her spirit has connected with you and enabled you to view events from her vantage point."

A deep knowing broke loose inside Cassandra and sent cold waves of certainty rolling through her. Why had it taken a stranger to point out what she should have seen herself?

"Hey. I didn't mean to upset you. It was only an idea."

"You're right." Cassandra slapped a hand on her leg. "It makes so much sense. How did I not figure it out myself?"

Excitement bubbled in her stomach and tightened her throat. "My entire life, I've felt strangely disconnected, but not only because of my psychic abilities. A part of me functioned slightly out-of-sync with the overall pace of the world around me. As if it didn't fit. I didn't fit. I assumed it was because my powers made me different." Cassandra's voice rose as she excitedly reasoned through a new understanding of herself. "As a child, I remember sensing an awareness of a constant pressure surrounding me. A hovering presence. I'd wake up during the night and hear a voice. I came to rely on that voice the same as I would a parent or teacher. It became such a part of my daily life I eventually accepted it as normal. That voice, that presence, must have been Ainevar."

Panic drove Cassandra to her feet where she stood facing the ocean. "If I can't figure out that one simple thing, then what good am I? How can I possibly expect to help anyone?" She ran her hands over the deck railing, taking comfort in the smooth, solid wood.

"Cassandra. I can't even imagine living with another person's spirit imprinting itself in every aspect of your life. You must have been a confused child."

"Ha. That's an understatement."

"Look, I understand your concern. I fought the same feelings of uselessness last year, but everything turned out fine. Until now. At least you have knowledge and a basic understanding of your powers. That already puts you ahead of where I was when I came to town." Skye stood and moved to stand beside Cassandra.

"I...my powers can't be depended on. I'm frightened of being responsible for people's lives."

"You're not in this alone. Samson's destiny and yours intertwine, past and present, and I can guarantee you won't find a better man to be at your side. Other than Jerome, of course."

"Yes, but you and Jerome get along so well. I don't think Samson even likes me."

Skye laughed. "The first time Jerome and I met, he practically accused me of being involved in his mother's murder. Believe me, it took time and a lot of patience for us to come together in any semblance of co-operation. Now look at us."

Cassandra smiled, grateful for Skye's encouragement. "I don't expect I'll end up married to Samson and pregnant with his child. But I'm sure I can handle working with him if it means saving lives."

"So, you're staying?"

"I'm not sure yet. I'll let you know when I decide."

"I have a way to help you decide. Hold on, I'll be right back."

Cassandra nodded. While waiting for Skye to return, she considered her situation. Leaving town offered the easiest path. Pack and leave. That meant she'd be letting Memnon down. Worse, she'd leave behind an evil born during Britain's turbulent struggle for identity and the Druid slaughter of those times. Religious cleansing. Seabhac had entrusted Ainevar with preserving Druid knowledge and the existence of a journal and knife proved she'd succeeded. Now, the objects had returned, bringing evil with them. Even if Cassandra was a present day incarnation of Ainevar, did that make everything her responsibility?

What about Seabhac? He'd sent his life force into the journal on his deathbed. Did the blank pages mean his soul had left the book and carried on to wherever souls went on their last journey?

Cassandra's thoughts rambled and raved over what if's and maybe's until she wanted to scream. That's the state she was in when the touch of Skye's hand on Cassandra's arm made her jump.

"Sorry. Are you okay?"

"Yes. Sure. I was thinking. There's so much to consider."

"I've got one more thing for you to fit into what I'm sure is a raging mass of confusion."

Skye raised her hand. In her palm rested a pouch of black silk sewn shut. She reached in her pocket and produced a small pair of scissors. "I'll open it so you can have a look, but just don't touch it."

Cassandra stared at the silk pouch and scissors, certain if she followed Skye's request, her life might spin into an unorganized, uncontrollable maelstrom.

"Hell." She swore in a forceful whisper as she watched Skye cut the threads. "It already has."

Carefully, Skye snipped the delicate threads holding the pouch closed. Shaking, yet breathlessly, strangely excited, Cassandra watched as the pouch opened to reveal dark shadows. A glint of light, then darkness.

The world stopped. Cassandra existed only during that moment. Hovered in the uncertain mist between past and present. Of its own volition, and despite Skye's warning, her hand lifted and reached into the silken cloth. Her fingers brushed across hard steel and Cassandra sucked in her breath as everything came rushing back to her in a blazing flash.

Frantically, she looked to Skye for help. Saw only the disappearing face of a surprised, worried woman. An unseen guide grasped Cassandra and threw her into the past, into the midst of a life-threatening situation.

Samson closed his living room curtains, effectively shutting out the view of the ocean and afternoon sun. He tried not to think too deeply about what he was doing because he'd advise anyone doing the same thing to stop being an idiot.

Oh, well. So I'm an idiot.

Striking a match, he lit a variety of candles. Silver for intuition, clairvoyance, and astral energy, and white for spirituality and peace. His plan was to gain access to the book's information using his astral self. Physical restraints of a human body might be the impediment to seeing the writing Samson knew existed on an ethereal level.

Not bothering with the distraction of music, he sat cross-legged on the plush living room carpet, cleared his mind of all outside thought, and focused on the area of his body located two inches inward from the naval. His martial arts training had taught him the body's central points and how important it was to keep the area open and filled with energy. A sea of energy.

He concentrated on fanning the flame he imagined at the spot. His mind's eye watched the flames burn brighter and hotter. Heat pulsed outward and spread through his body.

His innate sense guided him to take that energy and direct it outward, hoping to connect with the book. Time passed and the midday warmth faded, while car horns honked in a hazy distance. Sweat beaded on his forehead and his legs cramped, but he ignored the pain and continued to concentrate. When he thought his venture might prove unsuccessful, the book warmed in his hands and a barely perceptible vibration hummed at the tips of his fingers. Sound vanished and Samson felt himself wrenched from his body and dumped into the pages of the journal.

Flashes of time. Shadows and light. Glimpses of a life lived and a love unfulfilled.

He became Seabhac. Lived the book's creation and years of labor the Arch-Druid had poured into his writings. On a deep and shadowy level, awareness of the writings in the journal came to Samson, and he mentally scanned the pages, soaking in the knowledge. Until he came to the cliff top battle, where Vespasian, possessed by evil, jolted Samson from his path and thrust him into an even darker place.

In this place, time weighed heavily. Consciousness, a barely recognizable state. He ached for the death of innocent Druids and the knowledge of lifetimes. He battled a conscience so ingrained with the edict never to divulge the Druid secrets in script. He yearned for the forbidden love of a woman who held the future in her hands. And he screamed in silent agony at a death never-ending. Limbo. A captive of his own making, held prisoner by the bindings of the journal.

Afraid for his sanity and terrified of being stuck in such a place, Samson gathered all his remaining strength and focused it into his center. With a mighty effort, he let out a primal scream and forced himself into awareness. But the darkness didn't want to let go. Finally, like a boot pulled from greedy, sucking mud, his spirit found release and returned to his body.

Awareness rushed back and his stomach gurgled with immediate hunger. He sat briefly and gathered strength to stand. Shuffling to the kitchen, he snatched an apple from the fridge and bit into the tart, tasty fruit. With heart pounding, his mind ran over his experience and categorized his findings as if he were writing a police report.

Found a point of entry. Lived a lifetime of emotions. Read journal pages as intended. Was mission successful?

No. Damn it!

He tossed the apple core into the garbage and cursed again. He'd read Seabhac's journal entries up until the Druid's death, but nothing more. He was no further ahead than before. If the book contained the Druid's essence, Samson had seen no evidence.

An icy shiver rippled down his spine. Briefly, upon his return, barely a glimmer of a moment in time, he'd felt the eyes of evil upon him. His wrenching gut told him his journey into the journal had provided a link from the evil to him.

Chapter Twenty-Five

The acrid smoke burned Ainevar's nostrils. She ran for her life while her heart bled at the thought of her possessions burning in the flames of a fire set by her enemy. She tripped in the darkness and drew a sharp, hurting breath. Sobs tore through her.

Relentless in its quest to claim the knife and journal, the evil had pursued her across ocean and time, claiming people with a glimmer of darkness in their soul and susceptible to the whisper of greed. Under the guise of rooting out witchcraft, the latest fear-monger manipulated the townspeople into a frenzy, and accused Ainevar of magic.

They'd torched her home, and now she fled. Grasping the bleeding wound in her side made by the swipe of a knife blade, Ainevar swept branches from her face with her free hand. She fumbled in the darkness of an unfamiliar forest.

Shadows, dimly lit by the barest slice of moon sitting high in the sky, danced in and out of the trees. The lack of moonlight should prove a hindrance to Ainevar's pursuer, who did not possess her extraordinary senses. Yet, as the crashing of the underbrush drew closer, despite Ainevar's hurried pace, she realized the futility of such hope. Evil lent magical abilities to the human who should have fallen behind by now.

After centuries of running, the calendar year had ceased to matter to Ainevar. Now, as her death drew near, she became painfully aware of the passing of time, and Seabhac's dying words burned into her, much like the raging fire burning behind her.

...you are the Guardian of the Druid knowledge. It is your place to ensure the safety of these objects until you can find a worthy recipient. Only when Druids can again practice in light and freedom, will we be free.

She'd failed. In all the years of flight, she'd helped many people, but never had she felt ready to bestow the gift of ancient knowledge.

Now it was too late.

Death waited in the dark of the night.

Born in the wild hills of Britain, trained by the most powerful Arch-Druid ever, able to claim Avalon, the land of mists, as her home, Ainevar seemed destined to draw her last breath in a nowhere town called Salem, Massachusetts. Despite her best attempt, the culmination of Seabhac's knowledge and trust would die here.

No. She must trust the Fates. Though her visions foretold a horrible future for the tight-knit community of Salem, a time when hysteria overcame the most sane and reasonable person, Ainevar sensed a deep reverence for life in many townspeople. She'd befriended one such woman and needed to trust her now, with everything.

She grasped for Seabhac's journal and knife to make sure they were still safely strapped to her back. Prompted by a precognitive flash, Ainevar had hidden them in a hollowed out space among the roots under a nearby tree and retrieved them on her flight from danger.

Weak from loss of blood, her breath coming in short spurts, Ainevar spied the faint outline of the small house belonging to the woman she knew as Annie. Driven with a desperate desire to fulfill her task, she surged forward.

The slash in her side burned, and blood spattered the ground, leaving a dark trail behind her. Her nostrils tingled with the coppery scent of blood, and she gagged. Her strength wavering, Ainevar used her body weight and the last of her energy reserves to push open the door. The decrepit wooden door opened with the squeal of warped wood. She fell onto a dirt floor, her abrupt entrance eliciting a scream from the sole occupant.

"Thank the Fates, you're here." Ainevar whispered. Her voice raspy from smoke damage to her throat. "No, don't." She waved when Annie moved forward. "Bring me your boline.

Annie's hesitation prompted Ainevar to grit her teeth and hiss. "Hurry. Time runs short."

Moving as fast as her aged body allowed, Annie shuffled to the crudely constructed altar perched in the back corner. Her movement sent flecks of dust to dancing in the flickering candlelight. Taking the white-handled ritual knife in hand, Annie returned to Ainevar's side and knelt to the floor with a groan.

"Ah, I fear age creeps up on me."

Ainevar might have smiled at the complaint if she hadn't needed to conserve what energy remained.

"I would give all for the luxury of growing old."

Annie patted her shoulder while tears traced a pattern down her wrinkled cheeks. "You are too young to think of death. I'm sure we can heal your injuries." She placed the knife on the dirt floor and ran her hands in a seeking motion over Ainevar's body.

"No." Ainevar brushed the hands away. "I am older than you can imagine. I will not live out the night."

With an effort, she picked up the knife. Its white handle shimmered in the glow of the candles. With Annie lending support, she stood. Fumbling with the leather strap, Ainevar pulled the pack off her back. It dropped to the table with a loud thump and spilled its contents into the dim light. Palpable in the small room, the sense of death mingled with anticipation. Intent on her task, knowing the preciousness of time, Ainevar took Annie's hand, more gently this time, and pinned the woman with her gaze.

"What I am going to do will bind you and yours from now into an uncertain future. Nothing and no one will be more important than protecting what I am entrusting to your care. Do you accept this task?"

Annie stared at the book and knife on the table before her. Candle wax sizzled. A tiny mouse scampered across the floor. All else was silent. Hesitating only slightly, Annie raised her gaze to Ainevar and nodded.

Satisfied by the surety in the other woman's eyes, Ainevar lifted her hand and drew the sharp blade of the boline across her palm. Blood welled and flowed. She placed her hand upon the top of the book. The words poured into her mind, and she spoke them aloud.

"The tide of Life ebbs and flows continuously
Ever shifting, ever searching in its quest
A force sown from the elements of the earth
That must eventually return from whence it came
But with each ebb of a life, a new flow begins..."

Ainevar's breath faltered and her heart fluttered an irregular beat in her chest. "Give me your hand." She took Annie's hand and with no warning drew the blade in a swift motion across the startled woman's palm. Annie's hand shook and her face drained of color, but she remained quiet. Guided by instinct, Ainevar continued the blood oath ceremony by placing Annie's bleeding palm on the book.

"...so, as blood of the past returns to Earth's womb
This sacrifice of blood, offered freely, creates a bond
Once spoken, never to be broken, never to falter
Upon this day, I charge thee and yours this task
Guard and protect this book and knife."

Warmth spread to her limbs and blood mingled with blood. Shaking with the fatigue from fighting death's approach, she dropped Annie's hand and sank to the floor.

"It is done. The book will guide you. The knife will protect and empower you." The room wavered as her vision faded. Shadows and mist rose from the floor to envelope her in a soft and warm embrace.

"Go, now. Evil approaches."

Sound receded and Ainevar's last vision was of Annie opening the door before fading into the night with the book and knife clutched to her breast.

Within her mind, she cried. "Seabhac, I have failed you."

His face appeared before her, contrasting pale against the darkness of death's blanket. She reached a hand toward him. Her mind cried again. I have failed you.

"Come to me, Ainevar."

Spoken so distantly, she wasn't sure she'd heard him call.

"Come to me."

Seabhac's face faded. Ainevar panicked. Terrified of losing him, she ran faster. All she found were dark, dancing shadows, taunting her with whispers of failure.

"Come on. Wake up."

"I failed you," she whispered, and closed her eyes. Tears rolled down her cheeks. Tired, weakened, she sank back into the oblivion of death.

The insistent voice prodded. Dragged her back to awareness. "What are you talking about? You have failed nobody."

The mist faded to reveal the face of a stranger. No, not a stranger. She strained to remember, but flashes of flame blinded her and searing heat drove her. The man moved swiftly, dark eyes blazing with hate. She whimpered. A scream gathered in her throat at the glimpse of silver steel clutched in his hand.

Nooooo!

Sharp pain pierced her side and the scream died. She swayed. The world spun and dipped like a roller coaster. Too weak to stand, she fell to the ground. Hard. She blinked, expecting to see the inside of the dusty, dim hovel where she'd fled for her life, and was shocked at her surroundings. Her fragmented thoughts strained to understand. Her trembling hand touched her side where a knife had sliced. Nothing. She was healed. Even Druid knowledge couldn't heal that quickly.

"Hey, are you okay?"

"I..." She gazed into the most gorgeous eyes of blue with a hint of purple. "Blueberries."

"What?"

"Your eyes are the color of blueberries."

That's when everything hit her. Her hand flew to her mouth, and she frantically re-adjusted her mind to the present. Skye and Jerome stood by the deck railing, while Samson knelt beside her, his forehead creased into a worried frown.

When Skye noticed she was awake, she ran to kneel by Cassandra.

"Are you okay? My, God. You touched the knife and then fainted. You were unconscious for so long and moaning. It sounded as if you were in pain, so I called Jerome and Samson. I didn't know what else to do." Tears flowed down Skye's face and she ran her hands over Cassandra to reassure herself all was well.

"I'm fine. I think." Cassandra gently prodded her side where the knife had slashed Ainevar. "But I had one hell of a dream."

"No doubt." Samson held her gaze and then gave a definitive nod. "You're fine. Here, let me help you up."

His touch sent a shot of heat through her. Not the ravaging heat of flames that had nearly taken Ainevar's life. Rather, flaring warmth that spread and left her limbs weak and quivering.

"I think I need to sit." Cassandra avoided looking directly at Samson, but noticed the slight smile lifting the corner of Skye's mouth. Oh, God. She hadn't thought she was so transparent. To cover her discomfort, she quickly related the details of her dream while the others listened and nodded and hummed in the appropriate places.

When words failed her in describing Ainevar's death, Samson squeezed her hand lightly and said. "Take your time."

His calm manner helped Cassandra, but relating Ainevar's last thoughts and emotions proved too much for her. And the tears fell as she finished her tale.

"She died believing herself as a failure. She gave no consideration to the centuries she spent dedicated to preserving the Druid knowledge, or all the people she helped with her healing skills. Her final, gut-twisting thought was that she'd failed Seabhac."

"She didn't fail him." Samson declared. "According to your earlier dream, Seabhac's words to her were, 'It is your place to ensure the safety of these objects until you can find a worthy recipient.' She did that. She passed the knife and book on before she died."

"Yes, but you're forgetting the rest of his speech. 'Only when Druids again walk in light and freedom, will we be free.' As far as Ainevar was concerned, she hadn't fulfilled that part of Seabhac's last request. At the time of her death, the Druids, as with the witches of the time, still practiced in secret."

"But not anymore." Jerome leaned closer and gave Cassandra's arm a reassuring pat. "Because of her sacrifice, the knowledge was preserved and can be used without repercussion."

"She didn't know that. Clearly the Fates agree with her, or the book wouldn't be blank."

"But it wasn't blank until..." Skye flushed and stopped talking.

"Until I came to town." Cassandra's voice dripped with bitterness.

Silence followed her statement, and she wanted to melt into the deck and disappear into a void. She stood. "I think I should leave." She wasn't sure if she meant to leave and go back to Memnon's house, or leave town altogether. As if sensing the duality of her emotions, Samson immediately stood and took her arm.

"I'll walk you back. We can talk."

She wanted to argue, but the steely glint in his eyes halted any protest she might have made. "Fine." With a quick glance at the offending knife and with Skye's comment to call her no matter what time of day. Cassandra bid a hasty goodbye.

The walk home only took a couple of minutes and no one spoke. But Samson's presence set Cassandra's nerves on end.

Samson leaned forward and whispered, "Hey, relax."

"I am relaxed," Cassandra muttered.

Samson chuckled, and Cassandra risked a quick glance in his direction. The words, ruggedly handsome, came to mind. A barely visible scar cut through his eyebrow, uniquely colored eyes, his chin with the slightest hint of dark stubble, and lips to drive a woman crazy. Samson turned to her. Palpable tension, hot and sexual, blazed between them. Samson's nostrils flared and Cassandra flushed.

"You're no more a failure than Ainevar was."

His words caught her off-guard.

Shame and guilt battled within her. "I'm not sure what you mean."

Samson spoke softly. "Your parents."

Cassandra's throat constricted, and she fought the urge to flee. "They died in a car crash when I was young. I'm not sure what that has to do with me."

"No? What about the misplaced guilt you suffer because you predicted the crash and couldn't stop them from leaving."

Cold prickles rushed through Cassandra, and she froze with mortification. Years of guilt burned in her stomach. Her limbs weakened. Then the anger struck. She slammed her hands on her hips and glared at Samson.

"How dare you?"

Damn him. How dare he resurrect her pain! She wanted to scream at him and demand he apologize for invading her life.

Hot blood rose to her face, and without thinking, she raised a hand and slapped him. The resounding crack echoed in the stillness of the late afternoon, and Cassandra immediately recoiled from the uncharacteristically violent act.

Cassandra waited for him to yell at her, or make a retaliatory move, but he only flared his nostrils and lifted a hand to touch his cheek. When he spoke, his voice rumbled low, and he forced the words through clenched teeth.

"I dare because people are dying." Aloof and distant, he continued as if reciting a speech. "There was another dog slaughtered today, so I'm guessing there'll be another murder tonight."

He stared at her. Waiting.

"I'm sorry. I don't know what I can do. I can't tell you more than I already have."

"Fine. Then give me your sketches so I can study them for clues."

Cassandra retrieved the sketches and handed them to him.

"Next, you need to decide if you want to stay and fight, or run for the rest of your life and live with actually being responsible for someone's death. I've got a long night ahead of me, so goodbye."

Having answered her unspoken question, Samson turned and strode back up the driveway, leaving Cassandra alone and shaking on the front porch.

Chapter Twenty-Six

Joshua slunk through the darkness. He scrambled into the bushes from behind the garage, hoping no shuffling footsteps or rustling clothing gave him away. Once in place, he shifted on the hard, uneven ground and stifled a sneeze. He waited. Patience ran short while waiting for Randy to return home. Technically, he'd only make it as far as the back door.

His thoughts returned to the stab of discomfort he'd experienced earlier in the day. A sharp sense of danger. Encroaching, stifling, the awareness of the archaic nemesis so near it had almost made Joshua cancel his mission. Failure and frustration flashed into his mind, but he would not be defeated.

Laughter drew Joshua forward, and he peered inside the window he'd squirreled himself under more than an hour ago. A woman, as radiant and golden as an angel, spoke on the phone she held in her hand. She moved around the kitchen with grace and beauty that belied her earthly chains.

The spicy scent of spaghetti sauce drifted out the partially open window. The woman hummed a haunting, soft melody, evoking distant, hazy memories of comfort that Joshua struggled to recall. The voices raged at him to forget. The nagging memory disappeared in the swirl of shrieking phantoms.

Whore. She mocks you. Teases. Discipline her.

Joshua growled at the insistent demons. Heat knifed his groin. Beauty was a tool of the devil. Meant to weaken and blind a man to the truth of a woman's nature. The woman strutting in the kitchen needed to know she hadn't beguiled him. She needed a lesson in a man's right of supremacy. Joshua's holy right of might, against the wiles of a woman.

His hand moved to his groin, and he rubbed hard, as if that might quell the lust flaming through him. The demons were right. The woman needed a lesson on the libertine practices of sexual blatancy. If the wench persisted in enticing him, Joshua would oblige her. Lust may be a sin, but using it as a tool to teach the sinner was assuredly acceptable.

The slamming of a car door snapped Joshua back to his current task. The crunch of shoes on gravel elicited a wave of excitement. Different from the sexual lust he'd felt, his instincts flared into visceral bloodlust and pious righteousness.

The woman had almost deterred him from his mission. Jezebel. Tempestuous bitch. He'd handle her later.

"I don't care if he's been with the company for fifteen years, his sales have plummeted. Fire him." Randy snapped his cell shut, cursing and muttered, "Damn every incompetent twit ever born."

Joshua glowered at Randy. His lip lifted in a sneer. He must smite such arrogance from the planet. Obliterate it from the presence of a worthy Lord.

Each crunching step brought his prey closer. Joshua's heart beat in time with each footstep. Thud. Thud. Thud. Anticipation heightened his senses until he could barely contain himself.

Randy moved closer, the breadth of his body a shadow outlined by the light of a nearby streetlight. Joshua waited. Clutched the ether-soaked rag in his hand. His quarry moved past him and reached for the door handle. Joshua shot from the bushes, grabbed a handful of Randy's hair, jerked his head back, and jammed the cloth over his nose and mouth.

He expected the man to melt to the ground, but the son of a bitch put up a fight. Randy grunted and rammed an elbow into Joshua's ribs. Pain sliced through Joshua, but he clenched his hand harder over Randy's mouth. The struggling man stomped down on Joshua's instep.

With a leaping motion, Joshua wrapped both legs around his quarry. Randy staggered. His breathing became shallow, and muscles slackened. Finally, Randy sagged, moaned, and sank to the ground.

Relieved, Joshua rolled off him and stood, his legs shaking beneath him. It took a minute for his breathing to even out. He had to hurry. If Randy's wife had heard the car door, she'd be expecting him in the house any second. Placing a hand under each of Randy's arms, Joshua dragged the inert man back to his car.

He anticipated the long night ahead. He'd enjoy every blood-filled minute. Unfortunately, Randy wouldn't be able to say the same.

Chapter Twenty-Seven

Samson spent the night staring at sketches and driving around town, comparing them to anything similar. That, as well as watching for unusual circumstances, exhausted him by morning. The phone rang a shrilling scream. Cursing, Samson wheeled his Hummer to the side of the road and answered the insistently ringing contraption.

"Sorry, boss. You're going to want to head to Salem Willows Park."

"The park?"

"Close to the same spot as the dog yesterday."

"I'll be right there." Christ. The park. The same place as the dog. That hadn't been the M.O. for the first murder. The murderer had laid out dog and human in different places. What did it mean? Did it mean anything?

Samson didn't ponder the questions because he arrived at Salem Willows Park. The scene was reminiscent of yesterday. Strangely still and deafeningly silent. The mood more somber because the corpse was human, not canine. In the distance, the ocean waters lay liquid smooth, not a leaf rustled, and no bird twittered. Samson soaked in the unearthly atmosphere. Mother Nature giving a quiet prayer for the dead.

Humph! Too sappy even for me.

He wondered where all the reporters were and why no police cruisers or police tape marked the scene. He strode to Jaks, ready to blast him for not following procedure and not being in uniform.

Seeing the reprimand he was about to receive, Jaks raised a hand. "Before you rant about proper handling of a murder scene,

I'm trying to keep things under wraps for now. There's no one around and as long as that's the case, we can keep the scene clean. Once the tape goes up, so does the curiosity of the public. Then we get bombarded with media."

"Who found the body? And how did we get so fortunate for the crime to go undetected so far?"

"I found the body on my morning jog. No one else knows yet, and it's early in the morning so we might have an hour or two before confronting the media and public curiosity."

"Have you notified the C.I.D.?"

"I told them to bring their equipment, get here quick, and keep it quiet."

"Okay. Let's get through this and get the scene cleaned before anyone knows what's going on."

He doubted such luck, but one could hope. Pulling Cassandra's crumpled sketches from the pocket of his windbreaker, he walked to where Jaks directed him. It didn't take long to find the sketch that matched the scene. The body lay sprawled in drunken sailor style on one of the bench seats in the merry-go-round. Smeared dirt and tattered clothing led Samson to believe the person might have been homeless while alive, but a closer inspection revealed manicured fingernails, tanning salon tan, and the faint odor of hair gel mingling with the sharp tang of blood.

There was a lot of blood.

Someone with money who'd been dressed in tattered homeless clothing. Why? Another look at the sketch clenched in his hand, gave Samson his answer. Scrawled across the top of the paper was the word, Pride. The murderer had deliberately staged the scene in a manner meant to show contempt for the victim.

However, Samson didn't see the word Pride anywhere. He perused the scene and squinted against the rising sun. With the warming of the day, he yanked off his windbreaker and tossed it over a bench.

"Hey, boss, over here."

Jaks motioned Samson to the far side of the merry-go-round, where Samson noticed a pile of clothes laid out beside the word Pride. Written in blood, same as the first victim.

"Once the C.I.D. is done, check the clothes for identification so I can notify the family."

The thought of telling the family incited an acid burn in Samson's stomach that rose to his throat. He jammed the palm of his hand against his diaphragm and pushed.

"Jaks, you got any Rolaids?"

Jaks patted his uniform pockets. "Sorry, no."

Who the hell did this guy think he was? Coming into Salem and disrupting the even-keeled, peaceable environment Samson worked so hard to ensure.

"Chief?"

"Damn it, Jaks, when we catch this bastard, he spends every waking minute of the rest of his life in jail, and I get to choose his cellmate."

Then he remembered. He wasn't after a regular criminal. His quarry was an ancient evil born in a time practically before the civilized world existed. His throat tightened with an onslaught of doubt.

He better stop thinking like a cop and start thinking like a witch. *Faerie Enchantments and Sorcerer Magick* held the key. He'd have to try accessing the pages again. Lives depended on his success.

"Great. No pressure here," he mumbled.

"Pardon?"

"Jaks. I've gotta go. It's all yours."

Jaks's face whitened. His gaze darted to the body and back to Samson. "But..."

"You know what to do. Do it, Jaks." If the situation weren't so dire, Samson would have laughed at the nervous shock on Jaks's face. He left the park behind, but a heavy sense of wrongness stuck with him. Hell, it was a grisly murder. What did he expect?

Cassandra rested a hand on the gnarled bark and peeked around the tree trunk. Her stomach roiled at the macabre scene of butchered body splayed on a children's merry-go-round.

Oh, God.

Her sketch matched the grisly scene perfectly. She fought to stay upright and not puke her breakfast energy bar in the dirt. Sweat broke out on her forehead, and she dug her fingernails into the tree. Tired and achy from driving the streets all night, her legs trembled with fatigue. Transfixed, she stared at the morbid contrast of merriment and death.

Samson barked orders, his voice carrying across the park to snap Cassandra from her mesmerized state. He moved with a grace that exuded surety in himself and his abilities. No doubts about his place in the world would swirl around in his mind. No way. Each fluid move, each order given, pumped self-assured authority. Cassandra envied him. Her emotions were roiling with uncertainty, while inner turmoil ruled every thought.

When Samson pulled the sketches from his pocket and studied them, Cassandra's throat tightened with a familiar knot of guilt. She should have stopped the murder. For God's sake, she'd sketched the scene. Why couldn't she have known the location of the murder?

The quiet of the early morning and the seclusion of the slightly out of the way park lent an eeriness to the air. Aside from the obvious horror of the murder scene, a sliver of unease mingled with the gently drifting ocean breeze. Unable to resist the urge, Cassandra took a quick, covert glance around. A couple of squirrels cavorted by a nearby tree, a crushed coffee cup lay on the ground, and the occasional glimpse of a car passed on the nearby street. Other than that, the place was empty. Well, except Samson, the other officer, and a bloodied body.

So why did the grim sensation persist? It must be the proximity of death.

She rubbed her hands on her pants. Noticed Samson leaving. The glare on his face could have frozen boiling water. What had sent him into leaving with such purpose? Should she follow him?

No. She was tired and doubted he'd welcome her company. Besides, he had her sketches, which was the extent of her ability to help, so there was nothing else to do but go home and try to sleep.

As she walked back to her car, a large truck with the words C.I.D. on its side passed her by. Hopefully, they found evidence at the scene to nail the murdering son of a bitch. Maybe then her life would go back to normal. Whatever normal entailed.

She reached her car and climbed in. A cold draft rolled over her, increasing the grimness of this place. She shivered, cranked the key, and left the park behind her as quickly as possible.

Joshua trembled with rage. He watched the police chief snooping around and recognized the man's energy as the same disruptive force he'd sensed last night. The unwelcome intrusion of an old enemy. Even more interesting; he'd also spied a woman peering out from behind a tree. His first thought had been to dismiss her as a curiosity-seeker. Until memories slammed through him and he sank to the ground, clutching his head between his hands as a vision of fire seared his mind. He fought the memories of a figure fleeing from the roaring flames. Branches slashing his face as he hunted her through the night forest. She'd eluded him and passed

Seabhac's journal and the knife to another. She'd died before he could make her suffer for her defiance.

She'd considered herself better than he, because she'd eluded him and kept the knife and journal from him. But he'd used blood, fresh from her still warm body, to perform a ritual to ensure the journal remained useless to her if she found it again.

Now she'd finally returned.

Bitch.

Stupid bitch.

She'd not regain the items for herself. His soul ached with their nearness and in his desire to possess them, and he would risk anything. Do anything.

Once they were his, he could dispense with these short-lived, useless human bodies. Instead of merely inhabiting a body, he could transfer his force into a suitable recipient, meld body with soul, and become corporeal. Immortal.

This time, he was unstoppable.

Think. Think. What needed to be done?

He jumped to his feet, frantically peered around the corner of the concession stand he hid behind. Samson yelled commands at the man who'd found the body. Joshua's pulse raced. His nostrils trembled. The police chief reeked of magic and the Arch-Druid's presence oozed from him like sewer stench.

Samson stopped yelling. His gaze raked across the park. Joshua slammed his back against the concession stand and prayed that he remained undetected. Better to wait a minute or two. He steadied his breathing, while animalistic instincts honed over centuries set his mind racing with possibilities. He'd beaten the woman once, he'd do so again. Samson was a danger, but the death of a police chief would warrant an in-depth investigation, so the situation called for a more otherworldly approach.

Samson's angry voice drifted across the park and Joshua sighed with relief. He was safe. Exaltation lifted his spirits, and he almost screamed in triumph. Dropping to a crouch, he tilted his head and peaked around the corner. Power wafted off Samson in near palpable waves. Cold streaked down Joshua's spine. He'd use dark magic to destroy Samson, and no one could stop him. His only opposition lay with ancient foes that practiced true magic and understood how to manipulate elements of nature. Fortunately for him, even in Salem, people were woefully ignorant of the darker realm of magic. Many played at being witches and dabbled on the lighter side of an ancient art of which they had no true understanding.

The roar of an engine jerked him from his reverie. Samson's Hummer sped past him and Joshua's heart flipped. He sank into the shadows and cursed himself for almost getting caught.

He stood and brushed dirt off his pant legs. That's when he saw what Samson had left behind. Thrown over the back of one of the carousel horses was Samson's windbreaker. A ritualistic connection to his enemy. Stepping from behind the small building, Joshua slunk toward the merry-go-round. The arrival of C.I.D. caused confusion and allowed Joshua to go unnoticed, always keeping a tree, garbage can, or hydro pole between him and the police.

The jacket was within his grasp. He reached out to grab it. As he laid his hand on it, a voice hollered at him from the other side of the merry-go-round.

"Hey, this area is off limits. You'll have to leave."

Joshua froze. Lifting the jacket, he clutched it to his chest and pasted a smile on his face. Turning to the approaching officer, he said. "I'm sorry, I didn't see the police tape."

"You wouldn't have, but we're setting it up now. You'll have to leave."

The officer's gaze raked Joshua. Suspicion lit his eyes when he saw Samson's jacket, but the white collar around Joshua's neck changed suspicion to trust. "Sorry, I didn't realize...ummm, is that Chief Wilder's jacket?"

Keeping his voice low and friendly, Joshua replied, "Yes, it is. He left it behind and since I'll be seeing him later today, I figured I'd bring it with me and save him a trip back here." He extended the jacket to the officer. "If you have a place to put it until you can give it to him later, that's fine."

The officer frowned. Joshua prayed for the right answer.

"No. You keep it, Pastor." He waved a hand at the jacket. "You might as well hold on to it, thanks. You really should leave now."

"Of course." Joshua held his prize loosely by his side nonchalantly, but his insides roiled with triumph. He strode across Salem Willows parking area, nearly running into a jogger who threw a curse and a scowl at him. Joshua fumed at the disrespect and considered showing the jerk a taste of the Devil's discontent.

Maybe it was the connection the jacket gave him to Samson, or just the next logical step, but Joshua had a sudden realization that Samson meant to access the book. He clutched the precious jacket to his chest, its importance suddenly increasing to incalculable value. Joshua quickened his pace. Ritual preparation took time. He'd better hurry.

Chapter Twenty-Eight

Samson got nothing. The book lay on his living room table and taunted him with its cold indifference to his best efforts. Damn! Success was crucial, or more people might die. Jerking to his feet, he strode to the window and yanked the curtains shut. He turned to face the book. His heart pounded. Palms began to sweat. He wiped his hands on his jeans, gathered his emotions, and prepared to conquer the book's invisibility issue.

Driven by memories of bloody bodies and the grief-stricken acceptance on Randy's wife's face when he'd told her of his death, Samson lifted the book and placed it on his lap.

It's time.

He brought his emotions under control, and he jolted when the book warmed under his palms. Tiny sparks snapped in his belly and worked their way up his torso to spread out his arms. Sticky threads connected him to the book, and Samson kept his breathing slow and deep so as not to disrupt whatever was happening.

He imagined himself as Seabhac within the pages. Using his sparse knowledge of Britain's earlier history, he set the scene in his mind.

It was dusk, and the dimming light filtered through a small opening in a rudimentary structure of canvas laid over a stick frame. The rustic tent's only furnishings consisted of a narrow feather mattress laid on the floor, a chamber pot, a rickety wooden table and short, wooden stool. Scents of earth, leather, and peat from a nearby cooking fire tickled Samson's nostrils, and he heard voices and the stamping of hooves nearby.

Seabhac sat at the table, making entries into the journal. The scene seemed real, yet possessed an otherworldly dream quality. Samson's heart beat quickly with the thrill of his success.

Next, he needed to place himself in the scene from Seabhac's viewpoint. His view wavered between a bird's eye angle to one of sitting at the table, staring at the book in front of him. Each time he tried to solidify his entry into Seabhac angle of vision, something thrust him back up to the higher angle.

Damn!

The moment he lent thought to his frustration, he found himself thrust from his meditative state and back to his living room. Damn, again. He stood and stretched. He wasn't giving up. No way. He'd been so close.

He sat, crossed his legs, and was about to close his eyes when the book glowed. A shimmering mist of cream-colored light rose from the worn leather book and surrounded Samson. The mist welcomed him with a warm embrace, and as simple as breathing, Samson melded with the book.

It wasn't what he'd expected.

Joshua picked up the newspaper article with Samson's face displayed so perfectly in ink. Flickering candlelight danced shadows across the newsprint and illuminated the tiny basement room. Black candles, altar complete with knives and incense as well as an inverted pentagram etched in blood, fleshed out the macabre scene.

Carefully, Joshua laid the newspaper scrap onto the altar and sprinkled grave dirt across Samson's smiling face. He repeated the incantation three times, each time tying a knot in a piece of black thread he'd torn from Samson's leather jacket.

"I cast you away with the earth of the dead
Forever bind your spirit to a realm beyond
You shall remain, not of this world, yet undead"

He imagined Samson and the book together and bound as one. Each knot elicited a rustle of otherworldly whispers in the darkness surrounding Joshua. Power, dark and potent, tore through him. Belief in his immortality and utter control over the universe and all who inhabited it gave him a godlike sense of supreme right. When he laid the knot upon the newspaper clipping, raging forces drove him into a lusting scream of pure might.

Drained, yet assured of his success, Joshua doused the candles, leaving the newspaper and thread on the altar. As long as they lay undisturbed, Samson and the book remained bound as one, which left Joshua free to find the knife and claim the book. Once he possessed both, he'd rid himself of any opposition and continue to kill.

An insistent whisper began in his brain. Words not quite spoken, yet a vortex of such intense emotion that Joshua had no trouble deciphering the dark voice's message of intent.

The woman. She reeks of the scent of the female, Ainevar. The knife will find its way to her. Use it to destroy her.

A ripple rose through Joshua. Swirling, bubbling, growing, it burst from him in an ironic twist of merry laughter. Yes. What better way to destroy the life force of the Druid bitch he'd chased across centuries and continents? He'd kill her with the instrument her beloved had created to protect her. Supreme, satisfying retribution for daring to oppose his goals and desires. He'd make her wish she'd chosen to stay in the past when she'd died. With thoughts of triumph arcing through his mind, Joshua ascended the rickety stairs into the daylight.

A dark bolt appeared from nothingness and speared the warm light surrounding Samson. A battle ensued, and voices screeched with both pain and triumph. Agony flared in Samson and tore at him as the light gave way to dark and faded into a distant horizon. Swelling and roaring with triumph, a whirling vortex sucked him into a wild descent into darkness. Pressure on Samson's chest forced the air from his lungs and he gasped for breath.

Panic pumped his heart erratically.

He grasped at his surroundings, hoping to slow his movement, but found only emptiness. Then, a glimpse of a taunting presence visible in the darkening haze. Before he reacted, the presence disappeared with a hiss of satisfaction.

The cramping in Samson's legs disappeared. But that wasn't necessarily a good thing, because they'd gone numb. He'd lost sensation in his entire body. In a strange way, he had become part of the mist engulfing him and the darkness surrounding him.

Barely capable of cognitive thought, Samson sensed a hesitant presence hiding at the edge of the haze. Different from the previous one, this entity felt familiar, hesitant, and ancient. Even while his mind wavered between memories of Salem and memories of a life that ended centuries earlier in a place called Avalon, Samson became darkness, and darkness became him. The essence that was Samson became less as he drifted into oblivion.

Chapter Twenty-Nine

It was strange getting ready for bed with the blaze of the morning sun beginning. Cassandra stifled a yawn as she shrugged off her sweater and threw it on a chair near the bed. A brief vision of dark hair and blue eyes flashed in her mind and gave her a pang of regret she was going to bed alone. She tried ignoring the unfamiliar loneliness. It had never bothered her before, so why should it now? Alone was better. Safer.

Besides, she wouldn't be staying in Salem long enough to develop any kind of relationship. Better not to fantasize about Salem's hot Police Chief.

She unzipped her jeans and was sliding them off when the doorbell rang.

It couldn't be. No, of course not. That would be far too coincidental.

"Probably someone selling magazine subscriptions," she mumbled as she readjusted her pants, zipped them up, and went downstairs. When she opened the door, it wasn't a salesperson standing on her front porch.

"Hi, Cassandra. I hope you don't mind me stopping by."

"No...I...of course not, come in." She stood aside and let her neighbor into the house. When she realized what Skye carried in her hand, Cassandra's heart jumped.

Her reaction didn't pass unnoticed. Skye smiled and held out the silk wrapped knife. "I'm here to return what belongs to you."

Cassandra took a step back. "I can't touch the knife. You know what happened last time."

Skye kept her hand extended. "Keep it wrapped and you'll be fine. Trust me."

Cassandra reached for the knife. Her hand wavered midair, but curiosity took over and she brushed the silk with her fingertips. It was cool. Relieved at the mild reaction, she opened her hand, palm up, and nodded to Skye. It wasn't as heavy as she remembered, and this time, she actually remained conscious. She switched the knife to the other hand and rolled it back and forth. Still nothing more than a minor tingle.

"I meant for you to have it yesterday, but you were so upset after your trance, I figured I'd wait."

Motioning to Skye, Cassandra moved to the living room and sat down. She stared at the object in her hands. "I don't know what good I can do." Visions of the body on the merry-go-round sped through her mind, and tears threatened. Voice wavering and raspy, she said, "Have you heard? There was another murder last night."

"I know. It's all over the news. That's why I brought the knife to you. Jerome went down to the station to ask if he can be of any help to Samson. In an unofficial capacity. Cassandra, I understand how scared you must be."

Cassandra laughed. Hysteria threatened. "Scared. That's the understatement of the year. People are dying and I'm supposed to be the one able to stop it." Tiny balls of jagged glass rolled around her stomach. She leaned over, clutched her arms across her midsection, and rocked. It didn't help the pain, so she stood.

"I've been there, remember. And you're not in this alone."

Beads of sweat broke out on Cassandra's forehead and a wave of heat washed over her. Her trembling legs forced her to sit.

"Damn it, Cassandra." Skye's voice rose with frustration and a touch of anger. "You are not responsible for your parents' death. You need to get over the past and focus on what's happening now. If you panic and leave Salem, more people will die and that will be your fault."

Cassandra barely heard Skye's tautly given censure, because she was too busy fighting the urge to puke. She must have looked sick, because Skye put a hand to Cassandra's forehead.

"You're burning up. Oh, my, God. Here, let me take the knife." Skye relieved Cassandra of the knife and set it on the couch. "I can't believe it's affecting you this much. You must be more sensitive than I realized."

"Not the knife." Cassandra choked the words out.

"Then you're really sick, and here I am berating you. I am so sorry."

"Not sick, either." The room spun around Cassandra, and she struggled to remain conscious. She closed her eyes, trying to stop the spinning, but that action prompted a vision. A brief glimpse of a face. Distorted, as if covered by thick plastic, it was barely recognizable, and as Cassandra realized whom it belonged to, the face disappeared along with all Cassandra's discomfort and nausea. She gasped with relief and grasped Skye's arm.

"Samson. He's in trouble."

Without hesitation, Skye snatched her cell phone and entered a number. They waited. "No answer at his place. I'll try Jerome."

"No, we need to get to Samson's. You can call Jerome on the way."

The short ride consisted of a frantic phone call to Jerome that went unanswered and a lot of honking as Cassandra wheeled her car through lunch hour traffic. When they reached Samson's condominium, they didn't bother waiting for an elevator. They rushed madly up the stairs and pounded on his door. No answer. Skye rummaged around in her pocket and pulled out a ring of keys.

"Here. Let me." With shaking hands, Skye inserted the key and turned the knob. In answer to Cassandra's raised eyebrow, Skye explained, "After last year's events, we thought it best to keep keys to each other's home. Just in case."

They entered the apartment and peered into the dim room. Everything appeared normal, although slightly dark because of the closed curtains.

Skye spoke, her voice low and shaky. "I can't see much. Let me get the curtains."

While Skye padded across the room, Cassandra scouted the room again, but saw nothing out of the ordinary. If she had run Skye over here in a panic for no reason, the woman would never believe her again. She'd be right not to. With prickles of doubt stabbing her, Cassandra didn't notice Skye had moved to kneel beside the couch and now waved frantically.

"Cassandra. Cassandra, I need help."

At first, Cassandra couldn't tell what Skye was hovering over. When she realized it was Samson's prone body stretched out on top of the journal, she panicked. He was dead. Nausea rose in Cassandra's throat. She shouldn't have hesitated about helping. He wouldn't have been alone, and he'd still be alive.

"Cassandra. He's alive, but I need help to get him up so I can get a better idea what we're dealing with."

Cassandra rushed to help Skye move Samson to the couch. Once he stretched out, the two women glanced at each other and Cassandra asked, "Now what?"

"I better try Jerome again."

"Shouldn't we call 9-1-1?"

Skye gave a tense laugh. "I guarantee that modern medicine won't do any good in this circumstance."

While Skye tried her husband again, Cassandra went to the bathroom and wet a facecloth to put on Samson's forehead. For whatever good it would do, at least she'd be doing something. While Skye mumbled into the phone, Cassandra let her gaze wander, hoping to figure out what Samson had been doing. A dozen candles burned to pools of hard wax. A cushion where Samson had been sitting, and the journal lay strewn on the floor. The journal's blank pages silently mocked her. A spicy aroma hung in the silent room. Cassandra sniffed at the familiar odor and decided it was cinnamon, but couldn't identify the exotic flower scent mingling with the cinnamon.

"Cinnamon for protection and power." Skye knelt beside Cassandra. "Also rose geranium to enhance protection. A double shield. He knew he was placing himself in a dangerous situation, but didn't care. Damn him."

The last two words came out as a raspy whisper, and Cassandra realized Skye was crying. Fighting a stab of envy, she reached out and patted her shoulder.

"You're fortunate to care so much about the people in your life."

Skye sniffed and raised her gaze to Cassandra. "You must have people you care about."

"My brother, Memnon. He plays the role of brother, friend, family, Friday night movie date, and sounding board." Other than Memnon, Cassandra couldn't think of anyone who would blink if anything happened to her. No one to shed a tear or stifle a sob. Cassandra wanted to cry. Without thought, she ran a finger across the piece of hair so stubbornly curled across the front of Samson's forehead. Silky soft, the contrast of dark hair against unnaturally pale skin lent urgency to the situation.

Nerves formed a knot in Cassandra's stomach. The life of a man she barely knew hovered in the pages of an ancient, magic journal and she realized how desperately she wanted to bring him back. To her. Emotion thrummed with each pulse of her heart. The desire to belong to someone, with someone, raced through her blood.

Skye touched her arm, startling Cassandra from the unfamiliar well of emotions. "It's up to us to save him."

More a question than a statement, Skye waited for an answer. Cassandra shifted from her knees to her butt and stared at Samson's face. The inevitability of life had brought her to this place and shown her a man who'd slipped his way into her heart with a smile and a flash of blue eyes. She had no idea what to do, but it was hers to do.

"I guess I'm staying."

"I knew you would." In a rustle of movement, Skye jumped to her feet and cleared the candles and other remnants of Samson's ritual-gone-wrong. "We need to cleanse the room and rid the area of any semblance of whatever went wrong. Jerome's on his way over, we'll decide the next step with him."

The two women worked efficiently and silently. Within minutes, Jerome made a harried entrance, immediately moving to his friend's unmoving body. Skye had shown grief at Samson's state, but the deep despair rolling off Jerome in waves choked Cassandra's already harried emotions.

"Son of a bitch. Idiot. Stubborn mule." Jerome muttered as he turned Samson's head and rearranged his limbs to ensure his friend's comfort. Satisfied, he stood and faced Cassandra.

"How did you know he was in trouble?"

"I don't know...it just hit me."

"Fine." His tone taut. "Can you tell if he's all right?"

"I have no way of knowing for sure, but I can try to find out." Cassandra inspected Samson's inert body, his large frame filling the entire couch. She focused on the rise and fall of his chest, narrowed all her senses to awareness of him and nothing else. For a split moment of time, she felt him like a warm river of water washing over her body. Then... nothing. But it was enough.

"He's okay. Wherever he is, he's okay." Relief gave her strength. "So how do we get him back?"

Skye and Jerome shared a look, and Cassandra sensed an entire conversation occurring without the use of words. The tension between them practically burst the surrounding walls.

"You're not going in." Jerome snapped the command at Skye.

Cassandra frowned, not sure what Jerome meant. Skye understood because she replied, "I have to. We might lose him otherwise."

A shadow flitted of a frown across Jerome's face. "I can't lose you, or the baby."

"But..."

"No buts. Samson would never allow you to risk yourself for him. We'll have to figure out an alternative."

"I'd appreciate you explaining to me what's so obvious to both of you?"

Skye and Jerome stared at Cassandra. Jerome spoke first. "That depends. Have you decided to stay?"

Cassandra bristled at his confrontational tone, but realized the strain Jerome must be feeling. She spared a glance at Samson's prone body, lit by the sunlight streaming through the now open curtains. His dark hair glinted with the odd strand of gray, and his lips twitched in his unnatural sleep. Even in his slumbering state, Samson exuded raw, intense, sexual energy that burned into Cassandra.

Without realizing her intent, she reached out and cupped his cheek with her hand. As quick as a breath, the connection grabbed Cassandra in a spiral of flight, and she lost all sense of herself.

Chapter Thirty

Samson adjusted to the strangeness of his new reality. The presence hovering on the outskirts of the mist intrigued him. Not aware of anything malevolent, he floated closer. Still nothing more than a gentle hum. Then, suddenly, a voice boomed in his mind.

"You are here because of your stubborn nature."

What the Hell? Samson squinted into the murky mist that drifted thicker than the fog rolling off the Atlantic on a stormy fall morning. A flicker of movement drew him onward. A flutter of blue punctuated the gray, a darker shadow of a person's outline. He stepped into the miasma. Wary of his footing and unable to distinguish what the cushy stuff was that his feet sank into with each step. Deep, quiet laughter punctuated his movement.

Anger burned in his chest and he yelled into the nothingness, "Show yourself, and we'll see who laughs then."

"Control your emotions and you control your situation."

"I don't need lessons from a wraith that doesn't even exist except in a netherworld that's probably a figment of my imagination."

More laughter sounded off to his left, so he changed course. He moved closer to whoever was taunting him.

"I assure you, lad, your imagination could not even begin to cover your circumstances."

Damn, the voice had come from behind him that time.

Samson spun around and faced the man who'd invaded his dreams night after night.

"Seabhac."

"None other." The Arch-Druid bowed from the waist, his midnight blue robe rustling in the surrounding quiet.

With powers of observation honed through years of police work, Samson instantly noted every detail of the man standing before him. Gnarled hands peeked out from beneath the sleeves of the flowing robe, and though neatly trimmed, Seabhac's long, white beard reached halfway down his chest while his hair grazed the top of his erectly held shoulders. Eyes of a blue so clear Samson swore he could see through them. Bright and sharp, those eyes threw a gaze that bore into Samson. Testing, searching, weighing, and deciding.

Seabhac gave one sharp nod. "You'll do. I chose well."

"You chose well? You have two seconds to explain yourself, then I don't care if you are an Arch-Druid, I'm coming after you."

Seabhac's chest rose with an exaggerated sigh. "Ah, the impatience of youth. Such a burden to overcome."

"Yes, it's kind of the same thing as the arrogance of age." Samson retorted.

Barking out a short laugh, Seabhac moved a step closer through the shifting mists. His face tightened with gravity. "Amenities dispensed with, we need to talk."

"Great, you can start by telling me what the hell is going on. And start at the beginning."

With a dismissive wave of his hand, Seabhac replied, "The beginning is too far in a hazy past. We need to focus on now. For instance, how dim-witted are you to allow yourself to be trapped in this place?"

Samson raised an eyebrow. "Me trapped? From where I stand, old man, I'd say you're stuck in the same situation."

"No. No. That's entirely different. I created the book and placed myself here to remain as a guide to Ainevar."

"Mmmm, hmmm. You're stuck here, same as me. Am I right?"

Seabhac blushed. "Ahem. Yes. Quite." In a move unbecoming to the stature of an Arch-Druid, Seabhac folded his legs and plopped onto the ground. Or whatever constituted a place to sit in such a place. Surrounded and highlighted by swirling mist, Seabhac appeared to fade and reappear with shifting shadows and light. Mystical, magical, he radiated such a sense of overwhelming force Samson marveled at anyone being able to hold the man here against his will. The existence of an entity capable of doing so terrified Samson.

"Events were not meant to happen in this manner." Seabhac's whispering voice drew Samson closer. "I should have destroyed him on that cliff top. Instead, I fled like a fledgling Druid novice and led him right to Ainevar and the priestesses of Avalon. It is because of my cowardly act that Avalon no longer exists and that evil has run rampant on the earthly plane for so many centuries. Killing, plundering—stalking Ainevar as one would a wild animal."

Samson's heart twisted with pity, but Seabhac raised his hand to stop Samson when he moved to comfort. "No. Let an old man take responsibility for his actions."

Samson stepped back. "Fine. It's your fault. But the question is, what are you going to do about it?" He threw out the challenge, hoping to shake Seabhac from his bout of self-pity.

It worked. Blue eyes sparked with anger and nostrils flared with indignation and fire. Literally. A flame of fire shot from Seabhac's nostrils, and a low growl rumbled deep in his throat.

"Impudent pup. You dare address me in such a manner?"

Samson folded his arms across his chest. "I believe I just did."

Pressure and heat built around Samson. In a movement so fluid the mist barely moved, Seabhac rose. Twice the size he'd been, he confronted Samson, who stifled the consuming urge to run. Seabhac pulsed with power. Samson stood in awe. Ancient magician against modern day police chief. Really, there was no comparison. Samson had no doubt Seabhac's ability to destroy him with a wave of hand or thought. He held his place, nonetheless.

After a tense moment of silent battle, Seabhac nodded with approval. "I told you I'd chosen well."

"There you go spouting nonsense again."

"You were correct in assuming my actions brought me to this place. Ensnared by the machinations of an evil force from beyond any worlds we know or understand. It craves power and feeds on terror. It came to our world at a time when the Druids were at their highest peak of power. It destroyed us. Sucked the life and energy from every one of us until I was the last one remaining." Low and raspy, Seabhac's voice pulsed with remembered pain. "I had to take measures to ensure survival. I could not act alone, so I took a young girl ripe with power and stole her from her family. I taught her everything. Entrusted her with secrets sworn to be shared with only other full-fledged Arch-Druids. But as history has proven time and again, circumstances dictate society's rules."

He passed a hand across his forehead in a weary gesture. "Over the years I fell in love with her spirit, her never failing desire to succeed and excel. I took her power to heights that one so young was not ready to receive. When I died, I left her with abilities beyond her understanding. I entrusted her with the preservation of all Druid history and knowledge. I told her that everything rested on her shoulders. Everything is my fault."

Samson waited for more, but Seabhac stared into the distance.

"What, exactly, is your fault? Finish your story before I run out of patience."

Seabhac turned his unfocused gaze on Samson. "It is my fault Ainevar died believing she was a failure. Because of me, she has spent lifetimes trying to right a wrong not of her making. My intent to preserve Druid knowledge allowed evil to walk the earthly plane. It is all my fault. How difficult is that to understand? Are you daft?"

Samson ground his teeth in frustration. "Fine. It's your fault, but what does that have to do with why I'm here? And how does that help us destroy the evil that's killing people in my town?"

Seabhac harrumphed. "Saints, people must be bred for stupidity these days. Ainevar's spirit has sought to correct what she considers her failure. She believes it is her place to destroy the evil force that killed her, and she won't rest until she does. She seeks and inhabits a human, using them as a conduit to the world, much the same as the evil does. The difference is that Ainevar merely guides the person, leaves them with free will, while the evil suppresses the human mind and soul and takes over totally. It's an advantage because that soul-sucking parasite erases all morality and the person it inhabits will do anything."

"So in all these years..." Samson began.

"Centuries."

Samson rolled his eyes. "Fine. Centuries, but that only makes it worse. In all these centuries, why haven't you written the solution in the book for Ainevar to read? Heck, if she only needed to develop a belief in herself, it shouldn't have been too difficult to relay that information."

"Daft. Daft. Daft." Seabhac punctuated each word with a stamp of a foot. "Her proclamation of failure upon her death and passing the responsibility of the book to another effectively blocked her from the information in the book. That, and an invisibility spell placed by the wretched evil haunting my every waking moment. No one Ainevar has chosen and guided over the lifetimes has ever been able to read the book." Desperation and defeat clouded Seabhac's eyes. "I believed Cassandra would be different. I was so sure she'd be the one. That's why I summoned her and chose you."

"There you go again. Chose me? How and why?"

"I have grown weary of watching from within this limbo of never-ending murky perspective and eerie silence." He waved a hand disgustedly and set the encroaching mist to swirling wildly in vaporous gray tendrils. "I pondered long and hard, trying to devise a way to effect change even with the disadvantage of Ainevar's inability to read the book. I decided to find an intermediary between Cassandra and the book. I hoped you could access the information within the book in case Cassandra couldn't." He snorted. "Apparently, I misjudged your ability to do me any good."

"Hey. Don't blame me for this, old man. If you'd clued me in to what you were up to, I might have been better prepared."

"I did present you with clues, but your mule-headedness prevented you from seeing what was right in front of your face."

Samson sputtered and indignation made him snap at Seabhac. "Now it's you who's being dense. What clues? You've done nothing to help me through this mess."

"I demonstrated to you how it began on a stormy, fateful cliff. I showed you firsthand the results of the evil's reign in Salem. I showed you Ainevar, and 'tis more than beyond me how you could not perceive her characteristics within Cassandra. I led you to the journal and let you hear the music, which is the key to guardianship of the journal. I even sent Cassandra directly to you to save you from searching for her. I gave you all you needed."

"Except the understanding of how to tie all those occurrences together. How was I supposed to know the visions you sent were anything more than dreams? How could I possibly have known that Cassandra was part of all this?"

"You knew. Think back to the first time you met her at the cemetery."

Samson remembered unease he'd experienced when he'd first seen Cassandra. He'd thought her a quirky nutcase sitting in her car, pinching herself. Then he'd experienced a thrust of sexual attraction when he leaned down and saw how stunning she was.

"Well?"

Samson snapped, "I'm thinking. Give me a minute."

Seabhac folded his arms, the long sleeves of his robe lifting and settling into place with a graceful flow. He tapped his foot and tilted his head.

Samson ignored him and remembered the unsettled, rippling energy bubbling through him when she raised her eyes to him. He knew then their destinies intertwined. He should have listened to his instincts and instead of playing macho cop. He should have trusted Cassandra.

His attempt to access the book alone illuminated his self-important male ego.

The encroaching fog circled his feet, snaked between his legs, and rose in tendrils around his body, simulating the embrace of a python. Samson kicked at the vaporous substance and sent it into a swirl of insubstantial gray.

"How do you stand this stuff? I can hardly even see three feet in any direction."

"You grow accustomed to it. There is really no choice."

"Sure. Well, I guarantee you I'm not spending centuries twiddling my thumbs in this desolate wasteland."

Seabhac wriggled his thumbs and frowned. "It is unclear to me what thumbs have to do with anything, but I am intrigued to know how you, a mere mortal with limited powers, hope to accomplish what I, Arch-Druid of all Britannia, could not during these centuries."

A part of Samson cringed at the haughty tone and inherent truth of Seabhac's statement, while another part of him recognized the facts. "If you're so almighty powerful, why did you have to send for reinforcements from a mere mortal with limited powers?

Seabhac flushed. At least Samson thought his face reddened, but it was hard to tell in the dull, drabness of the surrounding mist. Samson experienced a stab of regret for his taunt. It must be hard for a man of Seabhac's stature and personality to admit he needed help. Besides, now was not the time for petty ego. That was what prevented Samson from asking for Cassandra's help originally. He was mature enough to learn from his mistakes. Taking pity on the dejected Druid and knowing they needed to work together, he gave Seabhac the opportunity to regain his pride.

"Fine, since it's your ballgame, you tell me what we need to do to stop this evil."

"Ball game? Your speech continues to make no sense. Anyway, we cannot stop it. Must I explain everything?" Seabhac rolled his eyes.

Humph! So much for pity and regret. The man was simply an arrogant putz.

Seabhac shot Samson a narrowed, calculating gaze. Samson stared him down. Challenged him to say something. Seabhac lowered his gaze and continued speaking.

"Ainevar died with such intense belief in her failure, she created a shift of energy. In order for things to correct, the displaced energy must return to a normal cycle. Ainevar must believe in herself, which means the person she has chosen must believe in herself before they can accomplish anything together. Otherwise, the wheel spins a never-ending journey. Unfortunately, she chooses a person whose weakness is the same as hers. Lack of belief in oneself. I've seen it happen many times over the years. I fear it is no different now."

Samson thought of Cassandra and the fire of battle that lit her eyes when she argued with him. Though slight of build, her passionate beliefs lent her strength beyond her size. Samson didn't doubt her. Not for a second. With that conclusion, a warm sensation passed through him, flaming a fire deep within. His nostrils quivered when he caught a whiff of Cassandra's vanilla-scented perfume hovering in the air. He swore the briefest touch of her hand brushed across his forehead. For an instant, the petite outline of her body wavered within the confines of the pervasive mist.

Not believing his eyes, Samson blinked. Cassandra's veiled shape remained. Her arm uplifted, reaching for him. He needed to tell her. Had to help her understand the simple answer within her grasp. Gathering energy, pulling all strength from the depths of his abilities, he pumped his mind with one thought and speared it in her direction.

Trust and Believe.

Cassandra's barely there form startled as his fervent, empathic cry stretched across the distance to her. She lifted a hand. A snap of light illuminated her. Then she was gone. The suddenness of her disappearance jolted Samson. He turned to Seabhac for an explanation, but the Druid remained unaware of Cassandra's brief foray into the mist.

Futility jabbed Samson. Damn. Stuck in nowhere with a grouchy, cryptic Druid and only one thing in common. Each of them knew his only salvation lay in the hands of a woman. A woman who doubted herself yet must develop absolute belief in her powers in order to rescue him from the darkness.

Cassandra's simple touch set the air between her and Samson crackling with stars of brilliant light. She struggled to keep control over her emotions, but wasn't strong enough. Whispers echoed in her mind—chanting familiar songs and ancient rites of magic. Guided, driven, her soul grabbed the buried depths of her past and pulled it into the present. Waves of turmoil swept through her and she moved toward the source, radiating strength. Samson. So close. She felt him. Knew he was her salvation. Drifting in unfamiliar surroundings, she followed his earthy scent and moved closer. Each step triggered the mist into a shifting dance. However hard she tried, the pervasive barrier remained between her and Samson.

Frustration gathered until the reassurance of Samson's voice calmed her. She couldn't hear the words. She moved closer. Words blasted at her amidst the near-impenetrable fog. *Trust and Believe.* The simple statement gave all past doubts and uncertainties emptiness. Cleansed her mind, body, and soul, and left her weak. With barely a moment to adjust or attempt to reach Samson, reality spun her back to the living room in Samson's condominium.

With an effort, Cassandra attuned herself to her return. Sparks dimmed, and the connection to Samson faded. She realized her stomach-wrenching drop into the unknown had fired a primal urge to protect and a powerful yearning to bond with the man on the couch in every way possible.

With realization, came panic. Panic, because what she'd believed about herself had been an illusion. Years had slipped irretrievably past as she denied that which was inherent within. Argued with the voice alternately confusing and driving her from a young age. Now, she had a name for the voice. Ainevar. Her powers flowed and ebbed with the pulse of her heartbeat. Strong and unafraid, she distinguished the separation of her energy from Ainevar's. Gained relief from knowing and understanding the boundaries separating them.

Once the world solidified, Cassandra fought to regain her equilibrium. A shift of consciousness had occurred and left her a different person than she'd been before her foray into the misty world beyond. How long had she been gone? Not too long because Jerome and Skye stood where they'd been with furrowed brows and tapping feet.

She raised her hand at their questions of concern. "I'm fine." She snuck another reassuring glance at Samson's prone body. "Samson is fine as well. I saw him briefly, and he wasn't alone. Seabhac is with him and to answer your question Jerome, yes, I'm in for whatever it takes."

Jerome's stare burned into Cassandra. Measuring her on a soul-deep level, his gaze bit deep, shook her up and made her feel violated. Cassandra's instant reaction was to ward off his probe, but common sense and understanding of his motives kept her from interfering. She stood and allowed his intrusion. After what seemed an eternity, Jerome gave a nod of acceptance.

"We're talking about a retrieval spell Skye performed to bring her dad's soul back from the Netherworld last year. It was dangerous then, and it's even more so now." He shot a pointed glare at his wife's belly.

"Tell me what's involved? Is it anything I can do instead?"

Skye exchanged a look with Jerome, and Cassandra prickled with warm heat from the silent battle between husband and wife.

When their expressions reflected obvious stress, Cassandra decided to end the conflict.

"Hey." Her voice cracked with tension, effectively ending the standoff. "It doesn't matter what we want." Cassandra infused her voice with a certainty she didn't feel. "For whatever reason, Ainevar has chosen me to haunt with dreams of her life and Seabhac has centered out Samson as his advocate in this time and place, so it only makes sense I be the one who performs this retrieval ritual."

Besides, she agreed with Jerome that Skye couldn't risk harming their unborn child.

For a brief moment, the only sound in the room was Samson's steady breathing. Cassandra noted the rise and fall of his chest and gave silent thanks he was alive.

What had he been thinking? It didn't matter. He was in trouble, and it was up to her to get him out of the book.

Chapter Thirty-One

Joshua faltered. The earth shifted beneath his feet. At first, he thought he'd tripped on the rug. Breath caught like a ball of fire in his throat and his heart sped up to a fierce beat threatening to burst from his chest. Thankfully, he hadn't yet left the safety and anonymity of the church.

He fell to the floor in the vestibule, writhing in pain. His lifeblood boiled while visions of hellfire and death tore at his mind. Sweat broke out on his forehead. Memories of the centuries flashed in a backward timeline. Jagged cliffs. Raging water. A streak from the heavens striking and forging a human vessel into a heartless machine of domination.

Anger, virulent and consuming as the plague, fired Joshua into a frenzied state. Fighting the memories and cradling his head in his hands, he rose to his knees.

It couldn't be. It wasn't possible.

Locking the police chief in the book should have prevented him from reaching out to the woman, effectively leaving her vulnerable to attack. The same strategy had worked with Seabhac and Ainevar. He'd killed Ainevar and spent lifetimes inhabiting these measly human bodies and performing unspeakable blood rituals to prevent Seabhac and Ainevar from communicating while he attempted to claim the wealth of Druid knowledge for himself.

All wasted.

Samson had connected to Cassandra and sent the vital message. Simple words capable of setting her free from uncertainty and giving her strength. Joshua clutched the edge of the nearby table to steady his balance. Driven by rage and frustration, he grabbed the brass candle holder sitting beside the sign-in book and flung it at a porcelain statue of Jesus perched serenely within a built-in wall-recess. He found no satisfaction in destroying the representation of one of the world's holiest leaders. Even less in the shattering sound as it struck the floor and sent shards flying in all directions.

Licking a drop of blood from a cut on his lip where a sliver of porcelain had struck, Joshua contemplated the possibilities. The woman was vulnerable as long as she doubted herself. If she understood her abilities, or the power of the knife, he was lost. He'd grown weary of hiding in shadows, within the limitations of another's body. It was time to be reborn in his true and mighty form. Time for him to claim the book and knife as his own, and then he would slash the world with the bite of his unholy wrath.

Cassandra hoisted the box onto her hip and balanced it precariously as she dug in her purse for car keys. She pushed the unlock button on the key fob, but the resulting beep barely broke her consciousness. She stood in a contemplative daze before realizing the car was unlocked.

Hastening to cover her absent-mindedness, she opened the door and placed the box on the passenger seat. She'd handpicked the items from Skye's list and they weren't easily replaceable. At least not in time to perform the retrieval ritual planned for that evening.

With a sigh, she climbed behind the wheel and gazed into the distance. Once they'd decided Cassandra would perform the ritual, they'd mapped a course of action. Since Samson was so vulnerable and exposed, Jerome stayed to protect him against the unknown enemy. Skye wrote a list and headed home to grab specific items, while Cassandra went to the recommended stores to buy whatever else they needed. Hence the box.

Cassandra cranked the key and her car engine purred to life, but she didn't move. A wave of dizziness slammed into her and she shut off the car. With a hand pressed to her fiercely beating heart, Cassandra leaned back and closed her eyes. She'd meant it when she said she'd perform the ritual, but that didn't mean she wanted to do it. Heck, if she had her way, she'd turn her car toward the nearest road out of Salem and keep going. As reassuring as it was to know she wasn't crazy, how did one handle having another person's life force living inside them?

Had decisions she'd made over her life been hers, or influenced by Ainevar? If she brought Samson back and they defeated the evil, would Ainevar disappear? Would Cassandra be the same person without her?

Cassandra's breath became shallow gasps. Her original relief at understanding why she'd felt out-of-step gave way to fright at knowing nothing about herself.

"You are who you've always been. Who you'll always be."

The whisper brushed past her, barely discernable among the noise of people and traffic on the downtown street.

Now she knew the inner voice to be a separate entity, Cassandra wasn't sure how to react. If Cassandra was going to bring Samson back from the foggy place she'd seen him, she needed to reconcile the two parts of herself that had lived in a relative state of harmony until then. She tried something she'd never done. She talked to the voice.

"What do you mean?" Her voice croaked.

Nothing.

"Please, talk to me. Help me."

"You are your own thoughts, reason, and creation. Not mine. All life's trials have shaped you into the person you are. Pain suffered has molded your compassion for others, while desires and motivations have led you on the path meant for you alone. I am merely a spectator. A believer in the goodness that is you. A hopeful watcher who bemoans her own fate and implores your soul to help deliver her from a state of grievous sorrow."

"Is that all?" Cassandra mumbled. "Here I thought you wanted something nearing the impossible. Oh, wait...you do."

Cassandra started her car and revved the engine more than necessary. Slamming the shift into gear, she peeled rubber from the parking lot, all the while mumbling a response to Ainevar. Anyone seeing her probably would have thought she was a crazy woman. If the shoe fits?

Joshua lit another candle and chanted words unfamiliar to him a mere few weeks ago, but now crossed his lips as if he'd been reciting them his entire life. The sulfur odor of matches wafted through the small room, mingling with the beeswax scent of the lit candles. Scent or color didn't matter. The candles lent atmosphere and helped Joshua achieve a frame of mind to enable him to make a minor connection to the person he concentrated on. In this case, Ainevar's chosen one.

Cassandra.

The results of the forgotten form of mind control rested entirely on the ancient verse filling the darkened room with a pulsing throb. A woman had eluded him centuries ago, and a mere woman, untaught and unaware of what lay within her, challenged him again. This nowhere town that relied on a past of narrow-minded persecution and the horrors of death to sustain itself would not be his undoing.

Greater things beckoned him.

A return to the land of his creation. Rich in archaic forces buried within the layers of slaughtered warriors and annihilated civilizations, the land of Britain called for his return. Magic and sorcery drifted among the hilly terrain, while ancient rites and archaic beliefs lent substance to tales of legendary feats.

His desire to return to where his powers could be cultivated to their strongest manifested itself in a bellow that vibrated the walls of the room with a wave of surging energy. Fired with rage, the discombobulated thought forms wavered. Uncertain in their direction, it took but a single, direct image in Joshua's mind to send them where he wanted.

Cassandra.

Chapter Thirty-Two

Panic started in the pit of Cassandra's belly and burned up her chest and into her throat. Without a thought to direction, she drove a harried route through town, barely managing to avoid slamming into a pedestrian at a crosswalk. Her course was haphazard, aimless, and a vain attempt to escape her fate. She didn't want the responsibility. She never had. Look what had happened with her parents.

Her panic increased a notch. Her throat tightened into the rigor of pre-vomit burn. Her foot pressed on the accelerator harder. Hot air rasped across her arms from the open window, its sting attesting to her advancing speed.

The speed invigorated her.

The control of a four thousand pound machine set her blood to pumping with exhilaration. Usually, she obeyed the speed limit and was considerate of pedestrians and other vehicles, but putting the pedal to the metal and letting it rip invigorated her. Charged her more than she'd thought possible.

It was the round-eyed terror on a young mother's face when Cassandra tore around a corner that brought her back to reality. The mother snatched her child from a stroller just as the car bumper roared past with inches to spare. Suddenly aware of how she'd sped through the streets with no consideration of the consequences, Cassandra began to shake. With a gasp, she slowed the car to a crawl and searched for a place to park and calm her nerves.

She turned into the nearest driveway and parked.

She'd never driven so erratically before. She'd almost hit a stroller, and at the speed she was going, would have killed the child. The adrenaline rush of her uncharacteristic race through town left her weak as it faded. Scared, shaky, and unsure of what had happened, Cassandra took in her surroundings, hoping she wasn't blocking someone's driveway.

No. It seems her wild, hypnotic ride brought her to the city outskirts where slightly less than historically correct homes lined the street. The neighborhood was spacious, a feature not available in the downtown core, and a sense of peace contrasted sharply with the rapid pace of tourism that drove Salem.

Her gaze came to rest on the building she sat in front of and her inner peace shattered. Stark white with a black shingle roof, glimmering steeple-shaped windows, and a large wooden cross stabbed into the front lawn. The structure was clearly a church. It made her blood run cold, and she rubbed her arms to eradicate the ensuing goose bumps.

Scared as she was, Cassandra understood that she'd been brought to this quiet street with its stately homes and strange church. Despite the pervasive sense of foreboding, the church fascinated Cassandra. A glint of sun reflected off a stained glass window pane and threw out a beam of ruby-red light that near blinded her with its intensity. Crossing a hand across her eyes, she stepped out of her car and moved toward the steps.

The structure glared down at her. Each wooden stair creaked underfoot, reminding Cassandra she shouldn't be here. Samson needed her. She should get going. But she climbed the last step and stood in front of the door.

Okay, Ainevar, if you know something I don't, now would be the time to warn me.

The unspoken request went unanswered as Cassandra placed her palm on the door. Opening her senses, she sent a probe into the church and tried hard to tune in to any danger waiting beyond the door.

Unused for years, her abilities were understandably unstable at best. She had nothing more to rely on, though, because it seemed Ainevar had deserted her.

Taking a shuddering breath and reciting a silent plea for protection to whatever guardian angels might be guarding her; Cassandra opened the door and stepped into the church.

Samson paced the confines of his prison. Although the ubiquitous mist swirled in ever-changing patterns, the scenery remained the same. No sound permeated the thick shroud. Breathing was an effort as he tried to inhale the heavy, damp air into his lungs.

He suddenly realized he stood surrounded—by nothing. He must have wandered too far away, and Seabhac no longer remained visible. Fear licked his limbs and he moved automatically. Then froze. He cautioned himself to be careful because with no defining barriers, walls, or fences of any kind, he might wander endlessly into oblivion. As far as he knew, he'd need to remain close to where he'd entered this place in order to return home.

"Samson." Distant, urging, Seabhac's voice beckoned him.

"Keep calling. I can't tell where you are." Samson yelled, but the fog muffled his voice.

"Here. Over here."

Samson followed the voice. When he drew closer, he heard the Druid mumbling. "Brainless. Impatient. Thinks he knows better."

Samson's nostrils flared at the insults, and he burst through the encompassing mist to face Seabhac. "I know better than to get myself trapped in this infernal fog for centuries on end, old man."

"Bah! You don't know anything and I take offense to your words and your tone." Seabhac lifted his hands above his head and began to chant in a guttural, yet strangely sweet song that evoked a haunting sensation within Samson. He quickly realized Seabhac directed the chant at him. Sweat beaded Samson's brow and his chest tightened.

Crap. Serves him right for pissing off an Arch-Druid. When would he learn to keep his opinions to himself?

"Seabhac?"

One whispered word brought Samson's discomfort to an instantaneous end as Seabhac gasped and dropped his arms. Face ashen and hands clenched, Seabhac faced the person who'd spoken. Relieved of pain, Samson peered into the fog to determine who'd had bad luck to end up in this place.

The figure of a woman emerged. Her slow, hesitant movement caused swirls of mist to form and rise up her body in a protective gesture. The slender woman barely reached Samson's shoulder. Like Cassandra, she was stunning, ethereal, with blonde hair and jewel-bright blue eyes. The woman's entire focus rested on Seabhac.

The Druid stood rock still. His chest rising and falling in a rhythmic pace. "Ainevar?" The softest whisper of hope and disbelief. "How?"

Ainevar moved closer, still not acknowledging Samson. Hungrily, her gaze raked Seabhac. "I know not. Only that I was thrust from the chosen one and sent here." Her voice quivered. "Though I have craved even the merest glance upon your face and prayed for a single touch of your hand, I fear the meaning of our being here together."

"Yes. He grows stronger." He stepped toward Ainevar, pain written upon his features. Samson imagined the agony of spending centuries watching from a distance as the person you love lives and suffers through lifetimes. Not able to help. Not even to encourage or touch them in any gesture of comfort. He wanted to give them time alone. He should have walked away and left them alone for a time, but he couldn't.

"Hey." He broke Ainevar and Seabhac from their silent perusal of each other. "If he, whoever he is, has grown stronger, then I'm guessing Cassandra's in trouble."

"Yes. She's the only one who can use the knife and read the journal."

"That's just it. She can't. Read the journal, that is. She tried and saw nothing. The pages were as blank for her as for me."

Seabhac sighed and ran a hand across his face. "Yes, and I've explained to you what she can do to remedy the problem."

Samson rolled his eyes. "You've told me, but how do we fill Cassandra in on the update?"

"We get out of here." Ainevar replied.

Seabhac and Samson shared an expression oozing with masculine ego. Seabhac replied, his tone vaguely superior. "Ainevar, would I have been stuck in here for centuries if leaving were a simple deed?"

"Do not condescend to me, Seabhac. I lived numerous lives without your help and managed fine, thank you much."

Bitterness overrode the love painfully visible on Ainevar's face when she glared at Seabhac.

The Arch-Druid clenched his jaw, anger flashing in his eyes. "Yes, I have observed how fine you've done over the centuries," he snapped at Ainevar. Opened his mouth to say more and then snapped it shut and spun to face the blanket of fog.

Ainevar stared at his back, her lips quivering. Samson steeled his heart against what was assuredly an emotionally charged reunion and attempted to bring a semblance of order and purpose. "Look," he pleaded. "I can only imagine how tough this situation is for both of you, but, please, let's not snipe at one another. Cassandra's in trouble and we're stuck in this godforsaken place, while an archaic evil tries to take control of my city. We need to work together here, folks."

Seabhac snorted and glared at Samson and Ainevar. "Folks. I tell you, Ainevar, many of the words this man speaks leave me confused. Is it a form of new language? Have things changed that much since I left the world?"

Ainevar relaxed. Even provided a light laugh. "Yes, things have changed muchly, but the language he speaks is English." Her gaze ran a line up Samson's body from toes to head. "Even with his strange words, he is an attractive specimen. Think you not?"

United in their perusal and consideration of Samson, Ainevar and Seabhac moved together, fingers entwining and shoulders touching. Tiny sparks of blue and orange lent relief to the dingy gray permeating Samson's sight in all directions. They communicated on a level Samson doubted he'd ever understand. Luminescent light created a soft glow around them. The glorious light encompassed the darkness and spread into the recesses of the vaporous mist.

"Together, Seabhac. We have ever been strongest together."

He nodded and reached down to take Ainevar's hand. He lifted his other one and stretched it out toward Samson.

"Take hold. Unless you want to remain here forever."

Samson took the proffered hand. That's when the world began to spin.

Chapter Thirty-Three

Cassandra couldn't see a thing upon entering the church. Her eyes slowly adjusted from bright daylight to the dimness of the church until she could distinguish shapes and colors. A typical church with rows of perfectly positioned pews, raised dais, tortured statues of a crucified Christ, and brightly stained glass windows.

No sound permeated from the outside. Within the church came a strange, disorienting hum that Cassandra tried to pinpoint. It rose from below, deep within the bowels of the building. Chanting. Not the usual Sunday morning sort of hymn song you'd expect, but rather a wailing lament oozing with echoes of dark intent and sent a shiver up Cassandra's spine.

She stepped backward while the lamenting wail clutched at her. Clung to the bare skin of her arms and drew her into its haunting song. Hypnotized, she moved. Each step, a surreal gliding movement bringing her closer to the raised altar in front of the pews.

Not knowing where she was going, Cassandra moved toward the back of the church, behind the altar. Lifting a heavy, embroidered wall hanging, she stepped into a recess leading to a narrow, dark hallway. Palpable tension clung to her. A faint glow at the end of the short hall beckoned. She came closer and saw stairs leading down to a doorway. The glowing light changed to a flicker. Candlelight? Strange.

Knowing she should turn and flee, she placed her foot on the first step and paused. Her brain screamed to run, but a force beckoned her to the basement. Cassandra descended. A familiar, indistinguishable scent assaulted her, and she fought the urge to gag. She took another step down. And another, until she stood on an uneven dirt flooring. The glow of dozens of candles illuminated the small room with shifting shadows and arcing images of the lone figure in the room.

Rising from where he'd been kneeling by a badly stained wooden altar, the man turned and faced Cassandra. Her heart thudded an irregular beat in her chest as she found herself unable to turn away. Every detail of him burned itself into her mind. Dark hair, narrow nose, high cheekbones, and lips pressed in a thin line that hinted at distaste. What stood out the most were his eyes. Dark pits of roiling anger. Cassandra recoiled from the raging sense of hate emanating in waves from those eyes.

Yet she moved forward. Those eyes compelled her, pinpointed her insecurities, and battered them into uselessness. Power pumped through her veins. She was free from the plaguing doubts and guilt she'd lived with since her parent's death. They had decided to travel despite her warning. The accident was their fault. They should have listened to her. Whom did they think they were causing her years of doubts and suffering? They'd deserved to die. All these thoughts crashed into Cassandra's mind, and she believed them.

Then she saw the cross. The blood. A replica of her dream.

With a gasp, she recognized the white collar around the man's neck before she noticed the dog pinioned upon the small altar. Blood ran in a rivulet down the altar and slowly, threateningly, toward Cassandra.

That's when she screamed.

The woman's scream incited Joshua. He ran to catch her when she fainted. He carried and positioned her on the hard-packed dirt floor by the altar. Led by a force beyond his reasoning, he picked up the knife from the altar and lifted the blade to his chest.

Chanting permeated his mind. Overflowing, compelling, the voice recited in an unidentifiable language and it tore through him, directing the movement of the knife. He lost all control over his intention and actions. In a sudden flash of clear thinking, he realized the foolishness of thinking he'd ever been in control.

Harsh, painful reality took hold. The comprehension of being a pawn in a scheme of evil. Sweat beaded on his body, and he wrestled with the unseen force that dragged him down in an ever-spinning vacuum. Fearful for his life, he screamed for release. No one heard. The voice turned to taunting laughter, and Joshua recognized the Devil's work. He fell into a dark abyss and struggled to remain awake and aware. It was a battle lost, and he plunged the knife into his chest, directly into his palpitating heart.

Joshua Parris died. In a darkness of his making.

Cassandra rose from the floor and brushed herself off. Whispers in the dark snaked into her head and began to babble. She cocked her head and listened.

Yes. I understand.

With a single glance of disdain, she stepped over the body on the floor and moved up the stairs. She emerged into the light of the upstairs nave and readjusted her eyes. Disjointed brain waves clashed with rippling internal voices. Car. Oh, yes.

Compelled by the voices, Cassandra strode outside and down the church stairs toward the waiting car. Soon the knife and the journal would finally be where they belonged.

Samson slammed into an immovable object. Not sure of his location, he cursed and opened his eyes. Consciousness brought recognition, and he realized he was lying on the couch in his condominium. Every inch of his body ached and when he ventured to move, pain roared through him like a flame of fire.

"He's awake. Oh my God, Jerome, he's awake!" Skye's excited proclamation evoked a confusion of movement as both she and Jerome rushed to Samson's side.

"No, don't try moving. We want to make sure you're okay." Jerome insisted, pressing Samson back onto the couch.

"No." He pushed Jerome's hands away. "Cassandra's in trouble, there's no time to waste."

"I greatly fear that Samson is right." The heavily accented, yet familiar, voice came from the direction of the kitchen, and Samson snapped his head around in disbelief.

"Seabhac?"

"Yes." The Druid stepped into the living room. "Ainevar is also here."

"How? You're both dead. I mean, you're supposed to be dead. Not that I'm sorry you're here, but...how?"

Seabhac rolled his eyes. "Cease your rambling. I swear the modern world breeds such inferior examples of the human species."

"Look, old man, I don't have to put up with your insults anymore. We're in my world now."

Seabhac gave an airy wave of the hand, which jolted Samson back against the couch with a hearty thump.

"Hey, no fair." Samson rose to his feet, teetering precariously. Once he regained his balance, he made a threatening move Seabhac's direction.

Ainevar effectively stopped him with a raised hand. “Now is not the time for banter, Seabhac. I do not understand how we came to be here, in this corporeal state, but we must make full use of whatever time we have.”

Seabhac’s nostrils flared, and shards of light sparked in the depths of his blue eyes. He inclined his head Ainevar’s way. “You are right.”

Samson frowned. “Why are you surprised to be here? Wasn’t that what you were trying to do?”

Ainevar replied. “No, we meant to send you back. We hadn’t considered what would happen to us.”

“Would someone please explain?”

Jerome’s voice jerked Samson from his squabbling, and Skye’s pale face made him realize the shock his two friends must be feeling. Instinctively, he moved toward her, but Jerome beat him. Jerome guided Skye to the couch and made her sit while casting wide-eyed, surreptitious glances at Ainevar and Seabhac.

Samson didn’t wonder at the confusion. Hell, he barely believed two powerful Druids, born hundreds of years ago, now stood in his living room. The guttural tones and hard-to-navigate intonation of their speech and visual impact of their clothing garnered attention and confusion. Clothing was similar for both, soft-looking, earth-tone leather leggings, worn under dark purple, lightly belted woolen tunics and topped with fur-trimmed cloaks held together at the throat with jewel-encrusted broaches. Flowing and comfortable looking, Arch-Druid and protégée each wore the clothing with ease and grace.

Samson lifted a shoulder. “There is an explanation.”

“The important thing is that you’re okay.” Skye smiled tremulously. “But,” she spared a quick glance at Seabhac and Ainevar and whispered. “Are they really who I think? And how did they get here?”

Before Samson spoke, Seabhac gave a sedate bow. “Arch-Druid Seabhac of Briton at your disposal milady.” He straightened and took Ainevar's hand. "And this is the lovely Lady Ainevar, my most apt disciple and practitioner of ancient Druid arts."

Ainevar inclined her head, and Samson noticed the slight tightening of her lips.

Oh, oh.

He knew that look. Seabhac's introduction had not met with her approval. He snorted and didn't envy the Druid for that slip up. For now, though, Cassandra was his concern, and she was in danger. A fact on which they needed to refocus.

Samson strode over and yanked open the drawer for his service revolver. He lifted his 9mm and held it in his hand, enjoying the familiar weight of the gun. He also reached for his back up pistol, thinking Jerome would need a gun as well. Armed and dangerous.

Under normal circumstances maybe, but nothing normal existed in what they faced. The human part of the evil would die with a bullet, but that would leave the evil loose in Salem. Using a gun might be a mistake.

Cold steel against ancient magic. Samson stared at the guns in his hand. He'd never doubted their use before and considering Seabhac and Ainevar's failure over the centuries; he did have reason to doubt their usefulness. Arch-Druid. Right. Couldn't have been such a powerful Druid to be defeated so easily.

"There was nothing easy involved. My defeat came about entirely because of misplaced belief in my infallibility and an intense desire to protect those I love."

Ainevar's gaze narrowed, and she stared hard at Seabhac, who flushed and stammered as he continued to speak.

"Since then, I've had centuries to observe and plan a strategy should the opportunity ever arise to confront the devil responsible for my departure from this world."

"And, what have you come up with?" Hesitation gone, Samson holstered his gun and handed the backup gun and leg strap to Jerome, who took and strapped them on his leg under his jeans.

Noting Skye's frown, Jerome gave her a quick hug. "Merely a precaution, sweetheart. Samson here'll be taking the force of all the heavy artillery."

"If I understand your meaning correctly, and Heaven knows modern jargon is so hard to understand, Samson will not be the one taking the force of all the heavy artillery. This battle began with me and it will end with me." Seabhac finished his statement by jutting his jaw and folding his arms.

"Jeez, the male ego races out of control no matter what century they're from." Skye's proclamation elicited an unladylike snort from Ainevar, and they shared a laugh.

"Great, so now you've disparaged all men through history. Where is Cassandra?"

"She went to pick up items for the retrieval ritual we planned, but clearly won't be performing now." Skye replied.

"The same retrieval ritual you did last year when your dad got lost in the Netherland of lost souls?" Samson asked.

Skye nodded.

Samson glared at Jerome. "Don't tell me you were going to let your pregnant wife perform such a dangerous ritual? What were you thinking? Even for a woman not pregnant, the risks are incredible. For Skye. They're unfathomable. I can't believe you'd allow such a thing."

Jerome shared a wary glance with his wife. He swallowed and spoke. "Skye wasn't going to perform the ritual."

"I see." Samson's mind raced with possibilities. "No, I don't see." Clued in by Skye and Jerome's discomfort, Samson reached the only conclusion possible. "Crap. That's almost as bad. Cassandra couldn't even begin to understand the consequences of such a ritual. Not only that, but she's torn by guilt over what she perceives to be her part in her parent's death. Her self-doubt would have placed her in danger."

"I had self-doubt and managed fine." Skye bristled.

"Yes, you did. You'd also been raised to accept and understand your powers." Samson raised a hand to quell Skye's protest. "Your mother may have discouraged you from using your full abilities, but she never denied them. You didn't have to grow up with the belief that your budding powers killed your parents. You didn't build a shield around yourself as protection against getting hurt. If Cassandra performed a retrieval ritual, the resulting rush of energy would have been equal to instantly opening the gates of the Hoover dam wide and letting the water rip free. Someone would have died. Probably her."

Skye's face stiffened, and her pallor paled. Samson softened his tone. "So I guess it's a good thing I'm back, and no one has to endanger themselves."

Skye nodded and leaned closer to Jerome, who sat on the couch beside her.

"How long has Cassandra been gone?"

Skye frowned. "Too long, now that you mention it."

Samson didn't wait. He strode to the door and yanked it open. Fully expecting the others to follow, he wasn't prepared to slow down and almost sent the person on the other side of the door flying backwards when he rammed into her.

"Cassandra?" He grabbed her arm to steady her and recoiled at the shot of coldness up his arm. "My God, woman, where have you been? You're freezing."

Cassandra glared at Samson. He moved back a step, driven by the malevolent intensity of her gaze. Dismissing him with a sniff and a wave of her hand, Cassandra stepped through the doorway. "I'm fine. What did I miss?"

Chapter Thirty-Four

Samson moved farther away from Cassandra to escape the winter-cold wave cutting through him and struggled to remain coherent in the aura of conflicting emotions and energies wafting off her. Something must have pissed her off. He searched her face for signs of anger or distress, but found nothing. Her face appeared cut in granite, hard and unforgiving. Her usually generous, soft lips compressed into two thin lines of distaste, while her eyes shot shards of penetrating intent as her gaze swept the room. Searching. Barely acknowledging Skye and Jerome.

Samson's gut tightened into a hard knot. "I'm fine, by the way. Thanks for asking."

Cassandra frowned. Her wary gaze swooped across her surroundings. Then, as if coming to a realization, her blue eyes lit with warmth. "I am sorry. Yes. I should have asked how you are. You're out of your trance."

She didn't sound sorry. Samson noted her pinched lips, shifting feet, and darting gaze. All indications of impatience and frustration. Uneasily, he wondered if he'd misjudged the woman. It wouldn't be the first time male hormones had overridden logic. If she was this heartless and cold about his return from the Netherworld, she wasn't the woman he'd thought her to be.

Not the woman he thought.

Oh, no. Something was wrong.

Aware of the shifting of shadows from the direction of the darkened kitchen and fighting the knots in his stomach, Samson gave a subtle wave of a hand behind his back to signal Seabhac and Ainevar to stay put. He didn't want to betray their presence until his radar for danger settled down and their anonymity remained his only advantage for now.

Heart pounding, he studied Cassandra while she talked with Skye. He searched her face for familiar signs of the woman he'd come to know over the last couple of days. Even as she talked, her gaze roamed the room. Dissecting every shadow, every dark corner. Samson knew what she sought. A fist slammed into his stomach because he realized Cassandra wasn't the one behind the fervent, visual sweep of the room.

Shit. What should he do? Evil inhabited Cassandra's body. So malevolent it had survived centuries and leave death and desecration in its wake. Samson did not have the capability to challenge such a force. Especially since any interference might leave Cassandra in a perilous situation.

Another terrible thought struck him, and icy dread froze his veins.

He had no idea if anyone had ever survived possession by that thing. Was it possible for Cassandra to exist in there on an invisible level, or had the evil taken total possession and destroyed her soul? That question led his brain on an entirely new path. Since evil possessed her body, there must be a discarded body lying around, or a disoriented person wandering the streets.

Thoughts and possibilities tore through his mind until nausea roiled in his stomach. His fists clenched into hard weapons of bone and flesh. He fought the urge to smash them at the wall. He took a step toward Cassandra. Before taking a second step, a hand fell to his shoulder and a soft voice whispered in his ear.

"All is not lost. We can save Cassandra. It will take patience, and we must not strike until we are assured of the advantage."

As relaxed as the gentle breezes that wafted into shore from the Atlantic on a warm summer eve, Ainevar's words soothed Samson. A Siren's song. A whisper and a promise of things to come. He conceded and drew his emotions in check. Ainevar stepped back into the shadows and Samson spoke. A low, rumble meant only for the two in the kitchen.

"Old man, your hands are full with that one. Her silver tongue could charm a wizard out of his staff."

Seabhac's reply was a thread barely woven within the fabric of Samson's mind. He had to concentrate to catch the words.

"She already has." Shadows of pain colored the words. An infinitesimal inkling of what Seabhac suffered on a daily basis. The freshness of love clutched in the hand of evil and lost over centuries. A numbing ache that dulled your mind every minute of every day, yet hurt so deeply you wished never to endure it again. The helplessness of watching your loved one fight to survive and being powerless to intercede.

Samson gasped as Seabhac's mind snapped shut and he wondered how the Druid had dealt with such pain for all these centuries.

The Druid gave a bittersweet smile quite clearly saying, 'You endure what you must.'

"Samson. Are you okay?" Skye's question drew him back into the moment, and he made a quick perusal of his surroundings. A cop thing. Always be aware. Always be ready to act. Never assume anything. Once he familiarized himself with where each person stood in the room and the availability of weapons, he answered Skye.

"Fine. I'm fine. Sorry, I'm still recovering from my excursion into another realm."

Cassandra stood in the shadows created by the closed curtains. Apart from the others, she pretended to be interested in what was going on, but her gaze swept the room. Taking a couple of giant strides, Samson moved to the window and yanked the curtains open. Cassandra cringed and turned away from the light. Not before Samson saw.

He flinched.

Eyes of a demon. Face of a fiend. Dark eddies of contempt swirled in fathomless eyes, while features once so classically beautiful morphed into a mask of malevolent fury. Then the shell of Cassandra returned to normal. Not soon enough. The creature observed Samson's cringe of revulsion at his brief glimpse beyond Cassandra's facade.

No need for secrets anymore.

Chapter Thirty-Five

Discovery was at hand. The demon in Cassandra lunged toward the table where the journal had lain untouched since Samson's ritual-gone-awry. Samson leapt forward as Seabhac and Ainevar rushed from the kitchen. Confused, but driven by his police training, Jerome seized Skye, pushed her behind him, and snatched the gun from where he'd shoved it in the leg strap beneath his jeans.

Samson grabbed the journal. So did Cassandra. When their hands touched, he screamed as burning pain flamed up his arm. With a roar of satisfaction, the creature that was Cassandra clutched the journal with one arm while warding off the approaching Seabhac and Ainevar with another.

"You?" Confusion and surprise crossed her features. She spat. "You challenge me again. And you have brought your woman to help. Ha! I defeated you both easily before. I can do so again."

"Circumstances are different, Vespasian. I've had centuries to watch, learn, and plan your destruction." Fervor burned in Seabhac's eyes. His hair snapped and sparked, the gray strands lifting and coming to rest on his shoulders.

Cassandra lifted her chin and replied. "Vespasian was merely a vessel, just as the one I control now. You cannot grasp the scope of my being. Or my power."

Seabhac's face showed no emotion, his arms hung calmly at his side, but Samson saw the rage and hatred seething off the Druid hotter than waves of heat off summer pavement.

"Do you know how I killed your woman and left her spirit to wander aimlessly in search of penance?"

Ainevar moved closer to Cassandra. “My journey was of my choosing and not due to your influence or power.”

Cassandra waved the book at Ainevar. “Your destruction most certainly was my doing. No one would willingly condemn themselves to lifetimes in limbo.”

Ainevar smacked her hand on a tabletop. “It was not done willingly, but it was my choice, not yours. Obviously, you’ve been living under a serious misconception all these years. You are not as powerful as you imagine.”

Seabhac’s snort of laughter followed Ainevar’s taunt. It enraged the beast. With a twisted smirk on her face, Cassandra gathered her free hand into a fist. Pressure built in Samson’s lungs as the oxygen in the room disappeared. He couldn’t breathe, and the others in the room were in trouble as well. Skye’s face whitened, and she cradled her stomach with her hands. No. She couldn’t lose the baby.

Cassandra! His mind screamed the single word. Was that her voice he heard in the distance? Cassandra, you must fight!

Yes. There was no doubt. He’d heard her, felt her. She was alive. With hope renewed, he struggled to remain conscious. His hopes crashed when the evil controlling Cassandra’s body opened its fist and thrust it straight up. All the oxygen collected in the fist and tore through the room in a mini tornado. Shredding, throwing, whirling, it destroyed everything in its path. With barely seconds to react, everyone dove for cover. Everyone except Cassandra, who stood in the melee laughing like a mad hatter.

Caught in the mini-tornado and struggling with the extreme of no oxygen to too much, Samson’s slipped deeper into unconsciousness. The others had already succumbed and lay prone on the floor. Damn! Stars spotted his vision. Sweat beaded on his forehead. His lungs fought with the effort to adjust to extremes.

Darkness took him.

Each of them woke, rubbed their heads, and moaned about aches and bruises. Wrestling hazy memories, they scrambled to their feet and tried to orient themselves.

Desolation swept over Samson. "She's gone. She...he...it...took us all on and still got away unscathed. How can we hope to beat it? Especially without harming Cassandra's body?"

Jerome put an arm around Skye's shoulder and pulled her close. "I don't know, Samson." He closed his eyes and placed his cheek against her hair. "We might not be able to, or want to."

"No. We have to proceed as if she were alive, Jerome. I know she is." Her presence had washed over him in comforting waves. He'd heard her voice far too vividly for it to have been his imagination. Locked in a realm beyond the physical one they existed on, she'd be lost forever if she didn't return to her body. Samson hated to imagine her wandering forever in a place like the one he'd found Seabhac. But he didn't know how to defeat the evil that possessed her body without harming her.

"She's taken the journal." Ainevar pointed at the now empty table. "She'll go for the knife."

Skye's gasp filled the room. "Oh, no. It's on the couch at Cassandra's house. When she got the premonition about Samson being in trouble, we raced to get here. I didn't even think about bringing the knife."

Her stricken face mirrored the stab of fear that shot through Samson. His gaze flew between Druids and friends while his mind filled with possibilities that he discarded one after the other.

"What happens if she gets the knife? She can't use it, right? I mean, Ainevar, you're not...you know...part of her anymore and that connection is what allowed her to touch the knife. As far as

I remember, only a descendant of Sarah Good can see the knife when it's unwrapped. So there's no problem." The high pitch of his voice deepened with a hearty clearing of his throat. "Someone please tell me she can't use the knife."

No one spoke. The room throbbed while each person considered the possibility. Seabhac broke the heavy silence.

"I have no idea what is possible at this point. But I would highly suggest we arrive at the knife first."

"No. It's too late." Samson checked the clock on the wall. "She's had a five-minute head start, and that's all she needs."

"Not necessarily." Ainevar spoke. "I've seen this evil inhabit numerous people over the centuries, and there's one common occurrence each time. It takes at least a day for the melding of energies to fully take hold. Until that time, some memories and even bodily functions are awkward or non-existent. The usual procedure is to hole up in a safe place and wait for the transformation from intangible force to human." Bitter pain laced her voice, likely triggered by lifetimes of memories. "Many times that short period of transformation has been my only reprieve from pursuit. And I'm certain it's the only reason I avoided death for so long."

Regret and guilt shadowed Seabhac's face. Lifting an arm to Ainevar's shoulders, he laid a whisper of a kiss to her brow. Ainevar smiled and leaned close enough for her hair to brush across Seabhac's face. The barest glow of light shimmered around them and then disappeared. Samson allowed them a moment, but no longer.

"We've got to go. If there's any chance Cassandra hasn't made it back to her place, we need to get there first." He raised a hand before Skye and Jerome moved. "Not you two. You're going home."

"Like hell we are."

The thrust of Jerome's jaw and his clenched fists showed what he thought of that idea. Samson raised an eyebrow and inclined his head toward Skye.

Jerome flushed. “Fine, Skye goes home, but I’m with you all the way. That’s what we do. That’s how it’s always been.”

“Things change, Jerome.”

“Yes, but I want to help.” He pleaded with his eyes, as well as his words.

Samson understood the pain wrenching Jerome. They’d been friends since childhood and stuck by each other no matter what. Neither of them doubted the other would give up their life for the other without a thought. But Jerome had more than his life to consider.

“Take your pregnant wife and go home. That’s an order.” His soft tone lessened the blow of his words. “Look, I’ve got an Arch-Druid and his apprentice, both of whom have earned a fair amount of faith over the centuries. I’ll be fine.”

Their gazes met and challenged, but the touch of Skye’s hand on his arm drew Jerome from his confrontational mood. He lowered his eyes.

“Okay. But promise you’ll call if things get too rough.”

Samson agreed, knowing he wouldn’t.

Chapter Thirty-Six

Cassandra's transition must have been a quick one, because by the time Samson, Seabhac, and Ainevar arrived at Cassandra's house, the knife was gone.

"Damn, she beat us here." Samson slammed his fist into his hand. Took a panicked look around. A brief wave of bleakness passed over Samson and he wished he hadn't turned down Jerome's help. Thirty years of having Jerome as a friend and being able to rely on him no matter what, made it hard to be alone.

"You are not alone." Seabhac's voice broke into Samson's self-pitying mood.

"Old man, I asked you before to stop reading my mind."

"Yes. You did." Seabhac folded his arms across his chest and fixed his unapologetic gaze on Samson. "I do not take orders well."

"Cease, you two. Now is not the time for flexing your male egos." Ainevar tugged on Seabhac's sleeve, the motion easily dragging him back a couple of steps. "Have you no idea who this evil inhabited before Cassandra? With the certain knowledge we'd come to Cassandra's house, it would return to familiar surroundings. I'm sure a ritual room and altar await there as well, ready for use."

Before answering, Samson reviewed the information he'd gathered. The ritualistic murders, Cassandra's dream about standing at the foot of a cross, her sketches portraying the seven deadly sins, they tied together and pointed one direction.

"Religion. Seabhac, you mentioned that when this evil possesses people, it twists their values and beliefs into a reason for killing."

"Yes. It finds their weaknesses. Uses their beliefs to control them. This person has killed people he, or she, believes to be sinners. The last person probably possessed inherently strong religious beliefs."

"Ah. So we look for a person who is affected most by blasphemy against God and the Church." Seabhac frowned. "A person you would refer to as a minister or priest."

"Yes. That makes sense." Samson paced the floor, his hands clenching and unclenching. "I'm not sure where to begin. We don't have time to search every church or talk to every minister."

"My connection to Cassandra might be an advantage." Excitement raised Ainevar's voice a notch. "So many years of two life forces living as one cannot be easily broken. Whenever I chose a person, I was unfailingly careful not to disturb their life force. I melded with them, shaped my own self to their thoughts and beliefs. I hid within and gave them guidance, never pressure. Made sure to cause barely a ripple of disruption to who they were at the root of their being. However careful, though, our essences have mingled and they will be eternally connected to a minor degree. If we get sufficiently close to Cassandra, I will perceive her existence here." She laid a hand across heart.

Samson understood everything but focused on the one statement bothering him the most. "What would have happened if you hadn't been so careful when inhabiting a person?"

The slight compression of lips and flicker of eyelids was not lost on Samson. His jaw clenched. "Don't bother, I can guess the answer."

"Take heart. I truly believe the displaced soul resides in another realm until their body dies. Cassandra can be returned, but..." Ainevar glanced to Seabhac, who nodded.

"She might be damaged. As she and I are bound by our closeness, so will she and the evil one be bound."

"Even if we kill it?"

Ainevar gave Samson a sad smile of regret. "I do not know."

"This gets better and better." Samson growled with growing frustration.

"Let us find her. Then we will determine what we can do to save her." Seabhac offered.

Samson's gaze swept Cassandra's living room one last time before leaving. He noted her sketchpad laid neatly on the table, pencils placed perfectly in order beside it, and a pale blue jacked folded and draped over the arm of a chair. Organized, but comfortable, the familiar room and muted colors calmed him. He knew he'd need that calming influence for what was to come as he turned and followed Seabhac and Ainevar.

Cassandra waved at the spiral of mist snaking past her face and curled its way down her body to slither across the unseen ground beneath her feet. With gritted teeth, she took another tentative step and cursed.

"I cannot believe this. Why me? Why do things like this happen to me? I would have been perfectly content living a normal life, like a normal person. Instead, the universe throws me into a mixture of magic, psychic premonitions and ancient, murdering, evil intent on taking over the world. Oh, and let's not forget the gorgeous police chief who, despite his protests that he can handle it alone, keeps dragging me into precarious situations."

Finding solid purchase with her feet, she took another step, uncertain why she bothered. "It's not as if I have a clue where I'm going or anything." She squinted into the miasma of mist. "There's nothing. I'm lost in limbo and I do not know what to do."

Then an encouraging thought struck her. Earlier, when she'd cupped Samson's cheek and found herself out-of-body and sensing Samson nearby, this was the place she'd been. There was no mistaking the ubiquitous fog. Maybe he was still here. If she went into a meditative state, she might be able to reach him.

A heavy-footed shuffle and nail-on-chalkboard scratching approached from an undetermined direction. Cassandra's heart thudded.

What shared the mist with her?

It didn't matter. Whatever hovered on the edge of the mist gave her incentive to attempt to reach Samson. Dropping to the spongy ground, she crossed her legs and put herself into a meditation as quickly as possible under the current circumstances. She breathed, focused her mind, and concentrated on Samson. His determined eyes, warm and welcoming. His square jaw, clenched in challenge when he'd made up his mind. She imagined running her hands down his shoulders and across the chest where she'd glimpsed dark curls of hair sneaking out from beneath his shirt. She squirmed at the thought of firm butt and powerful legs that molded his jeans into such a work of supreme art.

Screeeech!

Jolted from her increasingly hot thoughts, Cassandra jumped to her feet, her gaze jerking around her surroundings. Crap, whatever had made that wrenching blast was close.

Terror snapped at her with hungry teeth. Her body tingled with sharp prickles. Her heart beat fiercely and sent blood rushing through her.

Quivering with an onslaught of adrenaline, Cassandra plopped back on the ground and put her hands over her face. This was way beyond her abilities, and for the first time she regretted a lifetime of denying her powers.

A drifting waft of mist roiled around her, and Cassandra punched out at it in frustration. She hated being stuck in this nowhere place, while her body moved around the earthly realm inhabited by evil pretending to be her. There was a strong possibility the evil within her would be responsible for at least one death. This meant more guilt for Cassandra to deal with.

An unbearable realization struck her. What if she never left this place? She shot to her feet in panic. Any place would be better than here. She thrust aside her misgivings and ran into the fog.

Acting on a hunch, Samson called the station to check for any unusual reports logged recently. Told that a woman matching Cassandra's description had been seen driving erratically, Samson approached shopkeepers in the area. They provided him with lots of information—most of it contradictory, a common practice for eyewitnesses. Using his year of police interrogation experience, he weeded out the jumble and pinpointed the truth.

"Now what?" Seabhac asked. "You know which direction she has gone, but little else. It may take days, nay weeks to find her."

Samson smiled. "Seabhac, you do not know the wonders at our disposal in this century. Your magic has nothing on our modern-age computers."

Without saying more, Samson wheeled into an alley between buildings. "I'll be one minute. Don't go anywhere." He opened the Hummer door and stepped out, slamming the door on any protest from the two in the back seat of the vehicle. Fred, the barber, was more than happy to lend Samson the use of his computer for a couple of minutes. Samson found what he wanted with one search on the internet.

"Yes. That's got to be it." He gloated and wrote an address on a napkin he filched from beside Fred's half-eaten fries. Absent-mindedly, he commented. "Your wife knows you're eating those for lunch?"

Fred blushed, patted his belly, and changed the subject. "You got time for a hair cut?"

"Nope. Sorry. Got to go." Samson strode from the barber shop, leaving a flustered Fred mumbling something about how people were always in a such a hurry these days.

"Got it." Samson waved the napkin in triumph as he stepped on the Hummer's running board and climbed up.

"What, exactly do you have?" Seabhac's inquired.

"Cassandra's dreams hinted at a church, so I searched the ones in the direction Cassandra had driven. There's only one. It has to be the one we want." He silently prayed. Because, if his cop intuition failed him now, Cassandra was dead.

Samson pulled onto the road and frowned at the surfeit of rustling from behind him.

"I have no idea why you feel it necessary to conceal us in the rear of this contraption with no regard to our comfort." Seabhac complained.

Samson replied. "I told you, even in Salem, you two would stand out as different, and we're trying to fly under the radar at the moment."

"Did I not tell you he speaks strangely?" Seabhac mumbled to Ainevar loudly enough for Samson to hear.

"Look, can we focus on the task at hand instead of bellyaching about not being the one in charge for the moment?"

"I merely made a simple comment about being cramped. It does not bother me to let you take control of a situation thousands of years in the making. I am sure even though an Arch-Druid of Britain, nor his highly skilled apprentice, has been able to bring this malevolence to heel, you, a local officer of authority, barely dry behind the ears, should have no problems whatsoever."

Seabhac folded his arms across his chest and sat back with a definitive vocal harrumph. Samson slowed to a standstill for a traffic light. The old man did have a point. As usual, Samson's roughshod approach wasn't making him any allies. Rather than hide the two and hushing Seabhac every time he made a suggestion, Samson should respect their knowledge and experience. Hell, an Arch-Druid. A real one, not the phony kind you might find pandering spells and herbs in Salem these days. He believed modern Druids possessed powers, but their abilities would be minimal compared with Seabhac's. Jeesh, he was the original. Anyone would be a watered-down version.

He sighed. "You're right." Samson made a brief pause to allow Seabhac his self-satisfied snort. "What do you suggest?"

"We need to find your lady posthaste. By doing so, we shall find the current hiding place of the evil possessing her and probably where he performs his rituals. This is important for various reasons."

Pontificating puff of hot air. The ungracious insult jumped into Samson's mind. Aloud, he asked. "And those reasons, other than the obvious, would be...?"

"They would be none of your business if you continue to imagine me in such an unsavory manner."

Samson had the grace to blush. "Ya, ya. You can read minds. Sorry."

"Sorry you got caught, but not sorry for maligning my character."

Ainevar interrupted the tirade. "Please, lives are in danger. Let us put aside personal issues for now, and concentrate on finding Cassandra."

The hot rush of dread at the idea of losing Cassandra made him forget his petty arguments with Seabhac. "Yes. That's a plan I can go with."

"No. Going anywhere without us is not a good plan." Seabhac frowned and shifted.

Samson let the misunderstanding pass and said. "So, according to you, it's not enough to find Cassandra. We need to find the place this evil performs its rituals."

"That is what I said, yes."

"Why?"

"When we find its lair, we will also find the means to liberate Cassandra's soul. There will be an item binding her and the Netherworld. Usually an item as simple as a knotted rope completes the binding spell. With the combined power of a trio, we escaped. But Cassandra will not have that advantage. We will need to bring her back to this side."

Realization sank in and Samson had trouble swallowing. "You mean that's where she is? That horrible landscape of endless mist and slithering slinking in the shadows."

"Yes, she is. I thought you understood that."

Samson didn't reply. He was too busy imagining how terrified Cassandra must be in such a place. Alone. He'd have lost his sanity if he hadn't chanced upon Seabhac. He chanced a glance in the rearview mirror and wasn't surprised at the upward tilt in the corner of the Druid's mouth.

"Hey. Quit reading my mind. It's considered rude."

"Here!" Ainevar's slicing voice resulted in Samson jerking the wheel and grinding to a halt inches short of a hydro pole. Pain slammed into his shoulder when Ainevar jiggled the release latch, thrust the seat forward, and made a clumsy, hurried exit. Ouch! Samson rubbed his shoulder and frowned. He surveyed the surroundings to see what had Ainevar so frantic.

The street was quiet and sparsely populated with homes of indiscriminate heritage. Clothes on a line wafted in the breeze and a child's laughter softened the deadened silence. The church they'd stopped in front of sat unobtrusively recessed from the sidewalk. Stained glass windows darkened with shadows from surrounding trees, front steps led to a scarred wooden door that stood closed against prying eyes, and a weather-worn wooden exterior. All showed signs of age and recent, meticulous cleaning.

Despite the innocuous appearance of the building, Samson fought a sense of foreboding. Even without Ainevar's insistent waving from the uneven, cracked sidewalk, he'd have known this was the place.

Disapproval flushed Ainevar's face. "Come. She's in here. We must hurry."

Cassandra's safety replaced any extraneous thoughts about near accidents, the strange clothing of his visitors, or even concern for his safety. Banging his knee on the car door as he jumped out, he cursed and threw Seabhac a frown of disapproval when the Druid chuckled.

"Laugh at me again and I'll leave you there." For effect, he paused as Seabhac tried to figure out how to flip the release that would move the seat and allow him out.

"Fine. Get me out of this contraption and I'll not take such enjoyment from your discomfort again."

"Deal." Samson slid into the seat and stepped aside to allow Seabhac his freedom.

"Men. In any century, they are immature and prankish." Ainevar grabbed a fistful of her skirt and moved toward the church. "I guess it is up to me to save Cassandra."

"No!" Samson and Seabhac responded. "We go together. Just as we escaped the Netherworld together. Right?" Samson received a nod from Seabhac and Ainevar.

"Together." Seabhac declared as they moved across the sidewalk and took their first hesitant step toward the unknown.

Chapter Thirty-Seven

The landscape never changed. Mist clung to her clothing and created heaviness in the air that she sucked into her lungs with each breath. Sweat trickled between her shoulder blades and dripped from her chin, while her legs burned with the exertion of running for longer than she intended without a break. Finally, she stopped. Dropped her butt on the ground. Drew her knees up.

Her mind raced, and despite the heat, she shivered. Cassandra knew it was a reaction to fear that had driven her into an adrenaline-fired run into a gray horizon. If she wanted to get out of here, she needed to quell the panic and concentrate.

She couldn't. Her mind wandered all over the place. Work. Family. Memnon. He was her only family, but as supportive and close of a relationship as they shared, he was a busy person with a full life. One day he'd fall in love, marry, and have children.

That idea scared Cassandra, and she wondered if she'd be satisfied playing favorite aunt instead of having children herself. Tears welled in her eyes, and she swiped them with the back of her hand before they fell. She would not feel sorry for herself. She loved her work, possessed good health, and wanted for nothing. Or so she'd thought until she met Samson. His rugged self-assurance and steadfast morality filled a void within her she hadn't known existed. His laughter and deep-throated voice stirred yearnings for things she'd never missed before.

Her leg muscles stiffened in protest of inactivity, and Cassandra stood to give them a shake and stretch. Realizing she'd accomplish nothing by sitting still, she set off at a brisk pace, her mind racing. She'd allowed guilt to control her life. Instead of developing inherent abilities and using them to help others, she'd led a driven, organized, empty life. No, not empty...filled with guilt. Hot, acrid, debilitating guilt. And now, when her life depended on her accessing the deepest part of her soul and powers, she was useless. That's what her guilt had done for her. Well, no more. It was time to cast off the guilt and allow her true self to emerge, unshackled and ready to fight.

Unexpectedly, her surroundings changed. The air crackled with static. The heavy mist now shone lighter and charged with simmering energy. Whispers weaved themselves in the fabric of gray. Familiar voices, yet not. Invigorated with her newly discovered fulfillment of self, Cassandra called out.

"Hello. Is that you, Samson?"

The murmurs returned stronger, more insistent.

Cassie. Child. We can't see you. Come closer. Instinctual childhood memories made Cassandra hug herself like a child. "Mom? Dad?"

The surrounding mist spun around her feet and drifted up to her waist. A sob caught in Cassandra's throat. "Please. If you're here, talk to me."

We're here. We've always been with you.

The soft voices calmed Cassandra, yet created numerous questions. It might be a result of her imagination working overtime, prompted by the influence of this place. Since her parents had been dead for years, there was no logical reason for them to start talking to her now?

Cassie, you've finally let go of your guilt. Until achieving that, you'd never have become the person you were meant to be.

"What does that mean? Who am I? What am I?" Her previous confidence shifted and the familiar doubt crept in and began to shut down the part of herself that she'd finally managed to access. The voices of her parents receded. Retreated to nothing more than a mere wisp of sound in the distance.

"NO!" Cassandra screamed in desperation. "I won't lose you again." Frantic, she ran in the direction the voices seemed to be disappearing. "Don't leave me."

We aren't leaving you. But what comes next you must do yourself. Trust and believe. Feel what you know to be right.

Silence. Total dead silence. They'd left her and Cassandra hoped she wouldn't have to wait for another twenty-five years to talk with them again? Trust and believe, they'd said. What she didn't understand was whom did they mean for her to trust? Other than Memnon. And what was she supposed to believe in? She groaned and fought the urge to wrap her arms around herself and wallow in self-pity.

This personal growth business was not easy. Wait. Wait. Wait.

"Me. I trust and believe in myself." Cassandra yelled at the abysmal gray. Nothing. No voices answered her fervent enlightenment. She sank to the ground. Defeated. Then she smacked her palm against her forehead and mumbled.

"Idiot. That's the idea." She stood and assumed a don't-mess-with-me stance. "They aren't going to answer. That's the point. It's up to me. I have to make things happen."

Her mind whirled. She needed to protect the people she'd come to care for. Once Jerome or Skye realized the thing walking around Salem was a shell imitating her, they'd try to find her. Cassandra dreaded the idea that her careless act might cause harm.

Damn it. Damn the force that had drawn her to that church. Damn the damn fog that clung to her. Damn it, she would take none of this sitting down.

Her life would not end in this godforsaken place. Driven by a surge of pure intent, she shot to her feet and thrust her arms upwards. A primal scream of freedom and self-awareness built in her belly and rose past her throat to release in the grim surrounding fog with the intensity of a battle cry.

A lifetime of denying her true self lent vital urgency to her cry. The echoes of her pain, barely broke the thick miasma surrounding her, but that didn't stop Cassandra from releasing every ounce of breath into a scream and expelling every bit of her former self. With a gasp, she drew in the warm, humid air and the new sensations revitalized her. Hot blood pulsed in her veins and she tingled with prickles of power. Full. The sense overwhelmed her. A door had opened and flooded her with boundless vitality.

She could accomplish anything. If she didn't succeed in finding Samson in this panorama of mist, then she'd find her way out and reclaim what belonged to her. It shouldn't be too difficult. The body belonged to her, and that had to count for something.

The church foundations rumbled and glass from one of the stained glass windows came loose and shattered on the floor. Samson put a hand on the edge of a pew to steady himself.

"What was that?" Samson whispered, cautious not to betray their presence inside the church.

Holding each other for support, Ainevar and Seabhac shared a knowing glance. Ainevar answered his question. "I would say we experienced a powerful witch finally claiming her legacy."

"Cassandra? How? I mean, if she's not even here, how can she have such an effect on the surroundings?"

"As I said, her powers are strong."

Seabhac swept through the dim shadows of the church as if a shadow himself, while Ainevar explained further. "Cassandra has spent a lifetime denying the essence of who she is. She has effectively suppressed her powers, but that does not mean they have remained stagnant. Instead, they've roiled and boiled beneath her self-imposed restriction, ready to explode in a volcanic eruption."

"A volatile volcano." Seabhac interjected, coming to stand beside them again. "I find nothing in this room. We need to search elsewhere. Ainevar, what do you sense?"

The woman closed her eyes and Samson studied her intently for the first time. Her face was unlined, yet emanated ageless wisdom. Silken strands of blond hair drifted across her forehead and she brushed them away with a slender hand and a frown. When she opened her eyes, their green radiance punched Samson in the gut. She smiled. A gentle lift of her lips. Samson's heart fluttered.

"Back down." Seabhac's voice rasped close to Samson's ear. "She is not for you."

Though he bristled at the warning, Samson understood the Druid's possessiveness. Ainevar was stunning. "Don't worry, Druid. She's way too old for me."

"I have warned you both before. Now is not the time to flex your egos. Please, we must find Cassandra. Even more important is to reclaim the knife and journal before this creature can use them."

"Exactly how dangerous are the knife and journal in the wrong hands?" Samson asked.

"Deadly. On so many levels, you have no idea. I created the journal as a record for all Druid knowledge from antediluvian times. I created the knife, as magical protector, and Ainevar enhanced it to transfer knowledge from one person to another instantly. Not only the written word, for that is the journal's purpose, but the inherent abilities and blood-deep understanding that take a lifetime to master. Together, they give the bearer knowledge and instant Arch-Druid power."

Samson blanched. "Back in your time, at the height of Druid power, that would have been scary. Today, it's terrifying. Not a person alive today could even begin to understand what you are capable of accomplishing. Someone with all Druid knowledge and the ability to transfer it from one person to another would reign freely in this world. No one could stop them."

"Yes. You grasp the situation quite succinctly." Seabhac nodded his agreement. "Now, I suggest we find the ritual room, where I am sure we will find Cassandra's possessed body, as well as the journal and knife. We'd best destroy whatever talisman used to bind you and the Netherworld as well. While it remains intact, there remains a chance of you being drawn back there again."

"Whoa. Why am I just hearing this now?"

"Most likely because I have only just informed you of the situation."

Samson itched to wipe the smug look off the Druid's face, but common sense and concern for Cassandra quelled any such action. Gritting his teeth, he turned to Ainevar, who stood wide-eyed and staring in the direction of the altar.

"Ainevar?"

Prompted by Samson's voice, she lifted her hand and pointed.

Not waiting for the others, Samson strode toward the altar and thrust aside a heavy brocade wall hanging portraying Christ on the cross. With shaking hands, he lifted the door handle to release the latch and yanked. A dark maw greeted him. The acrid scent of burning candles elicited a sneeze that he did his best to stifle. Determination burned within him to save Cassandra and destroy an age-old evil that had ravaged the world for centuries. All without allowing the Netherworld to draw him back into its stifling embrace. No problem!

Sensing Ainevar and Seabhac close behind; he took the first step and descended into the darkness.

Chapter Thirty-Eight

Samson's earthy scent tickled Cassandra's nose, so he must be near. If she concentrated hard enough, she might hone in on his location. She wove tendrils of energy and cast them in all directions to feel for Samson. Nothing. Frustrated, she pulled the tendrils back and peered into the mist. Despair threatened, and tears gathered. She wasn't fooling anyone. She'd be stuck alone in the place forever.

Swish.

Her heart thumped. "Hello. Is anyone there?"

Thwack. Swissssssh.

Cassandra reacted without thinking.

"SAMSON." He must be nearby, and if magic wouldn't find him, she'd do it the old-fashioned way.

"SAMSON." Her voice cut through the thick air and echoed with lonely appeal. She tried again, this time inhaling and sending a belly-deep plea brimming with every shred of emotion she could gather from her toes up to the top of her head. "SAMSON."

Cassandra.

A barely perceptible whisper, but definitely Samson's voice. Which direction, though. Tears welled, and her nerves jerked with the need to run. The need to find safety. Fear of being forever alone in this place threatened to tear down her hard fought for sense-of-self.

Oh, Samson. A whimper punctuated her thoughts. Where are you?

No voice answered her silent plea. Nothing sounded amidst the heavy mist, yet she knew. With bone-deep surety, she finally knew which direction she'd find Samson. So she ran.

They'd found what they were looking for. Samson wished they hadn't. The gory display of the sacrificial ritual turned his stomach. Previous events in his line of work paled in comparison. Accident scenes with blood-soaked pavement, pale white limbs entrenched in twisted metal, flashing sirens, wide-eyed innocents trying to make sense of what had happened.

He'd prefer an accident any day rather than face another repulsive, immoral scene similar to the one displayed in the tiny basement room. The deliberateness of the act sickened him. Dark red symbols smeared the walls. Likely blood, judging by the animal carcasses and blood-filled bowl on the dirt floor. Candles situated in the outline of a pentagram flickered ghostly shadows on the walls while a black cat lay sprawled in the center of the pointed symbol. Cliché, definitely, and Samson's thoughts on upside down pentagrams and black cat sacrifices were known by the witch wannabes that he arrested for public mischief. Usually on All Hallows Eve.

The shifting of a shadow and a low chant alerted him to another person in the room. Before Samson reacted, Seabhac surged forward. Ainevar's hastily muttered spell froze Seabhac briefly. Long enough to stop the Arch-Druid from acting in haste.

Samson breathed in relief when the Druid shook off the spell and snapped indignantly. "You use a spell of my making against me."

"Better that than have you die. Look!" She inclined her head toward the makeshift altar where the journal and knife rested beneath the splayed hands of a cloaked and hooded figure.

"I suppose there's no sense in trying to remain secretive now, is there." Samson shot the caustic remark at Seabhac.

"You defeated that purpose the moment you stepped into my church." The figure rose and turned to face them.

Even knowing whose face he'd see, Samson felt sucker punched when he saw Cassandra glaring at them from beneath the hood. Although the eye color showed more black than blue, and the facial structure appeared harsher and lined than Cassandra's creamy, smooth features, the enormity of the situation hit Samson. This was so not in his job description.

The creature snorted. "Your newest initiate is dumbfounded, Seabhac. I suppose it comes down to you and me. It began on a cliff top and ends here, in this hole."

"The only thing to end here is your life, dark one."

"You tried that once, and it didn't work. And even though your woman gave me a worthwhile chase, I also ended her life."

"But you didn't get the journal and knife from me. Never forget that, dark one." Ainevar's voice rumbled with unrepentant anger and straining power.

A black sleeve lifted nonchalantly. "You can see they are now in my possession. Your defiance only delayed the inevitable and cost numerous innocent lives and souls."

Ainevar gasped. Her face blanched. Samson wanted to comfort her, but still couldn't move. He realized it wasn't fear or disgust causing his immobility. He'd been spelled.

"It's for your safety." Seabhac whispered close to his ear. "This is not your battle."

What! You son of a bitch. Unable to speak, Samson screamed the words in his mind.

Seabhac tut-tutted at Samson and turned to face his nemesis. "I will kill you for the pain that you caused Ainevar. Then I will take back what is mine. You are not worthy to possess the knife and journal."

"Take them from me then, Druid."

The taunting challenge delivered in a voice no longer belonging to Cassandra. Layered with centuries of death and torture and laden with malevolent intent and horrible acts, the shout thundered within the room.

Ear-splitting and potent, it released Seabhac's spell on Samson, who immediately clapped his hands over his ears. He fell to his knees in pain. Reverberations resonated throughout the room. Bile choked his throat. Black spots blinded him. Samson tried to straighten, but dizziness overcame him. Minutes passed. Finally, his head cleared, and the agony ebbed away. He glanced at the others. They stood, staring at him. The onslaught of pain and discomfort hadn't affected them. Only him.

Impatience flitted across Seabhac's face and, though he didn't speak, Samson heard his words. We are powerful beyond your understanding. Leave this to us.

"Damn you, you arrogant bastard." Samson snarled at Seabhac's declaration.

"Stop." Ainevar sliced the air with her hand. "The enemy stands there. Not here."

Before Samson could agree with her logic, the evil inhabiting Cassandra's body struck. Thrusting two hands forward, fingers splayed, the creature sent a black cloud streaking their direction. Seabhac waved a hand and surrounded them with a thin bubble of light that deflected the oily substance.

"Bah. You cannot kill us so easily." Seabhac thrust off the now sticky bubble and waved it into oblivion.

"You don't understand, Druid, I'm not trying to kill you. At least, not yet. I will use the journal and knife you created to gain your knowledge and your soul. An eerie grin preceded the next words. "Then I will kill you."

One leap brought Cassandra's possessor across the dingy room and instinct had Samson reaching for his gun. Ainevar and Seabhac leapt aside. Their hurried act knocked against Samson and drove him against the wall. Despite the pain, his mind raced with alternatives.

How did you stop a person trying to kill you without hurting them?

If they weren't careful, Cassandra might not be able to re-enter her body. But the alternative made Samson queasy. Evil, with unlimited power loose in the world. No one person's life was worth it. Even Cassandra's.

With those thoughts scrambling around inside his mind, Samson stood to face the entity, but Ainevar and Seabhac moved quicker. They stood, hand in hand, glowing with the light of combined energy and an unflinching belief in their purpose. Chanting reverberated in the room, but no one's lips moved. The air sparked with unreleased magic. A wicked wind whooshed through the pathway and across the room. It slammed open the door at the top of the stairs, leaving behind a crushing pressure in Samson's chest. He gasped for breath. Turned to Seabhac for help. Something had gone wrong. Even though no one else struggled for breath, their brows furrowed with confusion.

Great. What the hell did it mean if none of them knew what was going on?

The candle-smudged, blood-tainted room shimmered with brilliance for a brief moment, and then faded to its former bleakness. That's when he heard the voice in his head, and this time it wasn't Seabhac's.

Samson.

He straightened up. "Cassandra?"

"Quiet." Seabhac hissed. "You know she cannot hear you."

"No. She's here. Look." Samson pointed at the stairway where Cassandra stood. More appropriately, she hovered. A wavering wraith.

Chapter Thirty-Nine

It wasn't possible. Cassandra had found Samson all right. In the church's basement, where she'd been attacked. Beside him, in the shadows, stood a man and woman, strangely dressed. Thrumming with magic. Her gaze swept the room and her shock tripled. She stared at herself, dressed in a dark cloak and standing in a predatory stance.

Samson had seen her. Relief flooded her, and she ran down the stairs to his side. At least she tried to run, but only managed a floating glide.

Why couldn't she move?

A terrified glance downwards showed an ethereal replica of her body. She lifted a hand and tentatively brushed her opposite arm. Her hand passed right through and out the other side. She screamed, but it came out sounding like a mini squeal.

"It's alright, Cassandra."

She glanced up, and even if she hadn't known the voice, Cassandra would have known the woman who'd moved forward into the candlelight. There was no mistaking the ethereal essence that she'd spent most of her life linked with. "Ainevar?"

"Yes, it is I." The woman stepped closer, and Cassandra gasped. "You're beautiful." Cassandra recognized her from dreams, but in real life, Ainevar was so much more striking with her creamy complexion, long blond hair, moss-green eyes. Which meant the male Druid with her must be Seabhac.

The fake Cassandra sneered. "Ahh, how sweet. A reunion."

The real Cassandra bristled. For whatever reason, fate had plucked her from the land of mist and dropped her here, and she wasn't going to waste time. Puffing her hand into a wisp of mist, her soft, intense voice echoed in the room. "I want my body back."

"I would consider your request, but since I'm going to destroy the Druid and his woman, I'll need your body. So, no."

Samson tensed and moved her direction, but he was stuck in place. Having issued her threat and been denied left Cassandra unsure what her next move should be. She knew she wasn't leaving this room without her body.

Seabhac drew her attention when he raised his hand and held it palm up. "I told you I would kill you for the pain you caused Ainevar."

A glimmer of light, no bigger than a pea, appeared in Seabhac's hand. Fascinated, Cassandra watched him round his lips and blow gently into his palm. The light grew into tiny bubbles that frothed over the side of Seabhac's hand and cascaded to the ground. They bubbled into a frenzied mass, roiling and expanding into a mass that engulfed Seabhac, Ainevar, Samson, and Cassandra. Soon, the foamy liquid covered their bodies. Seabhac muttered a few words in an unidentifiable language. The room around them burst into flames, scorching and flaming everything within the room.

"Nooooo! Cassandra and Samson screamed in unison.

Cassandra sobbed. Her voice ragged, torn. "My body. You're burning my body."

The white froth protected them from the fire. The journal and knife were spelled and protected. But Cassandra watched her body fall into the flames. Her heart wrenched at Seabhac's deliberately callous and brutal act. Hope died. Cassandra's destiny entailed wandering the world as a misplaced soul with no body. She drifted to the dirt. An ethereal substance of nothingness.

Samson moved to her side. He spoke, his words a low rumble of reassurance. "Cassandra, look."

She didn't want to. Couldn't handle seeing her body laying charred on the dirt floor.

"I am not so horrible that I would destroy your chances of returning to your body. Look, Cassandra." Seabhac prodded.

Not daring to hope, she responded to Seabhac's urging. What she saw astounded her. Based on the scorched walls, blackened dirt floor, and still flaming altar, the now dissolved foam had protected them from what must have been an inferno of flame. Amidst the grotesque destruction, her body lay undisturbed and pristine.

Her heart beat fiercely with relief until she realized she had no idea how to re-enter the now empty shell. "How...?" Wrought with despair, the unfinished question hung in the air. Cassandra choked back a sob.

"Imagine yourself there, Cassandra. It is as simple as the whisper of a thought." Ainevar's soft reassurance whispered close behind her.

"It's over?" Samson asked with a frown. "Hell, if it was that easy, why has it taken you centuries to take him out?"

"Arrogant impudence." Seabhac muttered. "It is not over yet. Hurry, Cassandra, you must return to your body. I cannot complete the next step without your help."

"But..." Confusion slowed Cassandra's thoughts.

A sound, like distant waves rolling onto the shoreline, reverberated across the room. Each second brought it closer, louder, until it resounded with the force of thunder.

Seabhac's mouth moved, but Cassandra heard nothing. He motioned toward her motionless body. Ainevar's familiar spirit melded with her, the female Druid's calming influence giving Cassandra the ability to act.

Imagine yourself there.

Following Seabhac's instructions, Cassandra imagined herself looking at the room from her body's vantage point. Closing out any image or sensation from where she stood, she imagined herself into her body. One second she wavered midair by the stairs, the next instant, sucked by a powerful vacuum force, she slammed into her body with a gasp.

Overcome by the sudden denseness of solid form, it took her a minute to recover. She was cognizant enough to realize the thunder had subsided, and she took the moment of calm to adjust to her solid form. The adjustment was difficult because everything felt different. Not in a bad way, though. She tested her movement by waving her arms and taking a couple of steps. Yes, all was working. So, what made her feel like a foreigner in her own body? Then it struck her. She was alone. That strange sensation she'd always thought to be part of herself, the part that in fact was Ainevar, was gone. It was disorienting. She was strong. Full. Alive. Reborn.

Before fully adjusting to her solid form, a shout from the others alerted her to danger. With the awkwardness of a child learning to walk for the first time, she stumbled toward them, but was too slow.

A whirlpool of darkness rose amidst the subsiding tide of thunder. Ever growing, the eddy of dark power grasped Cassandra and threw her against the wall. Pressed tightly against the hard surface, she sucked in a shallow breath. Her frightened gaze turned to the others for help. Samson yelled something and lunged at her, but Seabhac caught him in grasp strong enough to bring him to an abrupt halt. The two men struggled briefly while Cassandra's breathing became more difficult.

Come on, I need help here.

She didn't think they'd hear her thoughts, but they must have, because they stopped struggling. While Cassandra struggled against the encroaching evil trying to force her from her body, Samson and Seabhac indulged in a brief, harried argument.

Pressure on her chest forced the last breath of oxygen from her. She didn't want to die. Not now. Not before exploring the possibility of a relationship with Samson. Not without a final farewell to her brother, Memnon.

I can't breathe. Help.

Inevitable defeat was her final thought as she slipped into a semi-conscious state. Ainevar's voice drew her back to awareness. The softest of a whisper reached into her subconscious.

Together. We can do this together. Stay with us, Cassandra.

It fired Cassandra's willpower. She would not give up. The strength of an Arch-Druid, his apprentice, Samson, and herself, should be sufficient to defeat the darkness threatening them. Threatening Salem.

Ainevar's words must have reached the others, because as Cassandra's awareness increased, the trio stood hand in hand. The combined effect of their bonding created a glowing circle that engulfed them. Shards of light shot from within the circle to touch the journal, the knife, and Cassandra. Bound with the others, strength and renewed resolve burned through Cassandra.

Words weren't necessary as Seabhac wound a connection. Bound them together. Weaved a spell brimming with the sum of each of them. Tenfold stronger than they'd been alone. Cassandra sucked in welcome air as her blood coursed with an empowering force.

Together. It was possible to battle the threat of ancient evil. Together.

Freedom reigned, and darkness screamed a fiery protest. Flames licked over her in a battle for supremacy, but laughter rose in Cassandra as through the dark veil that separated them, Samson's eyes shone with reassurance and caring. His phantom caress connected them together and burned a pathway which allowed Ainevar to send a blast of energy. The darkness recoiled into a ball. Immediately, with a force beyond reckoning, darkness unfurled and shot dark clouds at Cassandra. She choked on the creature's need for possession of her body.

"Not in this lifetime," she cried defiantly. Breathing deeply, she drew every ounce of power from the earth beneath her. With a thrust of her thoughts, she threw it at the glow created by the others. Trickles grew to tingles, which turned into pulses. Cassandra almost burst with the fullness of being alive and connected.

When darkness reached her, a deafening clap of thunder cracked. Earsplitting, near soundless with intensity, it echoed through the essence of the glowing light connecting them. Energy, individual to each person, melded and created a shimmering gossamer strand. Cassandra didn't understand how such a flimsy thing could defeat the roiling mist of evil, but Seabhac knew what he was doing. With a graceful wave of his hand, he directed the strand toward the darkness. Winding, weaving, stretching, never breaking, the strand wound around the dark until nothing remained except a glowing ball.

Seabhac's shoulders slumped. "Now it is over."

The absence of darkness released the pressure in the room. Cassandra began to shake as sight, sound, smell, and touch all returned to normal. She hadn't even realized how her senses had suffered being out-of-body as she'd been. Add to that the outpouring of physical and mental energy used to defeat the evil, and it was no surprise her legs turned to rubber and she headed for the floor.

She expected hard dirt to slam into her, but found herself scooped up and held in a hard-body embrace, her nose pressed against Samson's chest. Trembling, she lifted her arms around him and held tight. Tears threatened. Relief overwhelmed her.

"You're here. I looked all over, but you weren't there. I saw nothing but that damned mist."

Samson's heart thumped steadily against her ear, and Cassandra detected the scents of spice and cinnamon. She snuggled closer, totally satisfied to remain there and liking the sheer freedom of depending on someone other than herself.

"I know. I was there, but I found Seabhac and Ainevar and they helped me come back. Without them I'd still be in that place." He pushed her away from him and stared into her face. "I am so sorry I got you into this mess and I'm even sorrier you ended up in such a horrible, dismal place."

"And the world revolves around you, does it?" Seabhac's sarcastic comment cut the tender moment.

"Oh. I forgot about them." Cassandra rubbed her tears away and extended a hand toward Seabhac and Ainevar. "It's a pleasure to meet you."

Even to Cassandra that sounded too formal, but old habits were hard to break and at this point, she was too exhausted to analyze her actions or make any changes.

Seabhac's lips twitched into a half-smile, as if knowing her thoughts. He took her hand and bent a formal bow over it. "The honor is mine, lady."

Ainevar was not so formal. She stepped closer and hugged Cassandra tightly. "You did it, Cassandra."

With a tearful smile, Ainevar stepped back. "If you hadn't accepted the essence of yourself and fought back with every fiber within you, we never would have defeated the evil. It took all of us, but you were the connection."

Cassandra blushed, not knowing how to respond, so she remained silent.

"So what happens now?" Samson fixed his gaze at the offending ball, no bigger than a golf ball, resting so innocently on the ground. "How long will that hold the evil encased?"

Seabhac shrugged. "Forever, one would hope."

"You don't know?" Samson exclaimed.

Seabhac's chest rose with a deep sigh. Whether of resignation or tiredness was not obvious. "Of course I do not know. I've never performed such a spell before."

"You've never...you..." Samson sputtered.

Samson's muscles tensed, and Cassandra put her hand on his arm to calm him. With a snort, he snapped his mouth shut and glared at the Druid, who smiled serenely.

"I do believe you will miss each other, despite your constant verbal battling."

It took a second for Ainevar's remark to register. When it did, Samson was the first to speak. "Whoa, you can't go anywhere. There are explanations to give, police reports to fill out, and an enormous mess to clean up."

A quick examination showed a blood-soaked, fire-burned room with charred altar and dismembered animal remains.

"I do not believe any explanation you can concoct will explain this to your modern day law enforcers. Best to close the room off so it is never found again." Seabhac declared. He leaned over and picked up the journal and the knife.

"These are not safe in this world. We will take them with us, as well as the ball." He picked up the ball with two fingers, as if afraid that contact might contaminate him, and placed it in a pocket.

Cassandra wasn't sorry to see the last of the journal and knife because they'd brought trouble and disruption to her life. Ainevar, though, had been part of her for so long. Tears shimmered in her eyes. "I will miss you, Ainevar."

Seabhac reached out and took Ainevar's hand in his. The resulting glow lit the dingy room with a warm, golden glow. They shimmered into sparks of light and disappeared. Before they were gone altogether, Ainevar's voice carried across the threshold of two worlds.

"You do not need me anymore, Cassandra. You will be fine."

Ainevar's absence left Cassandra sad. The way a friend leaving would make her feel, nothing more. Her sense of completeness remained.

Chapter Forty

"So they disappeared into thin air?" Skye asked for the second, or possibly the tenth, time.

Cassandra laughed at the disbelieving frown on Skye's face. "Yes. Poof. Into nothing." She spared a glance outside at Jerome and Samson, who sat on the back deck with Second Chance rolling around at their feet, sucking up for attention.

"Where would they go? Will they come back? Did they take the ball of evil with them? What will they do with it? Have they destroyed the journal and knife?" Skye asked, and not for the first time either.

Cassandra laughed. "I'm sorry, you don't sound happy that you missed the action and now you're living vicariously through me."

"I am sorry I missed it, but don't tell Jerome. He'll go all logical and tell me I have to consider the baby now." Skye turned up her nose and, with a defiant snap of her hand, flung her long hair back over her shoulders. "He treats me like a child because I'm pregnant."

"He loves you and wants what's best for you. You're lucky." She fought hard not to send a wistful glance toward Samson, who threw a stick for the dog to fetch. The rumble of laughter melted her usually reserved emotions.

"He is handsome, isn't he?" Skye sipped innocently at her lemonade while eyeing Cassandra over the rim of her glass.

"Yes, you married well." Cassandra played innocent as well.

"That's not what I meant and you know it." Skye chided. "So what happens between you two now?"

Cassandra shrugged. She didn't know what to say. After yesterday's battle, Samson had taken her home and spent the rest of the day and night in the office writing a creative police report, as he'd called it. He'd mentioned nothing more about a relationship between them.

The front door bell rang and Skye went to answer it. Cassandra closed her eyes and relaxed. With recent events rolling around in her mind and keeping her awake, sleep had been elusive last night. Fatigue threatened to drag her into slumber, but a familiar voice broke into her peace.

"I'm not paying you to sit around and do nothing."

Her eyes flew open and she squealed. "Memnon." She launched herself off the couch and right into his waiting arms, causing him to drop the briefcase he held. As always, he caught her. His familiar hug soothed her wired emotions and settled her nerves. "Memnon, you wouldn't believe what I've been through."

"Maybe not, but the vibes you've sent my way give me a good idea. That's why I'm here." He peeled her arms from around his neck and set her back on the floor. "I'm also thinking you better quickly explain that I'm your brother, or that surly looking man over there is going to challenge me. And he's got a gun, so I don't want him upset with me."

Cassandra turned to Samson, who stood at the patio door with a dark scowl on his face. A glare he directed at Memnon. She took a step between them and offered introductions.

"Samson, this is Memnon. Memnon, Samson, Skye, and Jerome. My friends."

Memnon laughed and whispered in her ear, "Sis, I don't imagine Samson enjoys being referred to as a friend."

Her brother was right. Cassandra wouldn't have believed it possible, but Samson's scowl had deepened as he glowered at her.

Keeping his gaze on Cassandra, Samson said, "Nice to meet you, Memnon. Cassandra, it's time we had a talk."

Ever the brat, her brother answered cheerfully. "You can talk later. First, I'd like to know why an earthquake woke me from a sound sleep. What, exactly, has been going on around here?"

Samson's posture stiffened. His gaze locked with Memnon's, and a silent measure of character took place. Cassandra wanted to protest the male challenge for supremacy, but Skye laid a hand on her arm and whispered.

"Leave them. They might as well get it over with right away."

"Get what over with? I'm quite capable of making up my own mind, and have been for years."

"Honey, my guess is Memnon has let you go your way, but has watched over you to make sure you didn't get hurt. And in case you haven't noticed, Samson is about as alpha male as they come. Sorry, but I doubt you'll get to make decisions without considering him ever again."

"But..."

"No, buts. I suggest you learn to be like water and go with the flow. Eventually water can wear down a rock." She sent an appreciative glance at Samson. "And Samson is relatively rock like."

Cassandra giggled at Skye's rather appropriate comparison and realized Samson and Memnon must have worked out their male territorial tendencies. The two men shook hands, and the tension in the room calmed to a more acceptable level.

Samson turned to her. His eyes sparked with love, driving need, and desire. Drawn to Samson, she moved across the floor to stand in front of him. He lifted a hand and cupped her face. This time, his voice resonated with patience.

"We need to talk." He scowled at Memnon. "I suppose we can put your brother's mind at ease first."

Skye clapped her hands. "Great. Let me make sandwiches and mix more lemonade, then we can all get the full story."

Cassandra groaned. "You've heard the full story a dozen times already."

"I know, but I want to hear it again. Jerome, can you help me?" Skye disappeared into the kitchen and Jerome followed with the reassurance there would be beer and lemonade.

The remaining trio stood in uncomfortable silence until Memnon reached down for the briefcase he'd dropped. Looking around for a place to set it, he decided on the coffee table in front of the couch. He opened the lid and pulled out a stack of papers.

"I need your signature on these papers. That's the other reason I've come." He held a pen out for her.

"Papers?" Confused, she took the pen and frowned at Memnon.

"Yes. Papers for the house next door."

"I'm only the designer. What papers do I have to sign?"

"I'm afraid I wasn't honest with you, sis."

"Oh, like that's a first."

He grinned, and Cassandra knew she'd forgive him for virtually anything. "My intuition told me you had to come to Salem, but I also knew I'd never get you here without good reason. So I built the house."

"You mean you didn't discover the house and fall in love?"

"Yes, but not for me. I knew it would be ideal for you, a house that you would love to live in. I bought it for you. Getting you here to design and decorate for me to move into was merely an excuse to get you here."

Cassandra sat, stunned. She smacked his arm. "You manipulative bugger. Do you have any idea what I've been through? I had my life turned inside out, fought an ancient evil so powerful an authentic and ancient Arch-Druid had difficulty destroying it...I came this close to dying." She put her thumb and forefinger centimeters apart to demonstrate.

Memnon's face blanched, but Samson reassured him. "Don't worry. It wasn't as bad as she lets on."

"Not as bad?" Cassandra's mouth dropped open. "How can you say that after what we went through?"

Samson smirked. "Take note. That's how it's done. Now she's mad at me, not you."

Cassandra was too tired to argue with either of them, especially if they were going to gang up on her.

"Food's ready." Skye saved the day as she set her tray of sandwiches, crackers, and cheese on the table. "What did we miss?"

"I found out my sister has quite a story to relate."

Cassandra stared him down. "And I found out my brother has more money than he knows what to do with."

"Oh, oh." Skye handed out plates. "I think we need to unwind and relax. And in my experience, eating is a great way to achieve that goal."

"Sure. Words of wisdom from someone who eats like a cow." Jerome snorted.

Cassandra enlightened a confused Memnon. "Skye is pregnant and Jerome is a brat."

"Ahh, the eating like a cow remark makes total sense now."

Memnon reached for one of the bottles of beer Jerome had brought from the kitchen and tilted it forward. "To Skye, Jerome, and their unborn child."

Glasses of lemonade clinked with bottles of beer.

Samson shifted on the couch. His leg rubbed against Cassandra's. Warmth flooded her, and she realized she'd never been happier than sitting here with family, friends, and Samson. Though yet undefined, she had a good idea of where things were headed between them. She raised her glass and offered a toast.

"To letting go of the past, without denying its effect on us. To trusting and believing in ourselves. To my new neighbors, Skye and Jerome."

Skye smiled and sipped her lemonade. "I'm delighted you're moving next door. I think we'll become great friends."

Samson shifted on the couch and leaned forward, wineglass in the air. "I have a toast as well. To Ainevar and Seabhac." His blazing gaze burned into Cassandra. "We owe them more than we can ever repay."

Warmth fluttered in Cassandra's stomach and she laughed with a freedom she hadn't allowed herself in a long time.

Afterword

I hope you enjoyed reading this book and would appreciate if you could leave a review. Reviews help an author with future sales and marketing, so it's a great way to support and motivate the authors that you like. You can find me online at these places:

Website:

https://cathywalkerauthor.com
FB Author Page:

www.facebook.com/cathywalker.author

Author Bio

Books have fueled my imagination since reading the Black Stallion series when I was younger. Never thinking that I could actually write a book, I sat down and began writing anyway. I now have multiple published books and more on the way. All of them with a theme of myths, legends, romance, or fantasy.

I am fortunate enough to live on a farm filled with animals to love and care for. Every morning my dogs, cats, goats, and horses greet me at the barnyard. Spending time with them helps motivate me to write.

Milton Keynes UK
Ingram Content Group UK Ltd.
UKHW021827310324
440371UK00007B/916

9 781519 588197